Acclaim for the authors of

Christmas Gold

Cheryl St.John

"Ms. St.John knows what the readers want
and keeps on giving it."
—*Rendezvous*

Elizabeth Lane

"I predict a long and successful career for Ms. Lane—
she is quickly approaching the top of my must-read list."
—*Romance Reviews Today*

Mary Burton

"This talented writer is a virtuoso, who strums the hearts
of the readers and composes an emotional tale."
—*Rendezvous*

Dear Reader,

Harlequin Historicals is happy to kick off the holiday season with the first of our two Christmas short-story collections of the year, *Christmas Gold*, by three of our best-loved authors, Cheryl St.John, Elizabeth Lane and Mary Burton.

From longtime author Cheryl St.John comes "Colorado Wife," the story of a feisty do-gooder and the wealthy businessman she's determined to reform. But when these two opposites need to come together for the sake of two orphaned children, anything can happen!

In "Jubal's Gift," author Elizabeth Lane brings us a touching tale of love and the powers of forgiveness. When an emotionally scarred ex-soldier bent on vengeance arrives at a small Arizona trading post, a woman from his past helps him find happiness beyond any he ever imagined.

And to complete the collection, we have a delightful story from Mary Burton. In "Until Christmas," a rugged mine manager will do anything to win the heart and hand of the one woman who wants nothing to do with him. Be sure to read on to see how this one turns out!

We hope you enjoy this wonderful collection celebrating Christmas in the Old West as much as we did! And in November look for our Regency Christmas collection, *Gifts of the Season*, with three beautiful stories from Miranda Jarrett, Lyn Stone and Anne Gracie.

From our family to yours, have a very happy holiday season!

Sincerely,

The Editors
Harlequin Historicals

Christmas Gold

CHERYL ST. JOHN
ELIZABETH LANE
MARY BURTON

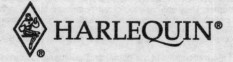

HARLEQUIN®

TORONTO • NEW YORK • LONDON
AMSTERDAM • PARIS • SYDNEY • HAMBURG
STOCKHOLM • ATHENS • TOKYO • MILAN • MADRID
PRAGUE • WARSAW • BUDAPEST • AUCKLAND

ISBN 0-373-29227-9

CHRISTMAS GOLD

Copyright © 2002 by Harlequin Books S.A.

The publisher acknowledges the copyright holders of the individual works as follows:

COLORADO WIFE
Copyright © 2002 by Cheryl St.John

JUBAL'S GIFT
Copyright © 2002 by Elizabeth Lane

UNTIL CHRISTMAS
Copyright © 2002 by Mary Burton

Visit us at www.eHarlequin.com

Printed in U.S.A.

CONTENTS

CHERYL ST.JOHN

A peacemaker, a romantic, an idealist and a discouraged perfectionist are the words that Cheryl St.John uses to describe herself. The author of both historical and contemporary novels says she's been told that she is painfully honest.

She says that knowing her stories bring hope and pleasure to readers is one of the best parts of being a writer. The other wonderful part is being able to set her own schedule and have time to work around her growing family.

Cheryl loves to hear from readers. You can write her at P.O. Box #12142, Florence Station, Omaha, NE 68112.

COLORADO WIFE
Cheryl St.John

This story is dedicated to you, dear reader.
May you have a joyous holiday season filled with love.

Chapter One

Needle Creek, Colorado
1875

"What are those poor bedraggled children doing out in front of your place in the cold?" Esmerelda Clark shook snow from her woolen scarf and hung it on a peg inside the front door of Home Street's Finest Eatery, then shrugged out of her coat.

Rosalyne Emery placed a basket of oven fresh yeast rolls at a table where four customers were seated, then wiped her hands on her apron as she hurried forward. "What children?"

"Those right there." Esmerelda pointed through the multipaned window that had been shipped all the way from Ohio. Outside, snowflakes drifted past the frosty glass and settled on the wood molding. Leaning close and peering out the window into the bitter December evening, Rosalyne's breath fogged the pane.

Sitting on the rough-hewn bench which sat at the front of her restaurant were two forms bundled in dark coats, thickly dusted with icy snow. One child wore a cap, the other had a strip of burlap barely covering blond hair. "What in the name of goodness are those children doing out there in the cold—and not dressed properly?"

"That's what I asked," Esmerelda replied.

Without pausing for so much as a shawl, Rosalyne opened the door and hurried to where the huddled figures sat leaning against one another for pitiful warmth. "Are you waiting for someone?"

The one who wore burlap for a head covering appeared to be the oldest and nodded. A long tendril of hair escaped the wrap and draped across the front of her snowy coat. Not really *her* coat, Rosalyne noted with dismay. Both of them wore oversize men's jackets with the sleeves crudely hacked off.

"Who are you waiting for?"

Teeth chattering, the girl glanced at her red-nosed sibling and shrugged, a barely perceptible movement inside the enormous coat.

"Is your mother or father inside one of the stores?" Rosalyne would certainly give that parent a tongue-lashing when she found them. How cruel for someone to leave these youngsters out in the cold while they went about their business. Surely the children didn't belong to anyone eating in her restaurant! "Or—" She jerked a thumb over her shoulder. "Your parents are *not* inside here?"

The girl denied it by shaking her head.

"Where then, dear? Where's your mother or father?"

Again the child looked at her younger sibling before she spoke. "Our pa's dead."

In confusion, Rosalyne glanced up and down Home Street, where glowing gas lamps had been lit against the early darkness. The few teams harnessed to wagons or buckboards seemed in order with the number of patrons in her establishment. Had there been an accident? A gunfight? She'd heard no commotion. She moved closer to the pair and knelt. "What's happened?"

"Got caught in the mud last summer. River drownded 'im." The anguish beneath that matter-of-fact statement was palpable, and Rosalyne's heart went out to the girl and her brother. How distressing to see someone of such a tender age initiated to the pain of life's hardships. These children's father had been another careless miner caught in the dangerous clay of the river. "Last summer?" she repeated, thinking of the months since then. "Where have you been until now?"

"The Thompsons took us in for a time," the girl replied. "But supplies get short in winter. They couldn't afford to feed us no more. Miz Thompson cried, but she said someone would find us here and take us in. She said sit tight right here until someone comes."

Rosalyne's whole chest ached at those pathetic words. She knew firsthand the abject poverty and destitute situations in the winter camps. Mining families helped one another as best they could, but hardships forced situations nobody could help. At least none they could help without turning their backs on their foolhardy dreams and going back to towns and cities with real jobs and secure homes. And miners were a blind bunch of fools.

"Come inside, then," she said quickly. "You can't sit out here and freeze."

"But someone might come for us!" the child said, fear in her reedy young voice.

In that moment, Rosalyne saw herself as a girl, felt the fear, isolation and hopelessness to her bones, and wanted to help. "I've found you, now, haven't I? There's a warm place right in here, plenty of food, too. Are you hungry?"

The smaller child came to life immediately and slid to his feet. "I am!"

The girl reached out a small chapped bare hand to grab the other's coat and hold him fast. "Matt," she warned.

"Matt's got the right idea," Rosalyne told her. "Come in out of the cold and eat. I have hot cocoa."

That did it. The reluctant girl released her brother's coat in favor of taking his hand and pulling him, and Rosalyne ushered them both into the warm eatery and past the now staring patrons. The appetizing smells of beef and rosemary and hot rolls permeated the inviting kitchen into which she led them.

White-haired, full-figured Mrs. O'Hearn turned from the stove, where she was removing golden-crusted beef pies, and spotted the newcomers. "Who have we here?"

"Two hungry children." Rosalyne removed their inadequate wraps. The youngsters were thin and unkempt, their blond hair lank and dull. Both wore threadbare flannel shirts and ill-fitting trousers with rope holding them up at their waists. Rags showed through holes in the toes and heels of oversize boots. The boy's stomach growled loudly, and his eyes opened wide with anticipation.

Rosalyne blinked back the threat of tears and placed a bright smile on her face, while guiding both to a wash basin. "Wash your faces and hands while Mrs. O'Hearn and I dish you up a hearty supper."

"We ain't dirty," the girl said with resentment lacing her tone. She cast Rosalyne a dark look.

"Of course you're not. It's just good manners for everyone to wash up before they eat. Why, I wash my hands before I eat my supper, and I've had them in dishwater all day. Go ahead now."

The siblings obeyed, but kept their attention on the food being served by the two bustling women.

"Where did you find such scrawny youngins?" Mrs. O'Hearn whispered. The woman had remained in Needle Creek after the death of her husband several years ago, and Rosalyne considered herself fortunate to have made her acquaintance. An excellent cook and Rosalyne's right arm, she'd become invaluable as a friend as well as an employee.

Before setting the table and pouring steaming mugs of hot cocoa, Rosalyne quietly explained how she'd found them. The widow woman clucked with sincere sympathy. Rosalyne kept her lips clamped lest she say something she shouldn't in front of the children. She had no use for miners and this was proof of why she was justified in her feelings.

She waited until the two were seated, then spooned

rich-gravied stew into bowls and buttered thick slices of bread. "My name's Miss Rosalyne Emery, and this is Mrs. O'Hearn."

The girl sat with her hands folded in her lap. She forced her hungry brown gaze from the food in front of her to Rosalyne's face. "I'm Zandy Baxter and this here's Matt. He's my brother, and I take care of him."

"Go ahead and eat," Rosalyne urged.

The two didn't need a second invitation. They lit into the food and didn't stop until Matt burped.

Zandy elbowed him. "Say 'scuse me."

"Ow! I mean, 'scuse me."

"You're excused," Rosalyne said graciously.

"Zandy is an unusual name," Mrs. O'Hearn commented, once their appetites seemed sated.

The girl wiped her mouth on the napkin beside her plate. Her delicate wrist seemed far too frail and bony. "It's really Alexandra, but Matt always called me Zandy and my pa caught on to it."

"You said your father died last summer," Rosalyne began gently, hating to ask, yet needing to know. "Was his last name Baxter?"

Alexandra nodded, and Rosalyne noted that the girl's lips were as chapped and dry as her hands. "Yes. Lowell Baxter was our pa's name."

"What about your mother?"

The girl's wide brown eyes seemed to swim with forlorn sadness. Her voice came out small and shaky. "She died when Matt was just a tiny baby."

Life in mining camps was difficult enough without the added loss of a mother. Rosalyne knew that all too well. "My mother died when I was very small, too."

Zandy's liquid brown eyes softened with sympathy. "Do you miss her?"

Once again Rosalyne's heart ached with kinship for these children's losses, and she nodded.

"What about your pa?" Matt asked bluntly. "Did he die, too?"

Standing then, she picked up a plate. "No. I imagine he's out there mining in the hills somewhere. I see him once in a while when he comes through for supplies." He usually asked for money, but she didn't mention that.

Obviously a kind family had taken in the children for as long as they could, but with winter full upon them and supplies running short, they'd had no choice but to make a hard decision for the well-being of their own. How long the two had been sitting in the cold, Rosalyne had no idea. She hadn't seen them that morning when she'd shoveled, or at noon when she'd turned over the sign from Breakfast Now Being Served to Dinner Now Being Served.

No one from the supper crowd had mentioned anything until Esmerelda, and thank goodness she'd spoken up.

"How old are you?" Rosalyne asked.

"I'm eight," Zandy replied. "Matt is six."

Rosalyne placed several of the caramel cookies she'd baked that morning on a plate and set it before the children, then refilled their mugs. "Help yourself to one of my porch cookies," she offered.

Matt took a huge bite of the cookie filled with raisins and nuts, chewed and swallowed. "These here are the best cookies I ever ate," he said. "How come you call 'em porch cookies?"

"Well, I don't know," Rosalyne replied, frowning at one of the treats remaining on the plate. "I suppose perhaps because people serve them on their porches in fair weather."

"Do you got a porch?" he asked.

"No, I'm afraid not. I have a small home just around the corner a ways. But no porch."

Matt seemed disappointed.

"Mrs. O'Hearn has a porch," she told him.

"She does?"

Mrs. O'Hearn nodded in affirmation. "My dear Henry built our home. He was a handy fellow with a hammer and nails. Could slap together just about anything you could ask for."

"He built a whole house?" Matt asked.

"He had a little help, but he mostly did the work himself."

"Our pa always said we'd have a house someday." A note of childish melancholy laced Zandy's voice. "Soon as we hit the big load."

Anger simmered in Rosalyne's belly. How many times she'd heard those hollow promises. How many times she'd wished for and dreamed of a solid home, rather than a drafty tent, prayed for a bed that didn't hold dampness and a floor that wasn't dirt or canvas and prone to bugs and snakes. She had gone after those things for herself once she'd been old enough. At seventeen, she'd panned a small bag of gold flakes and made her way to Needle Creek, where she'd bought a tent, a stove and supplies and started baking for the miners. But these youngsters weren't old enough to be on their own.

"We prob'ly woulda hit the big load this time," Matt said confidently, obviously speaking like a chip off the old block.

"Pa said that every time." Zandy seemed a lot less sure. "But he kept having to go back to Mr. Calhoun to get more food and stuff."

The name provoked Rosalyne's ire to a new pitch. Sam Calhoun was known far and wide as a rich mine owner who lived resplendently in town and grub-staked the poor placer miners. He now owned the Red Dolly Saloon, the Legal Tender Gaming Hall and the mercantile. It was men like him who made it possible for fathers to run after hopeless greedy dreams.

"You can sleep at my house tonight," she assured them. "I'll light the hard coal heater and we'll be warm and toasty."

"Last two meals," Mrs. O'Hearn said gently, gesturing with a ladle to the plates she'd just set on a scarred wooden counter.

"Thank you." Rosalyne scooped up the plates and delivered the suppers to her customers, pausing on the way back to take money and wish the diners a good evening.

It was quite late by the time the last customer had gone and Rosalyne and her helper had washed the dishes and started beans to soak for the following day. As she'd worked, she'd kept glancing toward the exhausted children who were now snuggled against one another on a pallet of flour sacks and blankets near the fireplace.

The more she thought about their situation, the angrier she grew and the more she cast about for someone to blame. The longer she considered, the clearer it became. Sam Calhoun was directly responsible for their destitute situation. If he hadn't repeatedly grubstaked their father, the man might have been forced to face his failure and make a home and a life for these young people. As it was, with someone to keep loaning money and supplies, these men could keep their pie-in-the-sky illusions alive at the sake of all else.

"Mrs. O'Hearn," she began. "I know it's late, and you've worked a long day."

"What is it you need, dear?"

"I want to go have a word with Mr. Calhoun."

The older woman raised a questioning brow. "Do you think that's wise?"

"I think I have no choice. Because he makes loans that he knows the miners can't pay back, he makes it possible for them to do things like this to their families."

"They pay him back with a share of their strikes." Mrs. O'Hearn hung a length of damp toweling to dry.

"Half!" Her shout had been too loud and she glanced to make certain she hadn't awakened the children. "He takes half of whatever the miners dig—if they find anything at all. Do you know what a percentage of profit that is?"

"I agree it's a terrible situation, and I know you

take this personally because of your own circumstances, but—''

''What person with a heart wouldn't take this personally?'' Rosalyne untied her apron and hung it on a hook. ''Will you please help me get the children to my house and into bed? I want to go speak with Mr. Calhoun.''

''I'll do whatever you wish, of course.''

Together they banked the fire, extinguished the lanterns, bundled Matt and Zandy into their inadequate wraps and led the sleepy children through the cold to Rosalyne's home.

She scooped coal in and lit the heater while Mrs. O'Hearn helped them wash and dress in shirts Rosalyne located. Tucked into the feather bed in the small room just off the dining room, brother and sister looked small and frightened as they huddled together.

''Don't you worry your little heads,'' Rosalyne assured them. ''I'm going to take care of everything.''

''I can take care of Matt,'' Zandy told her.

''I know you can. And you've done a good job.''

What she was going to do or how they would be taken care of, Rosalyne had no idea, she thought as she changed her dress and brushed and pinned her hair. But she was going to confront Mr. Calhoun and insist he make atonement of some sort before this night was over.

''I'll return as quickly as possible,'' she told her friend.

Rosalyne made her way along the snow-laden streets, her head bowed to stinging flakes propelled by the biting wind, her boots occasionally slipping on the layer of ice beneath the buildup of white. The Red Dolly was in full swing with yellow light shining from every pane of glass. The tinny sounds of the piano planking in the cold night air, laughter and an occasional whoop of gaiety broke the stillness.

Rosalyne took the path on the boardwalk across the street, avoiding the rowdy saloon and hurrying by with a skittish feeling nipping at her heels. She rarely traversed the streets at night, except to make her way home from work. The town had grown and prospered over the past few years until she barely recognized it.

Sam Calhoun's ostentatious three-story house sat at the end of the block on Main Street, and as she neared, lights and sounds of gaiety filled its walls, as well. What kind of tawdry entertainment did the man provide in his own home? The street and the walks had recently been shoveled, enabling her to brush the snow from her hem and walk over the bricks with a modicum of dignity.

A collection of well-appointed buggies and teams lined the yard, and Rosalyne hurried past them to make her way up the walk.

The door opened before she had raised her hand to lift the shiny brass knocker. In surprise, she placed her hand over her heart. "Oh, hello."

"Good evening, Miss." The burly bald-headed man who greeted her filled the entire doorway with his imposing size. He wore a tie and a jacket, but the gun in the holster on his hip made him more suited to horseback than a social gathering. "Do you have an invitation?"

"No, I don't. But I need to speak with Mr. Calhoun, please. It's important."

"Sorry, but no one's allowed in without an invitation."

"That's ridiculous. This is Needle Creek, Colorado, not Boston. I merely require a few moments of Mr. Calhoun's time, and then I'll be on my way."

"Sorry, Miss. This here shindig is for Mr. Calhoun's friends only." His gaze seemed to glance over her and dismiss her as unworthy of being one of the elite friends welcome at this function.

"And what makes you so certain that Mr. Calhoun and I are not friends?" She raised one brow in what she hoped was an imperious and aristocratic manner. "I happen to know Mr. Calhoun *very* well." She *had* seen the man in her eatery. She had even taken his order and brought his food once or twice.

His forehead wrinkled and he peered intently at her. "Aren't you the waitress from that eatin' place?"

At that moment the door was opened farther and a slender man in a crisp white shirt and dark jacket filled the space. "You're a friend of Sam's, you say?"

"Yes," she replied, encouraged that someone might finally let her have a word with the man. A tiny twist of the truth seemed a small price to pay on behalf of the two orphaned children at her house right this moment. "I never dreamed I would need a formal invitation. Why, when we spoke of it just this afternoon, he seemed to take it for granted that I'd be here."

The slender man poked the beefy one in the ribs

with an elbow. "He was with her *this afternoon,* Stoney."

The big man's brows rose in surprise. "*You're* the important meeting he had?" He glanced at the other man, "Hear that, George?" then back at her. "You're the partnership that's going to change his life?"

Caught off guard, but not willing to lose the ground she'd gained, Rosalyne nodded her bluff. "Yes. If you'll just tell him I'm here and allow us a few moments in private…"

The two men exchanged knowing glances.

George reached for her arm and guided her into an enormous foyer lit by hissing gas lamps. Swags of fragrant evergreen draped a polished banister and the holiday scents of cinnamon and clove hung in the air. He closed the door. "Let me take your wrap, Miss. I'm so sorry you were made to wait in the cold."

Just the mention of waiting in the cold assured her she was justified in what she'd just done.

"Stoney's sorry, too, aren't you, Stoney?"

"Er. Yeah. Sorry."

"Miss—I'm sorry, what's your name?" George asked.

"Emery," she replied, shrugging from her coat and removing her damp wool scarf.

"Miss Emery is a very close friend of Sam's, isn't that right?"

Stoney looked her over, his scornful expression plainly revealing his skepticism that a woman dressed in a plain dark-blue shirtwaist with no adornment to her hair and no jewelry was of a class to be mentioned in the same breath with Sam Calhoun.

Rosalyne raised her chin. "*Very* close."

Stoney cracked a grin.

George couldn't hide his amusement, either, and Rosalyne experienced a pang of unease that perhaps she'd gone too far in emphasizing her relationship to their employer. She certainly didn't want them thinking she was a chippy from the Red Dolly! She'd heard talk that Sam Calhoun frequented the place.

Just then a couple wandered past, arm in arm, both holding glasses of bubbly liquid. "Mr. and Mrs. Greene, I'd like you to meet Miss Emery." George politely performed introductions.

"How do you do, Miss Emery."

Stoney whispered something to Mr. Greene and the man's eyes bore into Rosalyne's. He turned and spoke softly to his wife. She smiled and took Rosalyne's arm. "Come with me, dear."

Rosalyne balked and held back. "I really need to speak with Mr. Calhoun."

"You'll have plenty of time for that," Mrs. Greene said with a sly smile. "For now you must meet Sam's friends and business acquaintances."

More introductions were made, and with each person she met, Rosalyne's confidence wavered. She was inappropriately dressed, feeling like a mud hen among the plumage of these socialite peacocks. All she'd wanted were a few private moments alone with the man who lived here, but she'd been drawn in and introduced as a guest at his elegant gathering. When she did run into the man, he would be furious at her ruse.

"This is such a surprise, dear!" A woman who'd

been introduced as Trudy made an exaggerated fuss in the midst of the gathering around Rosalyne. "How long have you known Sam?"

"Well..." She'd known his kind for a long time. "It seems like forever."

"How sweet." Feminine voices murmured.

"Sam, you sly old dog," a male voice called. "How cagey of you to keep this gem to yourself."

"You're naughty, Sam Calhoun," a young woman named Althea accused, waving a fan she had no need of. "Just plain naughty."

With a shiver of apprehension crawling up her spine, Rosalyne strained to see who they were speaking to. She had misconstrued her identity to gain admission, and now her lie was going to be exposed.

"What are you talking about?" The voice was like a beguiling melody she'd heard before, resonating, haunting, making the hair on her neck stand up.

"I'm talking about Miss Emery, here," Althea continued. "Your *fiancée!*"

Chapter Two

The word hung in the air like the heavy scent of candle wax and cloying perfumes. Rosalyne's heart stopped for a few precious beats, then resumed with the rapid cadence of a moth's wings against a window glass. Fiancée!

Heat rose up Rosalyne's chest and neck to scorch her cheeks. She swallowed the cry of panic that rose in her throat.

Frantically, she searched the faces in the crowd for the one that would be thunderously accusing her of the outrageous lie, and her gaze fell upon the dark, seemingly amused countenance of the tall man she'd occasionally served in her restaurant.

Sam Calhoun.

"You're a clever fellow, Sam," a distinguished-looking gentleman on his left commented.

Mr. Calhoun's gaze took in Rosalyne's clothing and hair, and she resisted the urge to reach up and tuck back stray tendrils. His wide bow-shaped lips, which were partially hidden by a softly curling black mustache, tilted at the corners in a secretly amused smile, creating charming creases in his high-boned lean cheeks. He wore a black suit and tie like other men wore chambray and flannel, as though he were completely at home and at ease.

Well, he was at home, and why shouldn't he be at ease? She was the one about to be cast out his door like a stray mutt!

"I—I can explain," she stammered.

"Don't worry your pretty head, darling."

Darling? Her mind went blank for a fractured moment. In two long strides he moved to her side, his imposing height and breadth rattling her even more. His black hair shone beneath the gas lights.

"I know how busy you are, and I did say to arrive at your convenience." Sam took her hand and raised her fingers to his mouth.

Rosalyne's heart fluttered crazily, amazed as she was at his forwardness. She tried ineffectively to jerk her fingers away, but he held them fast, all the while smiling into her eyes, daring her to make a scene and spoil her own charade. Her heart hammered painfully and heat rose in her cheeks. He drew her fingers closer to his lips, the moment drawn out until she thought her heart would burst from her chest.

His lips, surprisingly warm and soft, touched the backs of her fingers, his ebony mustache a gentle abrasion that shot a jolt of electricity up her arm.

Rosalyne's vision grew blurry. She drew a fortifying breath and managed to pull her hand from Sam's grasp without making it look as though she'd won an arm wrestling contest. Guests on all sides smiled and murmured and nodded. "I must speak to you alone,'' she managed finally, her voice sounding breathy. "It—it's about the children.''

A woman behind her gasped and another one tittered.

"Of course, darling. But please favor me with a dance first. I've been waiting for you.''

What was wrong with the man? Acting as though he'd been expecting her? "Oh, no, I—I couldn't.''

He was touching her again, this time with his hand on her upper arm, the heat emanating through her sleeve, his grip surprisingly firm compared to the gentleness of his tone. "I won't take no for an answer.''

He led her to a small area near the orchestra, where a few other couples glided and turned in time to the music. He moved his hand from her arm to the small of her back, and she found herself trapped within his commanding embrace as he smoothly led her through the steps. She'd never attempted to dance before, and desperately hoped she didn't stumble or trip or make a bigger fool of herself.

His chin was just above her eye level, the intimate nearness a breathtaking intimidation, but when he bent his head forward, his face lowered, closer and closer, though he kept a proper space between their bodies. The scents of starch and tobacco combined with a clean masculine tang and enveloped her as surely and as headily as his embrace. His nose was mere inches from her cheek, and she was almost sure he inhaled the scent of her hair deliberately.

She turned her face away as though she were gazing at the other dancers and felt his breath rustle the hair against her neck. "The lamps pick up half a dozen shades of gold in your hair,'' he said softly. ''I've never seen anything quite like it.''

Caught completely off guard, she made the mistake of glancing up to read his expression. Once his gaze locked with hers, she couldn't look away. His eyes were indigo black, with a mysterious depth, but a hint of mischief. He held her far too closely for her peace of mind, and another wave of heat climbed her neck and cheeks.

''If I'm not mistaken, you run Home Street's Finest Eatery. I found that name amusing first time I heard it, since it's the only place to eat on Home Street.''

Surprised that he recognized her, she ignored his comment. ''I'm sure you're wondering what I'm doing here.''

''I hired a cook for tonight, I thought you might be checking out the competition.''

''Of course not.''

The humor in his expression told her he'd been teasing and was delighted that she'd taken him seriously. ''Well, then I suppose you're going to tell me what you're doing here.''

''Like I said, it's about the children.''

His seductive gaze made her achingly uncomfortable. ''I think I would remember if we'd had children.''

She had to look away again.

''So you must be referring to someone else's. Are you soliciting for a charity? You could have come to my office during business hours.''

''No.'' How was it the man managed to tongue-tie

her with every sentence? "I'm talking about Zandy and Matt, the children of Lowell Baxter."

"Name's familiar. Do I know him?"

"You loaned him money."

"I loan a lot of men money."

Rosalyne braced her resolve with images of the two shivering children abandoned in front of her store. This man had been ordering servants and planning a party in his big fancy house while the orphaned Matt and Zandy had gone hungry. Mistake or no, she was going to make him take responsibility. "We need to speak in private."

"People will talk," Sam pointed out.

She raised what she hoped was a haughty brow. "People *are* talking."

Sam glanced around the room, then back at the lovely young woman in his arms. "Come to my den with me. I'll leave the door open."

Miss Emery resisted him minimally until he flattened his hand over her back and led her from the room.

He was lucky, no doubt about it. He ushered the golden-haired, blue-eyed little filly into his den and left the door ajar. There was something about her that drew him, *intrigued* him, even though he possessed a sneaking suspicion that her disposition could be as prickly as that of a cornered porcupine. No one but he would be lucky enough to fall into a fiancée as pretty as this one without a by your leave.

He had been enjoying her discomfort ever since she'd been introduced and began to search the crowd for him, and that probably said a whole lot about his character. But anyone with the brass to bluff her way into his private party either had something important to say or was a complete fool, and he'd like to know which.

"All right." He leaned his hips against his desk and nonchalantly crossed his ankles. "What is so urgent?"

"Two children were orphaned last summer when Lowell Baxter drowned."

The name and the incident rang a bell, but he couldn't place the man right off. "Baxter, you say?"

She nodded.

"I do remember hearing about that." He could check his account ledgers the following morning to see what his records indicated about the man.

"His children were taken in for a time by a mining family, but today they were abandoned on the boardwalk in front of my establishment."

"Did you send for the law?"

"They're not criminals, Mr. Calhoun."

"No, but the sheriff would see to it that they were cared for."

"And sent to an orphanage? I hardly think that's in their best interests."

He wasn't sure what the woman was getting to, but he did enjoy the way her vivid sapphire eyes flashed. He raised both hands in a gesture to show his confusion. "So why tell me this?"

"You're responsible for these children."

He uncrossed his ankles and straightened. "How do you figure?"

"You grubstaked their father."

His mind still hadn't made the connection. "He died owing me money, but those are the risks I take. I'm certainly not going to put a couple of kids to work to pay off his debt. If a miner dies, I have to write off the loss."

Her skin had been several shades of pink since he'd first laid eyes on her, but at this moment she looked as though she'd been left to bake in the sun all day. Anger swept her lovely features and she glared at him, a blue fire ignited in her eyes. "If you hadn't given their father money, he would have been forced to give up his foolish dreams and provide a home for his family. He might have found a decent job. As it was, you made it possible for him to starve and neglect them and get himself killed!"

Sam was standing at full attention now, his concentration riveted on this woman's ridiculous accusations. He moved away from his desk and took a step closer to where she stood. "Woman, you're nuts! I outfitted the man, just like I've loaned supplies to a hundred others. That doesn't make me responsible for their lives and their offspring. I make loans. They either give up or strike a vein and pay me back."

"Or die," Rosalyne added with contempt.

He shook his head in disbelief. "This is rough country. I'm just making a living."

She stood so rigid that she'd probably snap in two if he pushed her over. Her chin came up and her shoulders squared, and she took a step toward him as he'd just done toward her, and that small measure of boldness endeared her to him somehow.

"Just making a living?" Her voice dripped contempt. She turned her head and stared at the chunk of gold-veined quartz that sat atop his massive desk, a reminder to him of where he was and where he'd come from, and the day that had changed his life.

"You *miners* are all alike," she said with accusation lacing her tone. She spoke the word as though it meant something dirty. "You're just luckier than most."

"I am lucky," he agreed. "But I'm not a miner."

"Oh, really. You don't own three mines?"

"I own them." He didn't mine them himself. Maybe she had him on a technicality, but what difference did it make?

"All you can think about is finding your precious gold or silver. That comes before anything and everything else, including your children."

Sam leaned toward her. "Lady, I don't have any children."

Standing tall, she blinked and laced her fingers together primly. Sam stared into her sapphire eyes for a full minute while she appeared to collect her thoughts. He'd noticed her in her eatery, watched her efficiently handling customers. The woman knew how to run a business. Her way with people had impressed him almost as much as had her slender waist and the swell of curvy breasts and hips beneath her aprons.

He took a step back, for her sake or his, he didn't know. This was the first time he'd seen her without her apron, and he appreciated her feminine form in her plain blue dress. She didn't need fancy frippery to enhance her looks. In fact, anything that distracted from her exotic-colored hair and lovely features would be a shame.

"I was generalizing," she said finally.

Sam's thoughts veered back on track. This young woman obviously felt very strongly about her mission or she wouldn't have come to him. "Look, I'm sorry these kids lost their pa," he told her. "I don't think it's fair of you to blame me for it, though. I barely knew the man."

"They have nowhere to go," she told him. "They're orphans with no place to live and no one to take care of them."

"And I told you to report it to the sheriff."

"And send them to an orphanage?"

"I don't know what you expect me to do. Even if I knew, I have a feeling your expectation would be something I'm not going to do anyway."

"I want you to take some responsibility."

"I am not responsible. Now, if you've come here for my help, that's another matter. You want me to go to the sheriff for you, fine. I'll talk to him tomorrow."

"No, I don't want you to talk to the sheriff!"

"What then? You think I have money, so you've come to see how much you can get from me? I support the causes I believe are important, but I don't just give money to anyone who claims to have a need. If I did that, I'd be broke in no time. I'm sure your children are deserving, and I can give something to get them by until they have a place to live."

"*I* don't want a penny of your money, Mr. Calhoun," she said, her pretty feathers really in a ruffle now. "I take care of myself quite nicely and have no unrealistic dreams of sudden fortune. These children, however, are the victims of the way of life that I've managed to escape."

Exasperated, Sam took another step forward. "What exactly is it you want from me, Miss Emery?"

A pulse at the base of her slender throat beat above her plain collar. Color had risen high on her ivory cheeks.

"You want me to take responsibility for something I'm not responsible for. If I admitted I was at fault, what would you have me do? What is it you want?"

A frown crossed her features, only a momentary faltering of her confident stance and expression, but she collected herself and returned his stare. "I want you to admit you had a part in the fate of these children. Your business dealings propagate a hopeless way of life."

She had guts, he'd give her that. But he couldn't take on every person who had a problem. "I don't hold the future of every placer miner I've ever given a loan in my hands. What kind of crazy thinking is that? Now I have a party to return to, and a house full of guests who want to see more of my fiancée. We'd better get back."

She looked at him like he was the crazy one. "I'm not going back out there."

"What are you going to do? Hide in here the rest of the evening?"

Her gaze shot to the windows as though seeking a route of escape.

"You came in the front door. Walked through a

crowd. People would notice if you didn't leave the same way.''

''I wanted to speak with you.''

''Which you have.''

Her gaze raked over him with steely assessment. ''Which was like speaking to a bin of coal, for all the good it was worth.''

Sam took several steps toward the door and held out his arm in invitation. ''The food's good. Why don't you give me your opinion on the beef dish?''

Miss Emery glanced uneasily toward the door.

''What's your first name?'' he asked.

Her vivid gaze took in his features, roamed over hair and skin and eyes, all so different from her own, all attributes of his Sioux heritage, and he couldn't help wondering what she was thinking. Why did he care?

''*Ros*alyne,'' she said finally, emphasizing the first syllable.

''Rosalyne,'' he repeated. Feminine and yet sturdy, the name suited her. ''I ought to know my fiancée's name, don't you think?''

She lowered her gaze, lashes fluttering over those striking eyes. ''It was never my intention to mislead anyone,'' she said, almost contrite. ''I assure you, I did not tell those men at the door that I was your fiancée. That whole thing just—'' she raised her gaze to his, and this time it was apologetic ''—sort of snowballed, and the next thing I knew people were introducing me as your…your…'' A slack little wave of her hand substituted for the word she couldn't bring herself to say.

He really didn't mind people thinking he was promised to wed this lovely young woman. In fact, a fiancée might be just what he needed to get those matchmaking busybodies off his back for a while. Every eligible female from fifteen to forty had been shoved at him over the last two years. "Our acquaintance lacks trust so far, doesn't it?" he said.

She shrugged noncommittally.

"Seems you've made this situation and now you'll have to live with it," he said. "Do you really want your customers to know you've made fools out of them?"

Her expression showed her mortification. "You don't intend to let people continue to believe we're...engaged!"

"Unless you want to go back out there right now and say it was all a mistake and you just lied in order to get into my home, that's what they're going to think." He gestured toward the throng beyond his secluded office. "Go right ahead."

Her eyes widened and she shook her head. "I can't do that."

He strode forward and opened the door all the way. "Then you're my fiancée for the time being."

"I'm going home," she said, walking out ahead of him.

"But you've only arrived, sweetling." He took her arm, once again enjoying the feel of her beneath his fingers. Half a dozen people had already spotted them exiting the hallway. "I want to know what you think of the beef dish. It's almost as delicious as the pot pies you cook up in your eatery."

"They're just plain meat-and-vegetable pies," she said, but didn't resist his leading her toward the dining room where the buffet tables stood, laden with savory-smelling dishes and tempting desserts. The food had her interest, and before long she'd tasted a little of everything.

Sam wasn't the only one who found Rosalyne Emery an appealing young woman. He noticed the men, young and old alike, who smiled and greeted her, sneaking glances at her slender figure. One or two openly admired her striking mane of golden hair. Gathered into a loose knot, the precarious coiffure lent the sensual impression that it could cascade down her back at any moment.

Sam studied her as she balanced a plate on her palm and answered questions a portly banker posed, then pictured her hair flowing over her shoulders.

Catching himself, he looked away to compose his increasingly sensual thoughts and diffuse the physical effect that thinking of her in that manner was having on him. There. Trudy Billings, long-necked, gap-toothed spinster daughter of the banker from Carbondale; now she was enough to take the starch out of his libido. Trudy gave him a halfhearted smile, obviously disappointed at tonight's announcement, and he smiled back, truly pleased. With himself. With the reprieve from society's tiresome matchmaking.

With the idea that all these people thought he would be marrying Rosalyne Emery. Sam chuckled and joined her at the food tables.

"I'll see you safely home," he said to her an hour later, when she insisted she go.

"That won't be necessary," she replied.

"I can't let you walk home alone this late at night." George brought her coat as well as Sam's and then hurried ahead of them to a waiting carriage.

"That's George Randall," Sam told her as the man took the driver's seat. "He works for me."

"Obviously."

She wasn't sparing him an inch of friendliness, seeming only impatient to get away. "I'm glad you could make it this evening," he said as though she'd been invited. "I hope you enjoyed yourself."

Rosalyne pulled her collar up around her neck and ignored him.

"Where do you live?" he asked.

She gave directions and Sam relayed them to George. It was only a few minutes until the carriage pulled up in front of a small house where a dim light shone from a front window.

Jumping down before the horse had completely stopped, Sam waited for the carriage to settle on its springs and then reached up for Rosalyne. Even with her heavy coat, she didn't weigh much as he eased her to the ground. Snow blew in nipping flakes against their faces.

"I want you to see something." She walked ahead of him to her door. "Come in."

Surprised at the bold invitation into this young woman's home, Sam collected his thoughts, studying a tress of hair that had escaped her scarf. A spark of interest had definitely been kindled with this unexpected overture.

She took a key from her pocket and turned it in the

lock, ushering him into a tiny room where they knocked snow from their feet.

Sam took note of the simple furnishings, the homey touches and the warmth from a hard coal heater in the dining room. At the quiet intimacy, half a dozen sultry images rose in his mind's eye. His body reacted immediately.

She took his gloved hand and led him to an alcove beneath the eaves to the side of that room. His heart beat faster. He studied the plain wool scarf that hid her marvelous hair, imagined her long curls down and spread over ivory skin.

She tilted her head toward the bed, so he dragged his gaze away and looked.

There, snuggled warmly on a down mattress on an iron bed frame, lay two young children. Their cheeks were pink from slumber and their faces almost angelic in their youthful innocence. "You really do have kids here."

Rosalyne frowned. "What have I been trying to tell you? That's Alexandra," she whispered, pointing to the girl. "And that's Matt."

Naturally, Rosalyne Emery hadn't invited him in for a romp in her bed, as he'd deliriously imagined. She had a mission and she was nothing if not focused. How he had been chosen as her target for a helper, he had no idea. "Handsome children," he replied simply, unwilling to admit disappointment to himself.

Rosalyne drew off her scarf and in doing so mussed her hair. A long tress fell over her cheek. Without forethought Sam reached for it, taking the silken strand between his fingers and caressing it for a moment. He tucked it behind her ear.

Rosalyne brought a hand up to her ear where he'd touched her and raised eyes full of puzzlement to his. Her hair sparkled like gold in the light from a lamp on the wall.

The children's even breathing was the only audible sound in the room, but Sam's heart seemed to beat louder. If the children slept here, that meant she had a bed elsewhere. He shifted his weight and a board creaked. Rosalyne's eyes widened almost expectantly. Her gaze shot to his mouth and he felt the attention in his chest. Perhaps this was an offer after all.

Leaning forward, he lowered his lips to hers, and kissed her.

Chapter Three

Sam tasted her lips with inquiring gentleness. Surprisingly, she had closed her eyes and tilted her face. She drew a quick breath through her nose as though startled—at the sensation or at her acquiescence, he didn't know.

This close he could smell her...not perfume...faintly floral...more strongly, bread. And the clean outdoor scent of snow and cold clung to her still. He wanted nothing more at that moment than to enfold her in an embrace and feel her warmth against him, indulge himself in her womanly scents and textures.

One of the children made a mewling sound in their sleep and she drew away, her expression startled, but captivated nonetheless.

She'd liked it. She'd been a willing participant.

Sam smiled and took her hand. He pulled it to his mouth and kissed her icy fingers. ''Your hands are cold. Let's go into your bedroom and warm you up.''

Her eyes widened then, as though he'd slapped her.

She jerked her hand away and took a step back. "Leave!"

Confused, he tried to make sense of her behavior. "Isn't this what you asked me in for?"

"Certainly not! What kind of woman do you take me for?"

He'd turned away half a dozen women in the last month, all wanting something, all with their sights set on his money. At least this one was pretty, and there was something about her that drew him. He couldn't trust her, but he would sleep with her.

A snore erupted from a nearby room at that moment.

"Who is that?" he asked without replying to her question.

"That's Mrs. O'Hearn. You didn't think the children were here alone, did you?"

He hadn't known, hadn't wondered. He didn't know anything about kids. But Rosalyne's bed was apparently occupied, meaning perhaps she hadn't intended to take him there. Had he completely misread the situation?

She pointed to the door. "Get out of my house."

More confused than ever, he turned and opened the front door. A gust of freezing air blew in around his ankles. "Good night, Rosie."

She wouldn't look at him, didn't give him the satisfaction of knowing what she was thinking or of seeing her embarrassment. She pushed the door shut without a word and locked him away from her. Her heart thudded painfully, and she couldn't catch a deep breath. The entire night had gone impossibly, irreparably wrong, and her head had begun to pound.

Mrs. O'Hearn was sleeping soundly on Rosalyne's bed, so she guiltily left the woman to her rest and prepared herself a place on the divan. Her intentions of bringing Sam Calhoun to her way of thinking and convincing him to take responsibility for Matt and Zandy had been derailed to the point that she couldn't foresee a way to get them back on track.

She wished she could start the entire day over again and go back and change the mess that had developed. Head buzzing with distressing thoughts and images, she lay awake, unable to close her eyes without seeing something she didn't want to relive.

That horrible moment when she realized that those two men who worked for Sam Calhoun thought she was *involved* with him. Being introduced and hearing her name linked with his. Being called his fiancée. Getting nowhere with her pleas to his integrity. *Dancing.* His touch on her arm. Her ear.

Him kissing her.

Heat washed over Rosalyne's body at the remembrance of that sensation, and she kicked off the quilt. He'd been standing so close…so *intimately* close, and he was so painfully *handsome,* his features mysteriously dark and appealing…and she'd *wanted* him to lean over and place his mouth over hers…. Where had that innate desire come from?

Oh, my. If those lips on her fingers had been sensual and nerve-racking, the feel of them against her own had been more indulgent pleasure than one woman could bear in an evening. Firm and warm, like nothing she'd ever felt or imagined before. The kiss had been like an elusive dream, a sensation so vivid and exotic that it woke you and made you wonder if it had really been true.

She wondered now what it was she'd felt. What had happened to her in those moments? What spell had she fallen under that made her brain turn to mush and her body tingle and her thoughts be directed to things no respectable young lady should ever be considering, let alone doing?

But he'd obviously been thinking thoughts along the same line—and worse! He had been expecting much more! Apparently her behavior had been completely inappropriate and misleading.

She had to get her thinking back in line. Falling for his handsome features and coercing kisses wasn't taking her where she wanted to go, so she corralled her wayward thoughts and directed them elsewhere.

He had expected her to take him to her bedroom. The shocking realization paralyzed her. What kind of man accepted illicit invitations from women he didn't know? What kind of man thought every woman was out to seduce him?

A man like him, that's who. A man so full of himself that nothing or no one else ever entered his thinking.

That chunk of gold-veined quartz on his glossy polished desk had been enough ore to buy food and warm clothing for the entire population of a mining camp for the winter, and she'd never get the sight out of her mind. That's the kind of man Sam Calhoun was. Selfish. Concerned only with himself and his fancy lifestyle.

And by tomorrow the whole of Needle Creek

would think she planned to marry him. Rosalyne's heart turned over in her breast. What had she done?

"You did *what?*" Mrs. O'Hearn asked, leaning over to scoop enough flour from the barrel beside the stove to thicken a pan of gravy.

"It was a complete misunderstanding," Rosalyne hurried to explain. "I'm still not sure how things got twisted so badly. And I'm sorry that I was late last night. I'm glad you lay down instead of waiting for me."

"Think nothing of it. I got a good night's sleep. What have you decided to do about the children?"

Rosalyne had been worrying about the problem since last night. Right now Matt and Zandy were seated in the dining room, working their way through their breakfast. "Mr. Calhoun thinks I should go to the sheriff."

"Maybe you should."

"But I wouldn't want to see them placed in an orphanage."

"They are orphans, Rosalyne." Her tone wasn't unkind.

"But maybe the sheriff or Reverend Becker knows of a family who would take them in."

Mrs. O'Hearn shrugged, but didn't look hopeful. "Maybe."

"They're lovely children." Rosalyne paused in rolling out her last pie crust and stepped to the doorway to look out on them. "They seem awfully small and lost, don't they?"

"So maybe talking to the sheriff is a good idea."

Rosalyne wiped her hands on her apron. "Maybe.

I'll do it now, before we get busy. I'll just fill this last crust and stick my pies in the oven.''

Forty minutes later Rosalyne handed Seth Parker a covered plate holding warm cinnamon rolls. Eyes lighting up, the sheriff moved a stack of papers and a pair of spurs from the seat of a wooden chair and gestured for her to sit. ''Much obliged. What can I do for you, Miss Emery?''

She explained the situation while he peeled the napkin away from the treats and picked up a sweet roll to take a bite. He rolled his eyes and made an appreciative sound.

Rosalyne waited patiently while he finished the roll and licked each one of his fingers. ''You make bread and rolls just like my mama used to. Nothin' finer.''

''Thank you.''

''Shame about the kids' pa,'' he said finally. ''Happens more often than people'd think. Last winter a feller up the mountain got tossed off his hull and clean broke his neck. Had a wife and half a dozen kids holed up in a shack.''

''What happened to them?''

''I think she took a job at the Red Dolly. One of the kids died over the winter and maybe she sent the others to a relative. Can't recall for certain.''

His dismal story certainly didn't do anything to raise Rosalyne's expectations. ''What are the options for these particular children, Sheriff? Can you find them a home?''

''I ain't in the adoption business, Miss Emery. I can wire Denver, and they might send someone to take them off your hands.''

''And I suppose if they do have any relatives, the

authorities could look for them. What about until then?''

"I can put 'em in a cell, if you like.''

Aghast, she flattened her palms on her calico-covered knees and stared at him. "No, I wouldn't like! What a horrible suggestion. What about finding them a place to stay?''

"You can find 'em a place if you want to.'' He eyeballed the other roll on the plate. "People got enough mouths of their own to feed. Not likely anyone will want two more.''

"Well, I can feed them. Food is something I've got plenty of at my place.'' She stood. "I will try to find them a home on my own then. I'll ask around town.'' She paused on her way to the door as an idea came to her. "I'll place an advertisement in the newspaper.''

He shrugged and reached for the remaining cinnamon roll. "Whatever suits you.''

On her way to the newspaper office, Rosalyne drew up short on the boardwalk and stared blankly into the window of the dentist's office where a wooden Saint Nicholas smiled a red-painted smile. And what was she going to say? People purchased advertisements to sell things, to hire employees, to attract business, but they did not buy space in order to get other human beings off their hands. Did they?

Come to think of it, the papers published in the East sometimes carried wanted listings for brides. This would be a request for parents. Not so unlikely when one thought about it. A dire situation called for dire measures.

When she entered the newspaper office, Jack Tierney turned from a table where he was setting type and wiped his inky fingers on a rag. "Mornin', Miss Emery. Come to place an engagement announcement?"

She drew a blank for a moment, and then last night's debacle flooded her memory. The entire town knew already? They'd heard since only last night? Of course they had. Gossip traveled quickly in a town where everyone knew each other's business. "No," she said, heat climbing her cheeks. "I need to place an advertisement."

Jack took her information and her money without blinking an eye. "Yeah, heard about the pair o' curtain crawlers dropped on your boardwalk," he said with a shake of his head. "Shame, ain't it? 'Specially with Christmas comin' an' all."

If he felt such compassion, he could have given her the advertisement free of charge. Obviously his pity didn't extend that far.

He promised that her request would appear in the paper which came out on Monday. Only two publications a week were printed, and he'd already typeset the edition for today. "I could print a stack of flyers if you need them."

Rosalyne imagined flyers hanging on fences and how that would make the children feel if they saw them. She thanked Jack, but declined. Perhaps as a last resort.

Making a stop at the mercantile, she selected clothing, slates, chalk, two books and two pair of sturdy black boots, swallowing hard at the total amount charged to her account. She sewed all of her own clothing, but the children needed clothes immediately and she didn't have time to make them.

Back at her establishment, customers were filtering

in for the dinner hour. Rosalyne seated Matt and Zandy on the far side of the kitchen with crates for benches and desks, and instructed them to busy themselves with lessons. "After dinner we're going back to my place for a bath and a change of clothes."

"Do we gotta take a bath?" Matt asked. "It's winter!"

"I don't live in a tent," she assured him. "I'll stoke up the heater and warm your water, and you'll be plenty comfortable."

He didn't appear too certain of her promise, but fell to practicing letters on his slate.

"I can give myself a bath," Zandy told her. "And I can wash Matt, too."

"I'm sure you can," Rosalyne replied. "You're quite a capable young lady."

Zandy gave her a skeptical glance. "I took care of Matt all the time before...before..."

"Before your father died?" Rosalyne asked.

Zandy nodded, but she wouldn't look at her. "And I took care of him at the Thompson's, too."

Rosalyne knelt beside their makeshift desks. "I don't want to take away anything that you and Matt have together," she told her gently. "I only want to help both of you. I'm afraid the law won't let you take care of yourselves without an adult to help."

"I like you, Miss Rosalyne," Matt said with a charming grin. "I can prob'ly wash my own self, though. I'm a pretty big boy."

Rosalyne touched a finger to his freckled nose. "You are at that."

He grinned. Zandy avoided Rosalyne's gaze, and Rosalyne went back to her chores.

"You might as well send them to school," Mrs.

O'Hearn said as they dished up roast beef and potatoes for hungry patrons.

Rosalyne hadn't considered that, but school did make sense. The siblings would be in Needle Creek for at least several days or weeks, if not permanently, if no relatives were found, and they'd need something to do while she worked. They couldn't be expected to sit in a corner of the kitchen all day. "You're probably right," she replied. "I'll go speak with the schoolteacher after the dinner crowd leaves."

Carrying two meals through the open doorway, she caught sight of a pair of broad shoulders and a head of ebony hair. Dressed in a shirt, shiny black vest and dark trousers, Sam Calhoun was seated prominently at a table in the center of the dining room.

She placed the food before a couple she didn't know and hurried back to the kitchen for the coffee server.

"He's out there!" she said in a panic.

"Who?" Mrs. O'Hearn asked.

"That man," she choked out, heat engulfing her body and face. "Why can't he leave me alone?"

Mrs. O'Hearn peeked around the doorway. "You went to his home last night, dear. He's just here for dinner."

"He's not here for dinner. He's here to humiliate me."

Mrs. O'Hearn grabbed up two more plates filled with hot food, and swished past Rosalyne. "You'd better take his order."

Rosalyne filled everyone's cups before reluctantly threading her way back to the table where Sam sat waiting. In an angry whisper she asked, "What are you doing here?"

"Nice to see you, too, my turtle dove." He made no effort to keep his voice lowered, and the corner of his mustache tweaked up in an irritating smirk.

She glanced around, hoping no one was paying attention, but already the diners at the next table were staring. "Have you no conscience?"

"Should I be feeling guilty about getting hungry?" This smile was more genuine, flirtatious actually, the kind of smile a man would give the woman he planned to marry.

Rosalyne's face flamed. "What do you want?"

"The roast beef looks good. Do you have carrots?"

"Yes," she said through clenched teeth.

"Be prepared," he said seriously, and reached for her hand. Heat seared up her arm and she met his twinkling black gaze. "I'm staying for dessert."

Rolling her eyes and wanting to bolt in the opposite direction, she pulled her hand from his gentle grasp and walked away with dignity. The gall of the man, coming here when he knew she was being stared at and talked about and that all eyes would be on them. He was finding malicious pleasure in tormenting her.

An idea popped into her head as she was preparing his plate, and she turned. "Matt and Zandy, there's someone I'd like you to meet."

They placed their chalk aside and followed her through the doorway and into the dining room. Rosalyne placed Sam's plate of food before him. "Mr. Calhoun, these are the Baxter children. Alexandra and Matthew. Children, say how do you do to Mr. Calhoun."

The children greeted him politely.

"Sorry to hear about your pa," Sam said.

Matt nodded and Zandy blinked.

Sam's dark unreadable gaze traveled over their hair and clothing. "Miss Emery has a nice warm bed for you to sleep in?" he asked finally.

They nodded. "She buyed us slates!" Matt said excitedly.

"We have new clothes to wear," Zandy added.

"But we gots to take a bath afore we can put 'em on," Matt added, a frown showing his displeasure.

"You don't like bathing?" Sam asked. "Why, the washtub is a fine place for a man to think. And to sing."

Zandy giggled.

Rosalyne didn't know which reaction was more perplexing, Zandy's immediate acceptance of the man, or her own wayward thoughts. She immediately conjured up a picture of the big man before her, his sinewy body shiny and wet, lounging in a copper tub filled with sudsy water. Fire licked her cheeks.

"What's the matter, Rosie?"

"That's not a proper topic for the dinner table," she whispered.

Sam looked at Matt and shrugged. "You'd think we were talking dirty," he said with a grin.

Matt chuckled. "We was talkin' *clean*, wasn't we?"

"Soap-and-water clean," Sam agreed. He picked up his fork, then gave the children further consideration. "I suppose you two have already eaten your dinner."

Zandy shook her head. "Nope."

Sam laid his fork back down and glanced up at Rosalyne. "Miss Emery, will you bring them their dinner so they can eat with me, please? I could use some friendly company while I enjoy my food."

Rosalyne couldn't have been more surprised. The children scrambled onto chairs, and she hurried to fix them each a plate.

Zandy had been skeptical of Rosalyne, but she seemed to have no such hesitancy regarding Sam Calhoun. The girl had taken to him as though she'd known him all her life.

Rosalyne carried two plates through the doorway and immediately noticed half a dozen customers who had come in while she'd been in the kitchen. Taking note, she observed that they were all seated near the table where Sam was patiently waiting for the children's meals to be delivered before he dug into his own.

Staring straight ahead and feeling every eye on her, Rosalyne traversed the space to the table and placed their food before them.

"Thanks, Miss Emery," Matt said immediately.

Zandy looked from Matt to Sam, without picking up her fork.

Sam fixed her with a questioning look.

Zandy collected herself then and mumbled a thank you to Rosalyne.

"I don't suppose you have time to join us, sweet cakes?" he said, gesturing to the remaining chair.

The endearment tested her remaining shred of patience, and she struggled to keep her composure in front of the crowded dining room. "No, I don't, thank you. You may have noticed the sudden flood of patrons."

"Business is doing well, isn't it?" he replied conversationally, apparently blind to the fact that every eye in the place was focused on them.

"Remarkably well." The door opened as she spoke

and Jack Tierney, along with Chester Morgan who worked at the mercantile, removed their hats and hung their coats inside the door. Sam waved at his employee. "Unbelievably well," she added.

"Afternoon, Sam!" Chester called, striding to one of the last empty tables. The door opened again and a customer Rosalyne knew had already eaten earlier reentered the restaurant.

Apparently dinner hour had become the most popular entertainment in Needle Creek. Rosalyne hurried to take orders and instructed Mrs. O'Hearn to slice a ham while she peeled more potatoes. "I should be charging admission at the door," Rosalyne said in hushed tones.

Mrs. O'Hearn laughed. "Or charging more for the meals."

"That's right." Rosalyne plunked the last potato into the pot of boiling water. "From now on a slice of pie costs half a dollar."

"Do you think we'll sell any that way?"

"We only have three pies left," she answered, gesturing to the table where the remaining cloth-draped desserts sat. "It will sure narrow down who really wants a piece."

They shared a chuckle and Rosalyne hurried out to gather dirty dishes and silverware. They'd run out of forks with the last customer.

Zandy and Matt carried their own dishes to the kitchen. Rosalyne turned around after plunking a stack of plates into the dishwater and ran smack-dab into Sam. The plate he'd carried clattered to the floor, and he steadied her with his hand on her upper arm. "Whoa there, sweet pea. You're running around like a chicken with its head cut off."

"If you're not here to do dishes, get out of my kitchen," she replied, low enough so that only he heard.

"Noticed you're a mite backed up out there," he said and proceeded to roll up the sleeves of his crisp white shirt, exposing muscled forearms dusted with black hair.

"What are you doing?"

"Don't want to get my sleeves wet. Is the water hot?"

"I just added hot water and soap shavings," Mrs. O'Hearn replied cheerfully.

"Good." He plunged his hands into the basin and scrubbed at a plate.

Rosalyne gaped at the unlikely sight of Sam Calhoun washing dishes in her eatery.

Chapter Four

"**Y**ou might as well go wait on customers," Mrs. O'Hearn told Rosalyne matter-of-factly.

"Why are you doing this?" Rosalyne asked Sam with a puzzled frown.

He turned and his expression was as unreadable as ever, but his tone sounded contrite as he said, "It's partly because of me that you're overrun with customers today. I don't want you to make a bad impression on paying guests. This is a good business day. Make the best of it."

So he did know that all those people had come to gawk, and he was actually doing something to help. Rosalyne bit her lip and carried on with her work, distracted as she was by Sam's presence.

Another hour passed before the crowd thinned and people left to get back to their places of business. Sam hung a wet towel beside half a dozen others on a makeshift line between the stove and the back door and buttoned his cuffs.

"You goin' now, Mr. Calhoun?" Matt asked.

Sam knelt beside the sleepy child now lying on his pallet. "I have work to do this afternoon."

"Are boys asposed to do dishes?" the boy asked.

"Boys—and men—are supposed to do whatever it takes to get a job done," Sam replied.

"Oh."

Rosalyne finished cleaning the top of the stove and wiped her hands dry. Taking a calming breath, she managed to thank Sam.

He straightened and gave a nod. "Afternoon, ladies."

She noted his long legs and broad shoulders as he disappeared into the other room. A moment later the front door closed.

"I'd better go lock up until time for supper." Rosalyne hurried to the front of the building. Peering through the panes of frosty glass, she observed Sam Calhoun in his hat and coat, striding along the boardwalk on the opposite side of the street.

"Nice of him to pitch in," Mrs. O'Hearn said from behind her.

Caught staring, Rosalyne spun around. "I'll be going to speak with the schoolteacher now. Why don't you have a cup of that tea I brewed and put your feet up? Matt looked like he was ready to nap, and I'll find something for Zandy to do."

"That sounds like an ideal afternoon," her friend said with a smile. "I'll pull out my bag of embroidery work."

Rosalyne removed her apron, tidied her hair and shrugged into her coat and boots. During the brisk walk to the schoolhouse, she glanced around uncomfortably. It would be just like that annoying man to appear and further ruin her day.

Sylvie Anne Carter had been teaching school in Needle Creek for the past four years, ever since her husband had died of a fever and left her on her own. A reed-thin woman with warm brown hair and a pretty smile, she welcomed Rosalyne into her classroom.

Students of various ages glanced up from their books to observe the visitor.

"Eyes on your tasks, pupils," Sylvie Anne instructed them.

All of the children turned obediently back to their studies.

"What a nice surprise," Sylvie Anne said to Rosalyne. "Hang your coat on a peg and join me. I made myself tea, and there's enough for two." Apologetically, she blew chalk dust from a cup and filled it.

Rosalyne took a seat and presented her request in hushed tones.

"The Baxter children are most welcome," the teacher assured her. "They attended one winter a couple of years ago. As I recall, they were woefully behind the other students."

"I was afraid of that." Rosalyne had already surmised that their father hadn't cared any more about their education than he had about providing a home. "I don't know how long they'll be in Needle Creek." She explained that she'd placed an advertisement and that the sheriff had notified the authorities. It was no guarantee that a family nearby would take them. Or a family at all for that matter. So far, Rosalyne's efforts were based on hopes.

A sick feeling swelled in her stomach at the prospect of the law taking the situation out of Rosalyne's hands. Quashing those fears, she forced her focus back to the task at hand and thanked the teacher.

With the plans in place, Rosalyne set about giving Matt and Zandy the most normal life she could in the short time she would have with them.

That afternoon, with baths accomplished and both of them dressed in their new clothing, she told them about school.

"We getta go to school?" Matt asked, his expression one of pure pleasure. His fair hair had been trimmed and washed and slicked into order. "And I gotta new slate!" He flung his arms around Rosalyne's waist and hugged her tightly. "I *like* school! And I like you, Miss Rosie."

Rosalyne held his head against her midriff, his small ears cold from his bath, and experienced a pang of pleasure from his affectionate expression and sweet words, even if he had picked up an abbreviation of her name from Mr. Calhoun.

Zandy, who'd been admiring her store bought dress in Rosalyne's cheval mirror, turned her gaze to her brother and Rosalyne in the glass. She guarded her expression closely. "Thank you," she said stiffly.

"It's my pleasure, Zandy."

Matt released Rosalyne and picked up a carved horse Mrs. O'Hearn had given him. "I'm stayin' clean," he said before settling down to play.

"What about you?" Rosalyne asked Zandy's reflection, hoping to draw her out of her diffidence. "Do you like school?"

The girl quickly moved her gaze from Rosalyne's face to the new dress she was wearing. A shrug was her only reply.

With a swish of skirts, Rosalyne moved closer, but sat on the edge of her mattress. "Mrs. Carter said you'd been to school before."

She waited for a reaction.

Finally, Zandy said, "Didn't have a dress then. The other girls made fun of me."

A sinking feeling dipped in Rosalyne's chest. She understood only too well. "That was very unkind of them," she said.

Zandy shrugged again and didn't meet Rosalyne's eyes.

"Your hair is dry now. Let's brush it out." Rosalyne stood to find a hairbrush and stepped behind the child. Slowly, she drew the bristles through Zandy's shiny pale tresses. Her hair had needed only a good washing and detangling to bring out the rich texture. "You have beautiful hair."

In the mirror, the girl's gaze went to Rosalyne's hair. "Not as pretty as yours."

Rosalyne smiled, but disagreed. "Oh, yes, as pretty as mine. Prettier."

She parted Zandy's hair down the center of her head and plaited two perfect braids, tying each with a bright-red ribbon.

"I grew up in a mining camp, too," Rosalyne told her.

"You did?"

"Mm-hmm."

"You didn't have a house?"

"No. I didn't have a nice dress, either. I had old ones that someone cast off. I was ashamed to go to school."

"Did you? Go, I mean?"

"Not much. I got lucky when I was ten and one of the women in the camp taught school during bad weather days. The rest of the time I had to help my father. But I learned to read and write and I borrowed books whenever I could. I was eager to learn about all kinds of things."

Zandy tilted her head to better see her hair in the mirror.

"You have a nice dress now," Rosalyne told her. "And I'll make you some more. We'll pick out the fabric together."

"I like the dress," Zandy told her. "But I'm not smart. They'll make fun of me because I'm dumb."

Rosalyne took Zandy's chin and raised it until the child met her gaze. "You are not dumb. You are every bit as smart as any other child in this whole entire town. In all of Colorado for that matter! You may not have had the opportunities that the other children have had, but that doesn't make you any less smart. As soon as you've had a chance to read and study, you'll be the brightest student of all."

Zandy gave her a hesitant smile.

"And you're definitely the prettiest."

The girl's next smile was genuine.

"And," Rosalyne added, "anyone who says different will have to deal with me."

She still hadn't won Zandy's confidence or approval entirely, but in the days that followed, the child's will to make Rosalyne's predictions fact was strong. She attended school and brought home books and assignments and even helped her younger brother.

Rosalyne's advertisement appeared in the promised editions of the newspaper, but no one responded. Sheriff Parker arrived one afternoon just as the diners were thinning out. "Miss Emery," he said, hanging his hat and coat and taking a seat.

Rosalyne poured him a cup of coffee. "Would you like a meal?" she asked.

"I'd take one of those cinnamon rolls," he replied, and she hurried to serve him.

"Had a telegram today," he said. "Seems the Thompsons had been in touch with the law in Denver, too. They didn't turn up any family for the youngins."

Rosalyne sank onto a seat across from the sheriff. "You don't think they'll come now to take them to an orphanage, do you?"

"Nah," he said around a sweet bite of roll, and licked his fingers. "They didn't come when the Thompsons had 'em, they ain't gonna come now. Not unless we ask 'em to."

Well, then, she was just going to have to increase her efforts to find them a new family.

By the middle of the week, when she bundled up and trudged to the mercantile for her mail, she was euphoric over finding an envelope addressed to her.

Rosalyne stood in the store and tore open the parchment. The missive wasn't a letter at all, nor a reply to her advertisement. It was a formal printed invitation to a holiday party being given by the Greenes, the couple whom she'd met at Mr. Calhoun's.

After the initial disappointment had worn off, Rosalyne was filled anew with a measure of hope. Perhaps attending this social function and meeting a few more of the influential townspeople would be a means of finding a family for Matt and Zandy. She was becoming increasingly fond of them, but an unmarried woman wasn't the foundation they needed.

The same afternoon, she returned to the iron caged window at the mercantile and posted an acceptance reply.

The rest of the week she avoided Sam on the days he entered the eatery and deployed Mrs. O'Hearn to take over the dining room duties while she took over the kitchen. Rosalyne also hired a woman to come in for three hours over the dinner rush and help with the increased business.

Besides that, she worried. It would take a miracle to pull together an ensemble such as those worn by the women she'd seen at the Calhoun home. A miracle or more money than she could afford after having charged a tidy sum on her account for the children's necessities.

Mrs. O'Hearn provided the miracle. "I have a few gowns in my attic," she told Rosalyne. "I don't know why I've kept them all these years. I'll never fit into them again. You're perfectly welcome to make them over any way you see fit. I'll help you, in fact."

That night Rosalyne and the children went home

with Mrs. O'Hearn. Matt and Zandy were delighted to see the fireplace, and helped carry wood and sticks to build a cozy blaze. With books and slates, they made themselves comfortable before the hearth while the women hauled a trunk from the attic and Rosalyne exclaimed over the lovely gowns.

"I wasn't always a widow woman," her friend told her. "There was a time when I was young and pretty and my Henry cut a fine figure in a suit." Her expression and her tone were wistful.

"I love this one," Rosalyne said, running her hand over a gown in a shiny ecru and made of buff brilliantine.

"The scallops would have to go," Mrs. O'Hearn said, coming back to the task at hand and frowning at the outdated embellishments. "We could remove the collar and cuffs and add black velvet trim. Velvet is in fashion. Of course, you won't wear the hoop underskirts, so we'll have to take up the hem."

Rosalyne caught Mrs. O'Hearn's excitement and visualized the finished product, as well as how she would look wearing it.

After two nights of intense work, they had created a gown perfect for a holiday festivity. On Saturday evening, Mrs. O'Hearn, pleased to have company for the evening, kept Matt and Zandy with her while Rosalyne bathed and dressed and fashioned her hair.

The Greenes sent a carriage, and she accepted the ride with no little surprise. Apparently her supposed status of engagement to the richest man in town was providing her with a few amenities. Hopefully, she wouldn't have to address the fiancée quandary tonight.

But of course she would, she realized as the carriage drew closer and closer to the Greene's home. She'd been so caught up in making over her dress and planning to propose her cause to the well-to-do families that she had idiotically overlooked the fact that Sam Calhoun attended these fancy functions. A shiver of apprehension ran through her. It wasn't too late to change her mind.

She leaned forward, ready to tap the driver on the shoulder, when he drew back on the reins and guided the horse to a stop. Immediately, he jumped down and moved to assist her from the carriage. "Miss."

Rosalyne bundled her coat around her and took his gloved hand. "Thank you."

She paused on the walk, but the driver held her firmly by the upper arm, as though preventing a fall on the ice, and guided her to the door.

The door opened immediately. "I'll take your wrap, Miss."

Rosalyne relinquished her coat to a woman dressed in stiff black crinoline and a starched apron.

"Rosalyne, dear!" Mrs. Greene greeted Rosalyne and ushered her into a room where elegantly attired guests had begun to gather. "You are simply radiant this evening. The promise of matrimony is becoming on you."

Rosalyne thanked her with a skeptical smile.

"What an elegant gown," another woman said, moving close to admire Rosalyne's dress. "If I were twenty years younger I'd be insanely jealous." She stepped back as if taking in every detail of Rosalyne's appearance. "Not many women could pull off that pale color, but its very simplicity makes your striking hair and complexion decidedly breathtaking."

Rosalyne stroked the fabric of her skirts, somehow pleased with the effusive compliments. "Thank you. It was a gift."

A few more women had moved to surround her and together the crowd of females murmured and nodded.

"From my friend." She tried to clarify, but they'd made their own conclusions and were sharing sly smiles.

"I don't have to tell you what a striking couple you and Sam make," Althea Grady said with a wave of her gloved hand. "With his dark coloring and your unusual blond hair, why, I don't think there was a woman in the house last week who didn't sigh when the two of you danced."

"The way he looks at you," Trudy Billings said, her voice a combination of regret and admiration, "is the most romantic picture."

Rosalyne didn't know what to say, so she kept her silence and glanced toward the gathering of men, not seeing the black hair of the man she hoped to avoid. Thankfully the conversation turned to a couple planning an anniversary party. The women drew Rosalyne into their midst and included her in their whispered gossip and lighthearted teasing. From time to time, she scanned the room surreptitiously, relieved that Sam Calhoun didn't seem to be present.

When Mrs. Greene announced dinner was served,

Althea took Rosalyne's arm and led her into a long dining room with formal table settings.

"There you are," Althea said with a little push and started Rosalyne toward the table and the ivory card that bore her name in black script. Mrs. Greene had obviously worked hard to create an elegant table setting for this small-town gathering. Having grown up eating out of a bean pot over an open fire, Rosalyne felt decidedly like an outsider.

She smiled hesitantly at the gentleman who held her chair. He was mature with gray at his temples. Perhaps he had a son or daughter who would like to adopt two children. She hoped he would be sitting beside her so she could ask. She glanced at the place card beside hers.

The name printed there brought a roar of dread to her ears. *Sam Calhoun.*

Chapter Five

"**Y**ou look like an angel this evening, my bewitching sweetheart."

Sam's achingly familiar voice started a warm tingling deep inside, a tingling she didn't want to acknowledge...or allow. Instead of giving in to the first reaction that rose in her and firing back a saucy retort, she took a deep sustaining breath and shot his own ammunition back at him.

"Sam, oh Sam, my dear heart! What has taken you so long?" She reached for his hand and he stopped midway to a sitting position, his expression clearly revealing she'd stunned him.

Rosalyne hid a self-satisfied smile.

He lowered his weight to the chair and composed his handsome features. "I had a late meeting," he replied.

Belatedly, Rosalyne realized that by taking his hand, she had initiated a disturbing contact. His skin was warm against hers, his fingers engulfing. She knew three heartbeats ahead of the fact what he was going to do, and her heart hammered with anticipation.

With his black eyes boring into hers, he raised her hand to his mouth…and pressed his lips against the back of her fingers. She watched his mustache graze her flesh at the same time she felt the sensation. A corresponding thrill spiraled up from the center of her being and her breath caught in her throat.

He knew. His cocksure smile told her he knew the effect he had on her. He smiled against her fingers, his breath warm and damp, and the last thread of her composure snapped.

Rosalyne extricated her hand from his possession and glanced to see who had witnessed this embarrassing charade. When she unfolded her napkin, her hands were trembling, and she hid them in her lap. Focusing on the centerpiece of pine boughs and cranberries, she reminded herself of her purpose. She knew why she was here and why she would endure Sam's torment for another evening, but she had no idea as to the motivation behind his behavior. What could he possibly have to gain by this masquerade?

Rosalyne recognized the two young women who had been hired to help serve this evening. Both were granddaughters of the elderly woman who lived a few houses from hers. She had more in common with them than with anyone around the table, she thought ruefully, glancing from guest to guest, feeling like the imposter she truly was.

She considered the diners as possible parents for the Baxter children. Althea Grady and her husband shared a tiny home with her cantankerous mother, a situation that wouldn't be good for youngsters. Trudy

Billings lived with her parents, but Rosalyne had heard too much gossip about Trudy's father Robert spending all his evenings at the Red Dolly. That family was out. In moments she had rejected each guest as a possible guardian.

"How did the children do in school this week?" Sam asked.

Reluctantly, she returned her attention to him and calmed her betraying reactions to his nearness with a fortifying breath and a lift of her chin. "Very well. Zandy was hesitant because of past experiences, but she has courage."

"Did they tell you they'd seen me?"

She shook her head. "No."

He opened his napkin and placed it in his lap. "I stopped by the schoolhouse."

"Whatever for?"

"I always take a tree for the pupils to decorate."

She turned and looked at him. "Where'd you get a tree?"

He arched one ebony eyebrow before replying as though she were simpleminded. "The mountains are full of trees."

"I know that," she said, keeping her voice low. "I mean, how did you come by a tree?"

"I cut it down. Carried it."

Bewildered by the statement, she studied him in a new light. "You cut down a tree?"

"Yes."

Her gaze flicked over his elegant black vest and tie. "I'm having trouble picturing you with an ax."

Mr. Greene sliced a glazed ham and passed plates around the table. Sam held a glass bowl of spiced apple slices out to Rosalyne. "You don't really know me well enough to make judgments then, do you?" he asked, his voice audible only to her and his doting smile a complete contrast to the subject they discussed. Anyone observing them would think he was whispering endearments.

"I know your kind," she replied.

"Oh, that's fair-minded." He placed a serving of potatoes on his plate, a smaller one on hers, and passed the bowl. "I suppose I could say I know your kind, too. Would that be fair?"

"What do you care what I think of you?" Rosalyne asked.

He paused with his long fingers on his water glass. "I don't know. But your attempts to blame me for Matt and Zandy's circumstances seem rash and unfair. Forgive me if I take the accusation personally."

The woman on her other side touched Rosalyne's arm and spoke, and Rosalyne engaged in polite conversation for several minutes. When she looked back at Sam, he was speaking to Robert Billings about an upcoming local election.

By the time dessert was served, the men's conversation had wound down, and Sam turned to Rosalyne. "I hope our discussion didn't bore you, dumpling."

Mr. Billings was watching, so she smiled demurely. "Of course not, plum cake."

Conversation swelled around them, and Sam took the opportunity to lean toward her. "If you despise me so, why did you come? You knew we'd be seated together."

She wasn't about to admit she'd never been to a dinner this formal and hadn't realized the place settings would be prearranged. It had been dense of her to think she could avoid him. "I hoped to find someone willing to take the children. Now, I see that was a foolish thought."

"You don't see any prospective parents here?"

She shook her head and sighed. "No."

His plate was removed and he placed his napkin on the table. "What do you say we take them sledding tomorrow?"

She blinked. "Together?"

"You have something better to do?"

"Yes, well, Zandy and I were going to cut fabric and I'm going to show her how to use a pattern and sew a straight seam."

"I'm sure Matt will enjoy that," Sam commented dryly.

Rosalyne thought over his words and realized Matt would have a much better time getting out of the house and enjoying some fresh air than he would watching a sewing lesson. Zandy would probably enjoy the activity more, too. "Do I need to go along?"

Sam's crooked smile revealed his amusement. "Not at all. I'll come pick them up after dinner."

"All right."

"You're not worried that something will happen to them without you there to supervise?"

Truthfully, she wasn't concerned. She'd seen him with the children and had recognized, no matter how resentfully, the easy manner in which he related to them, as well as the way they had responded favorably to him. But some indefinable curious fascination spurred her to accompany them on this outing. "You're right. We'll all be ready."

"Dress warm," he told her.

If her body temperature while sitting beside him was any indication, heeding that instruction wouldn't be necessary. "Why do you want to take them sledding?" she asked, truly wanting to know.

"I thought they'd like to get out after their week of school...and getting used to the new routine." He lifted one shoulder in an expression of uncertainty. "I just thought it would be fun."

Fun. She considered his choice of words until he looked her way and she averted her attention.

The remainder of the evening went smoothly. Mr. Greene invited all the gentleman into his den for cigars and brandy, while in the parlor Rosalyne listened to the chatter of the women. Their world seemed a lifetime away from what she was accustomed to, and she felt more like an outsider than ever.

Conversation shifted to church activities, something Rosalyne knew a little more about. She'd kept to herself for most of her time in Needle Creek, but she did attend church services and help with special events.

"The children's practice is going well," Althea told the gathering. "They sing like angels." She turned to Rosalyne with raised eyebrows. "I understand you've taken in the Baxter children."

Rosalyne nodded. "Just until a family is found."

"Please make sure they come to practice tomorrow evening. There are only two more sessions before the Christmas Eve program."

"I'll have them there, thank you."

"A sizable Christmas donation was made to our agape box," Mrs. Greene said with a sly smile. "I think we should use a portion on the children, don't you, ladies?''

The women agreed wholeheartedly.

''And I'm sure the anonymous donor would approve of the cause,'' Trudy said with a chuckle.

The women laughed as though they were privy to a confidential joke. Rosalyne immediately felt even more out of place.

As the hour grew late, guests were given their coats and wished a warm good-night. Rosalyne stood on the walk beside Sam, staring at his carriage and his driver, George.

''I'll walk,'' she said.

''Nonsense. The Greenes expect me to see you home, and I will.'' Sam hurried ahead of her and brushed snow from the step.

She didn't want to speak to him, but the carriage was headed toward her home. ''The children are at Mrs. O'Hearn's. I need to go there first.''

Sam asked where the woman lived, then informed George. The driver guided the horses down the correct street and reined them to a stop.

Sam jumped down and accompanied her along the narrow path by walking behind her. He joined her on the porch.

Mrs. O'Hearn ushered them in with a smile and showed them the children sleeping on the floor before the fireplace. ''They've been asleep about an hour or so,'' she told Rosalyne. ''You could have left them for the night.''

''It'll be easier to get ready for church in the morning if I don't have to come for them,'' she replied, kneeling and tugging a bleary-eyed Matt into his coat.

Sam had gone back to the door and motioned for George to enter. ''George will carry Matt,'' he told Rosalyne. ''You go along and have a seat and he'll hand Matt up to you.'' Sam knelt and eased Zandy to a sitting position and helped her into her coat and hat before lifting her into his arms.

George covered the sleeping children with a blanket after Sam and Rosalyne were settled in the carriage. On the way to her street, Rosalyne looked over at Sam. The moonlight offered her a glimpse of his expression as he glanced from Zandy's to Matt's serene face. What was he thinking? she wondered.

Having children was an enormous responsibility and a weighty complication. In the short time she'd had them in her care, Rosalyne had discovered a dozen ways in which looking out for the Baxter siblings had changed the way she usually went about her life. The changes hadn't been bad, necessarily, but everything took more thought and planning.

Sam Calhoun's acquaintance, on the other hand, had been a burden she could have done without. The man drove her to distraction.

He and George took over carrying the children into her house, and Rosalyne instructed them to lie Matt and Zandy on their bed. She would tuck them in later.

George disappeared out into the cold and Sam wished her a good-night. ''I'll be by shortly after dinnertime.''

''I'll see you then.'' She closed the door and slid the bolt into place. Holding the curtain aside, she watched the carriage pull away and disappear into the night. It wasn't the children who had turned her world

upside down, she admitted to herself that night. It had
been Sam. And she had agreed to spend more time
with him tomorrow.

At least she wouldn't have to worry about carrying
on the charade on Sunday mornings, she thought the
following day; she'd never seen Sam inside the house
of worship. Long into the night she had wondered
how long this ridiculous caper was going to last. Already she was weary of the ruse.

While dressing the children in their clothes, Rosalyne promised them an afternoon outing. When they
arrived at church, the two were polite and well be-
haved, enduring introductions and Reverend Becker's
windy sermon that had even Rosalyne stifling a yawn
behind her gloved hand.

They ate a filling lunch of sliced bread, cheese and
tinned fruit, and then Rosalyne gathered warm clothing, extra socks and prepared jars of hot chocolate to
take along.

Sam arrived right on schedule, and Matt and Zandy
chattered cheerfully, pulling him inside and showing
him their new clothing and schoolbooks and the lessons they'd finished. Sam produced fur-lined hats and
mittens for the kids, as well as for Rosalyne, and
showed them his own.

Rosalyne accepted the gift with discomfort. She
didn't mind him giving the youngsters gifts, but she
didn't wish to be obligated. "You'll be glad you wore
them," he assured her, seeing her hesitation.

Bundled and carrying their supplies, the four of
them climbed into the wagon Sam had brought. A
long wooden sled with shiny metal runners had been

tied in the bed, and Matt climbed over the seat to sit beside it.

"You'd be warmer up here with us," Rosalyne told him.

"I'm warm enough back here." He held up his hands, covered with his fur-lined mittens. "I got these."

Sam guided the horses out of town. The day was bright and crystal clear, and a new snow had fallen overnight, making the countryside gleam.

"Where we goin'?" Zandy asked.

"You'll see," Sam replied. "I know of the best sledding hill in all of Colorado."

It took another half hour to reach their destination, and Rosalyne thought surely there'd been hills closer to Needle Creek than this one. But Matt and Zandy exclaimed over Sam's choice and vied to be the one to help him carry the sled.

An enormous sweep of unblemished snow carpeted the treeless section of hill to which Sam led them. Matt wanted to be first and Zandy acquiesced, as Rosalyne had noticed the girl did often where her younger brother was concerned. Matt readied the sled.

Sam pushed off, jumped to sit behind Matt, and the two sailed down the slope. Rosalyne couldn't help joining Zandy in a whoop of excitement as they watched. Their breath made white clouds when they laughed. Zandy's brown eyes sparkled with delight.

Zandy took her turn next, then when he thought they'd had enough practice, Sam let the two youngsters sled down the hill alone.

Rosalyne waved to them where they'd tumbled over into the snow at the bottom and picked them-

selves up, laughing. Sledding really was fun, just as
Sam had predicted. The children were having a wonderful time.

"They're having a good time," she said, acknowl-
edging Sam's wise choice in inviting them.

"They deserve to have a good time," he said, a
look of contentment on his face as he watched them
trudging up the hill.

The man was an odd mix of antagonism and kind-
ness, and Rosalyne had difficulty separating the man
she saw here from the one she'd always believed him
to be—a self-serving man, unconcerned about naught
but his own gain. "What are you getting out of this?"
she asked.

He glanced up at the wide expanse of blue sky, at
the conifers on the mountain ridges above them.
"You just have to enjoy some days without measur-
ing how much you're going to get out of them," he
replied.

Never in a hundred years would she have expected
that reply from a rich man like Sam.

"What are *you* getting out of this?" he asked. And
he turned his penetrating ebony gaze on her full force.

What indeed? "I get the satisfaction of knowing
Matt and Zandy are having a good time," she replied.
"That their physical needs are taken care of...and
hopefully their emotional needs, as well."

"And why do you care?" he asked, turning the
tables on her.

She glanced away and watched the smiling siblings
as they dragged the sled up the hill with red-cheeked
exertion. "I just do."

"Yet you want me to explain my every motive," he said.

She didn't reply.

"Your turn, Rosie!" Matt called. "Me'n Zandy are tuckered."

"Oh, no," Rosalyne disagreed.

"Come on, Rosie." Sam took her coat sleeve and guided her to the sled. "Let's show them how it's done."

Rosalyne's heart beat a little faster at the thought of whipping down that hill on those polished runners. She hadn't done anything so carefree in years. And it had looked...fun. "Well...all right."

She settled herself on the sled. Sam's arms came around her and he gathered the rope in his gloved hands. "Ready?" he asked, his breath warm against her cold cheek.

Her heart thudded. She nodded.

He shoved the sled forward and quickly leaped to sit behind her, his long legs on either side of hers, his entire body engulfing her from behind. The sled picked up speed and the cold wind whipped against her cheeks. Rosalyne shrieked with a combination of anxiety and delight.

Sam's laughter was a wonderful warm sound that echoed across the hillside on the tail of her scream.

At the bottom of the hill, the runners hit a dry patch of ground and the sled stopped abruptly. Sam and Rosalyne did not stop, however, and shot forward, tumbling and turning in a tangle of snow-caked coats and limbs.

When the sky above stopped spinning, Rosalyne became aware of the body moving beneath hers, of breathing as labored as her own. Frigid cold nipped her wrists and neck where snow had crept against her skin. Sam laughed again, and the chuckle built to a guffaw against her back. She was lying atop him, staring into the puffy white clouds. The children's delighted voices drifted on the crisp winter air.

Rosalyne pushed herself up and away from Sam, turning to look at him. His hat and coat were covered with snow, his eyelashes dotted with moisture, his cheeks red, his skin dark against the whiteness.

He looked so comical, she couldn't help laughing. He laughed, too, and she realized she must look every bit as funny as he, covered in snow from head to foot.

"Are you all right?" he asked finally, getting to his knees, then pushing to a standing position.

"I think so." She shoved herself up and he assisted her. She tested her arms and legs and found nothing except her dignity bruised.

Sam brushed snow from her coat, pausing before her to whisk the white dusting from her collar. She found herself staring up into his dark eyes, eyes filled with humor and…something more. Admiration? Appreciation?

"You're a beautiful woman, Rosie. How come no man ever snatched you up?" He leaned purposefully toward her, his face lowering seductively.

Chapter Six

A girl could drown in the depths of those dark eyes. "There are no men in this town that I'd want," she replied.

His gaze dropped to her mouth. Her attention riveted on his lips and the droplets of snow on his black mustache.

"None?" he asked.

Her heart dipped with delight at the prospect of the kiss she knew was coming.

She raised her mouth to his and he lowered his head. His mustache brushed her lip. His lips were soft, his breath warm against her cold cheek, a delicious contrast her senses were quick to respond to.

Rosalyne cast aside reticence and gave herself over to the pleasure of Sam's all-consuming warmth and passion. When his hot tongue took possession of her mouth, she curled her cold toes inside her boots and wrapped her arms awkwardly around his neck. An avalanche of sensation warred with her good sense and won.

Kissing Sam was the most delightful experience she could remember. Warm…sensual…fun…

Something hit her shoulder. Her leg took another hit, the blow an irritating distraction.

Frigid snow pelted the side of her face, and Sam released her abruptly, drawing back to consider the source of the interruption. Rosalyne looked up at him with disappointment sluicing through her veins, then followed the direction of his gaze.

Matt and Zandy stood several yards away, shaping snowballs and letting them fly.

After making sure Rosalyne had caught her balance, Sam moved away and bent to dip a handful of snow. "You asked for it!" he called.

Matt laughed and Zandy turned away as Sam let loose and tossed his first projectile. Both kids scooped snow and the playful battle was on.

The ardent moment having been interrupted, Rosalyne joined them. Eventually, when she saw that Sam was winning, she changed sides. They all grew weary and Sam gathered their tired little band into the wagon and drove them in a direction Rosalyne was sure wasn't taking them to Needle Creek.

They passed a canyon where cattle clustered together out of the wind, saw more cows and corrals and a barn before a log house came into view.

"Whose place is this?" Rosalyne asked, as Sam stopped the wagon in the snow-packed yard and a man walked from the barn to greet them.

"Mine," he replied, matter-of-factly. "Grab those jars of chocolate and we'll heat it up inside. Miss Emery, this is Frank Potter, the Double C's foreman."

"Miss," Frank said politely.

"How do you do," she said, then turned to Sam. "The children have to be back in time for Christmas program practice."

"I'll have 'em back."

She found the bag with the jars and handed it to Sam. He guided them into the house.

The children were tickled to learn that Sam had a house with a porch and a stone fireplace. "You live here, Sam?" Matt asked with childish enthusiasm.

"I've been staying in town mostly," Sam said.

"Do you got a dog?" the boy asked hopefully.

"There are a couple of cow dogs on the ranch," Sam replied.

"Can I see 'em?"

"Maybe another day. We're going to drink our hot chocolate and warm up and then you have to get back to town for your church practice."

Matt's face fell. "Okay."

Sam went about stoking the fire that had been banked in the stove.

Rosalyne found a pan and poured in the milk. The kitchen was well stocked and appeared as though someone worked in it often. "Who takes care of the kitchen?" she asked.

"Frank's wife, Jeannie," he replied. "She doesn't come over on Sundays, though. They have a little cabin to the south."

When the chocolate was heated, the four of them sipped from mugs in front of the fire Sam had built. Rosalyne's fingers and toes tingled as warmth crept back, and too soon it was time to go.

"Can we come back, Sam?" Matt asked.

"Any time," Sam replied. "Rosie, too."

Remembering their kiss, Rosalyne blushed and looked away.

Short of an hour later, Sam halted the wagon in front of the church and assisted all three to the ground. Matt and Zandy waved and ran up the stairs and into the wood frame building. A light snow had begun to fall, and Rosalyne glanced up through the flakes. Things with Sam had escalated out of her control, and she needed her security back. "We should tell the truth," she said. "Isn't it time we stopped this pretense?"

With a gloved hand, Sam brushed snow from her collar. One side of his lips curled into a seductive smile. "Maybe it's time we made it the truth."

Rosalyne's heart skipped a beat, and warmth crept into her cold cheeks. "You say the most outrageous things."

Turning on her heel, she hurried into the church.

Rosalyne barely listened to the children's practice, overcome as she was with the information that Sam owned a ranch. Maybe he'd bought it as another investment; anything else sure didn't fit into her idea of the man she thought she knew.

What did she know? He hadn't used a single one of those ridiculous endearments the entire time they'd been alone. Nothing about him was stacking up into a neat pile of facts she could reason over and dismiss. His behavior with the Baxter children had baffled her from the beginning. He truly seemed to enjoy them—

even care about them. He didn't seem like a man who sat at his desk counting the gold he was acquiring from down-on-their-luck miners who finally struck it rich. Nothing she'd seen had backed up her illusion of a devilish man who went about luring miners to exchange their souls for supplies.

His flirtatiousness, on the other hand, was shameless.

On Monday when Sam arrived at the eatery, Rosalyne took his order. Again, he dispensed with the phony endearments and gave her a smile that made her remember her cold toes curling inside her boots. Business was still good, but this week the rush of eager onlookers had slowed to a few curious gossips and a newly enlarged dinner crowd.

She wanted to insist they tell the truth about their fictitious relationship, but remembered his audacity the last time she'd brought up the subject.

People were now coming to enjoy her meals and not to gawk and whisper. Though Rosalyne would never tell him so, Sam Calhoun had actually done her a favor by starting this whole put-on and by persisting in eating his noon meals here.

"You said you couldn't picture me with an ax," he said as she poured him a second cup of coffee.

She rested the pot on a hot pad on the tabletop. Actually, after seeing him on the sled, the whole tree-cutting thing was easier to imagine. "Yes?"

"I wondered if you and the kids would like to go into the forest and pick out your Christmas tree. I'll cut it for you—I mean for *them*."

Rosalyne had never decorated a tree for her home.

She'd usually placed a small one in the corner of the dining room here. "Matt and Zandy should have a tree they can call their own," she said, thinking aloud.

"Saturday morning, then?" he asked.

She agreed with a nod. Mrs. O'Hearn and the new helper could handle the breakfast customers. "Saturday."

That afternoon, between dinner and supper crowds, Rosalyne bundled up and hurried to the mercantile for her mail.

"Nothing here for you, Miz Emery," Chester Morgan said, checking the pigeonholes on the wall behind the iron cage.

Disappointed, she leaned heavily against the counter. She shouldn't be discouraged. It had only been a couple of weeks. People were busy with holiday activities. Something would turn up after Christmas. This way she would have Matt and Zandy with her for this time of year, and she wanted that. It would be a treat to spend the holiday with them. Years past she'd attended the church service on Christmas Eve and then shared a quiet dinner with Mrs. O'Hearn the following day. This year would be special.

Rosalyne straightened and dug into her pocket. "I'll pay on my account while I'm here."

Chester let himself out of the post office cubicle and moved over to the counter where the ledger book lay open. He put on his spectacles, working the wire earpieces over his ears, then flipped the pages.

With one stubby finger running down the entries, he peered at the figures, then over at Rosalyne. "You don't owe anything, Miz Emery."

She took a few steps closer to see for herself. "That can't be right. I placed all of the children's clothing and boots on my account, and I've made only one payment since."

"Nope. There's nothing owed. You can see for yourself right here." He turned the ledger around.

Rosalyne read the neatly scripted list of clothing and supplies, the notation of a grocery order, a record of her payment with a balance. Below that another payment had been logged, the amount of which she knew she'd never paid. "I didn't pay this."

Chester shrugged. "It's paid. That's all I know."

Rosalyne tucked her money back into her pocket. Sam Calhoun owned this place and Chester worked for him. It seemed likely that Sam had made that payment, even if his employee wasn't saying anything or perhaps wasn't aware. "Thank you, Mr. Morgan."

Making her way out of the store and along the boardwalk, her first reaction was one of anger. Sam had denied responsibility for Matt and Zandy being orphaned, but he'd paid for their clothing—and for supplies for her eatery. There was no other explanation.

She glanced up and down Home Street. She didn't even know where Sam worked during the day—in the den of that enormous house? He owned the Red Dolly and the gaming hall. At one time she would have thought he'd spend his days in a saloon, but now she doubted it. Wait a minute, she thought, reining in her thinking. Confronting Sam had backfired in the past. Perhaps finding him wasn't even a suitable response in this case.

She had demanded that Sam take responsibility, and it seemed he had—to some degree, anyway. By absorbing her bill at the mercantile anonymously, he was able to maintain his denial of what she'd claimed was his duty. He wouldn't admit paying it, because doing so would be admitting his part in Matt and Zandy's fate.

Rosalyne didn't know what to think, but she chose to let this matter rest for the time being.

She didn't tell the children about the plans with Sam until Friday evening, in case something came up or he changed his mind.

Once they knew about the outing and the tree, they were ecstatic, questioning Rosalyne about ornaments and asking when Sam would be arriving. She tucked them into their bed and fingered their silvery-blond hair back from their foreheads. ''He should be here first thing in the morning, so go to sleep.''

''Rosie?'' Matt said as she turned away.

She sat back down on the edge of the bed.

''We never had a real Christmas tree afore. Will it be a big one?''

''My house is not very big,'' she replied. ''We'll have to trust Sam to cut us a tree that will fit under the ceiling.''

''Sam's a nice man,'' Zandy said. Her cheeks were pink and shiny from her washing.

Rosalyne couldn't disagree; Sam had treated the children well. She nodded.

''He doesn't have any kids or a wife or anything,'' Zandy informed Rosalyne. ''I asked.''

''And he gots a great big house,'' Matt added. ''I

seen it when Mrs. O'Hearn took me to the livery with her. Mr. David fixed a skillet for her."

"Maybe Sam wants youngins," Zandy speculated hopefully.

"You need a proper home with two parents," Rosalyne told them, not wanting them to entertain any impossible ideas about Sam as a guardian. "Sam has businesses to run and he's a very busy man."

"He has time for us," Matt argued.

"He could get a wife," Zandy suggested.

The thought disturbed Rosalyne in a way she didn't want to acknowledge. "There's plenty of time to think about that," Rosalyne assured them. "The right family will turn up, you'll see."

"Billy Morton said orphans got to live at the orph'nage with all the other kids what gots no mamas or papas," Matt told her, his lower lip quivering.

Rosalyne reached for him and he flung himself into her arms. His slender body was all knees and elbows, but he smelled little-boy good, and his hug filled her with tenderness. "Don't you let anybody tell you bad things," she said, caressing his hair as she held him close. "I won't let that happen. I promise."

Zandy gave her a teary-eyed smile and Rosalyne reached for her. The girl joined her brother in the comforting embrace. This first sign of acceptance gave Rosalyne a new surge of hope. She kissed her forehead and felt the beat of Zandy's heart against her own.

Rosalyne dashed away tears with her sleeve and tucked her charges in with a comforting smile. "No more gloomy faces. We're going to pick out our Christmas tree tomorrow.''

"Rosie?" Matt asked tentatively.

"Yes?"

"We get to stay here for Christmas, don't we? We don't gotta leave before that.''

"Of course you'll be here," she replied quickly. "We're going to spend Christmas together.''

"Sam, too?" Zandy asked.

Rosalyne didn't want to promise them something she couldn't deliver. But she did want to make them feel wanted and secure. "You can invite him, and if he's not already busy, maybe he'll come for a while. He may already have plans, however."

Her reply pleased both of them, and they didn't seem to hear her warning. She turned out the light and moved into her bedroom, the delicious slide of anticipation surging through her veins. She was as giddy as Zandy now, rashly hoping Sam would spend Christmas with them. It was just as silly for her to have unreasonable hopes where Sam was concerned as it was for Matt and Zandy. She was old enough and wise enough to know better.

But sleep evaded her as she thought about him coming early and spending the morning with them. Those kisses had shown her his interest wasn't only in the children. Rosalyne tucked her head under the covers and tried to hide from her thinking. She'd better find her good sense soon or she would be in a heap of trouble.

Chapter Seven

To Matt and Zandy's exuberant glee, and Rosalyne's secret pleasure, Sam arrived on schedule. Bundled against the frigid air, their little company set out for the forest that carpeted the mountainside to the south.

"Sam, will you come to Rosalyne's for Christmas?" Zandy asked as they climbed down from the wagon. "She said it was okay if you wanted to."

Sam glanced at Rosalyne, but she pointedly observed the scenery.

"Please, Sam?" Matt asked, jumping up and down.

"I'd like that a lot," he said, his voice soft.

Rosalyne darted a glance to see him smiling warmly at the kids.

"Are you sure?" he said to her.

Her stomach dipped. She nodded. The children wanted him there. "I'm sure."

"All right, then." Sam propped an ax over his shoulder and inspected more than a dozen trees that Matt energetically pointed out. A rabbit darted from a thicket of pine needles and Matt chased it up the hill while Zandy took over his job of selecting the perfect tree. "This one, do you think?" she asked.

Sam looked it over with a critical eye. "Looks just about perfect. Don't you think so, Rosie?"

Rosalyne nodded, thinking that it did indeed look like the perfect choice—a spruce with thick long needles and a round shape—not too high for her ceiling.

Matt returned to give his approving vote. Herding them several feet away, Rosalyne kept the children beside her while Sam chopped the trunk.

"Can I try it?" Matt called.

Sam let the boy try to lift the ax and take a few ineffectual swings, before assuring him he only needed a little practice and resuming the task.

Once the spruce was loaded in the back of the wagon, they clambered up and Sam directed the horse toward town.

"Rosie ain't gonna let us go to a orph'nage," Matt called up to Sam from his position in the bed beside the tree. "She promised."

The words reminded Sam of the situation they were facing. He turned and met Rosalyne's vivid-blue eyes. She'd made a strong promise there. He didn't know how she would keep it, but he had no doubt she'd do her best. Rosalyne Emery was a determined woman. And kindhearted and generous. Her concern and care for these two small people were proof of that.

She had taken them in and provided for them, all arrangements made with their best interests at heart. Once he'd gotten over his initial irritation at her storming into his home and demanding he do something, he'd come to appreciate the qualities that made her bold and feisty.

Any guilt resulting from the fact that he'd allowed the deception of their engagement to continue had been overrun by his unexplainable attraction to her. Keeping her close had become more important than letting her off the hook.

"Don't matter what Billy Morton says," Matt continued. "What Rosie says is what matters."

Sam raised an eyebrow in question.

"Billy Morton is a pupil who told Matt he'd have to go to an orphanage," Rosalyne explained softly. Zandy sat between them, and she cast Sam a silent brown-eyed entreaty.

"Rosie's right, as usual," Sam called back to the boy. "Nobody's going to let you go to an orphanage."

Zandy smiled and returned her attention to the road.

The two adults exchanged a look which hinted that this subject would come up again when they were alone.

Sam had shaken the snow from the limbs of the spruce and nailed it on a stand to hold it upright. He carried it into Rosalyne's house amid childish squeals of delight.

The tree looked so much bigger inside her tiny home, and he helped Rosalyne move a table and a sofa to get it situated just so.

"What do we put on it?" Matt asked. He'd discarded his coat and hat in haste and his hair stood up in tufts.

"We'll pop popcorn," Rosalyne suggested. "And make chains from colored paper."

She had to keep popping batches of corn, because Sam and Matt ate more than they got on the thread, but she did so with a cheerful smile. Sam's gaze was drawn again and again to the woman who talked and laughed so naturally with the children, and he wondered, not for the first time, why she hadn't married. He'd asked around some and had learned that she rarely had callers.

Rosalyne was a businesswoman, a successful one, and he admired that. Obviously she took her work, as well as most things in life, very seriously. He was sure this playfulness was a side not many men had been privileged to observe.

"Sam, will you come see us in the Christmas program?" Zandy's brown eyes were lit with excitement.

"Isn't it at church?" he asked.

Matt and Zandy both nodded. "Pu-leese?" Matt coerced.

Sam hadn't set foot inside the church since its construction. "I don't know...."

Rosalyne scooped fresh popcorn from the kettle into a bowl without looking at him. The children both gave him sad-puppy looks. What could he say? "Okay. I'll come."

Matt and Zandy cheered and knocked over the bowl of popcorn Rosalyne had just placed on the floor.

A pounding on the door startled all of them. Rosalyne wiped her hands on a towel and stepped to open it.

"Miss Emery, we got your pa at the jail."

Sam recognized the male voice as Seth Parker's.

"He's askin' for you to come," the sheriff continued.

Cold air rushed in with the sunlight. Sam got up and came to stand behind Rosalyne. Parker gave him a nod of recognition.

"What's he been accused of?" Rosalyne asked.

"Jumpin' Walt Wright's claim up Major Pass," Parker replied.

"Tell him I'll be right there." Parker turned away. Rosalyne closed the door and looked up at Sam, her cheeks bright pink. "I—I have to go."

"I'll stay here until you get back."

She took her coat from a hook, a confused look on her face, and hurried out.

Sam entertained the children for a while longer, but they were silent and Matt kept going to stare out the window. Raised in mining camps, they obviously understood the gravity of the accusation. To distract them, Sam bundled the children off to the eatery for lunch. Mrs. O'Hearn arranged a few tasks to keep them busy, so he left them in her charge and went in search of Rosalyne.

She was just turning into her walkway when he spotted her and called out. She waited for him to join her and let them into the house. He explained where the kids were.

"My father says he bought the claim," she told Sam, removing her coat and scarf and hanging them.

"Well, proving that should be easy," he said. "The

sale of a claim has to be witnessed by five disinterested parties. The sheriff can just ask the witnesses.''

"My father says there were no witnesses. He told me that Walt Wright signed the mine over to him for a pot of stew after they'd collected their traps one night and Walt was cold and hungry and ready to call it quits.''

Sam didn't have much trouble believing that. He ran a palm over his chin, while thinking. "Sounds like a logical story. I've heard of men who gave up and turned over their claims for less.''

"But he can't prove it," Rosalyne said. "Without any witnesses, it's likely he'll be convicted.''

Living in Needle Creek, they both knew the usual punishments for claim jumping: mutilation—or hanging.

Rosalyne had made no secret of her distaste for miners, and Sam was coming to understand her reasoning. She obviously didn't approve of her father's occupation, but the man was still her father. She wouldn't want him to come to harm.

"What do *you* think?" He leaned forward and touched her shoulder. "You know him better than anyone, right?''

She shrugged. "I don't think he'd steal anything. He'd sell every last thing he owned. He'd spend every cent and he'd borrow himself into debt, but I've never known him to be dishonest.''

Her opinion was good enough for Sam. "I'll go see what's coming together," he said, giving her shoulder a gentle squeeze. "A judge, jury, prosecutor and defender will be elected, and I'll bet they move forward right away, to have the trial over by Christmas.'' Maybe Sam could get himself elected as defender. If not, maybe just talking to the court would make a difference.

Rosalyne glanced around the small room. ''Thanks for the tree and everything,'' she said.

''You're welcome.'' Sam hesitated before moving toward the door. Rosalyne looked shaken over this latest incident, and she had every right to be. He came back and took her hand. ''I'll do what I can, okay?''

She nodded.

Unable to leave it at that, he reached for her and pulled her close. She came willingly, resting her head against the front of his coat, her soft weight molding to him as though she could absorb his strength. He regretted that he still wore his coat and couldn't enjoy the press of her lush body. Again, he noted that she smelled more like the fresh outdoors and vanilla than anything flowery or perfumed. He liked her simple feminine fragrance. He liked everything about Rosalyne Emery and he had ever since she'd barged her way into his house, her sapphire eyes spitting fire, and given him a piece of her mind.

Sam pulled off a glove and delved his fingers into the glossy thickness of her golden hair, loosening pins and knocking her chignon askew. Rosalyne tipped her head back and stared up at him, a question in her lovely eyes. He had no choice but to reply with a kiss.

Never a shrinking violet, Rosalyne raised an arm to drape around Sam's neck and hold him fast. He kissed her with all the tenderness and passion he was feeling, exhilaratingly alive to the feel of her soft warm lips, the texture of her hair, her sweet breath against his cheek.

"Sam?" she said, breaking the contact of their lips.

"What?"

She gazed into his eyes. "What does all this kissing mean?"

He touched his forehead to hers, but shook his head. He didn't know. And he had no idea where it was leading. "Hanged if I know," he said softly. "I just know it's good."

Rosalyne hugged him through his bulky coat. Stepping back, she repaired her hair. "I have to go to the eatery. Mrs. O'Hearn handled the place all morning."

"She was doing fine earlier."

"Nevertheless, I'll be joining her to feed the supper customers."

"Save me a plate. I'll be there after I find out what's going on." Sam turned and left.

As Rosalyne neared Home Street's Finest Eatery, a female voice called her name. Gathering her collar against the bitter wind, she turned, searching for the person bidding her.

"Rosalyne!" Althea Grady waved from the doorway of the mercantile.

Rosalyne waved hesitantly, then when Althea beckoned her, she hurried back several yards to join her.

Althea ushered her inside and closed the door against the cold. "I heard the news, dear."

Rosalyne glanced around the interior of the store. Chester Morgan was busy helping Robert Billings select a length of rope. "I suppose everyone has heard."

"No one doubts your father's word about buying the claim," the woman told her. "Old Walt Wright hasn't possessed all his faculties for some time now."

"Even so," Rosalyne replied. "The sale wasn't made legally, so that's my father's own fault."

"I'm sure something can be done."

"Sam is asking to be defender in the case."

Althea placed her gloved hand on Rosalyne's coat sleeve. "You can't ask for better help than Sam, as you know. Whenever he's involved, situations improve."

Rosalyne studied the other woman speculatively. "I don't know...."

"Sam's interest is the good of Needle Creek," Althea told her. "He'll help if he can. He helped with a mine dispute just last year. And he settled a problem with land ownership just last summer by purchasing the abutting section and donating it to the town council to divide as they saw fit."

"Sam gave land to the town?"

Althea raised both eyebrows. "My girl, Sam has given more than that little piece of land. He funded the church building. He owns both of the saloons, and even though the establishments are distasteful, Mr. Grady says they've increased commerce and grown the community. I know, I questioned the type of patrons who are drawn, but—"

"Sam Calhoun built the *church*?" Rosalyne said, having zeroed in on that fact and heard nothing else.

"It was my understanding that he'd never set foot inside the place."

"It's true he may have never attended a service," Althea admitted reluctantly. "But he contributes to the agape box and all the fund-raisers. Why he's the main benefactor."

"I had no idea."

"Well, he does it anonymously, but those of us on the committees know it's him. Mr. Grady also says Needle Creek's mercantile is the only one in a Colorado mining town that doesn't charge exorbitant prices for merchandise, and that's because Sam is a fair man who doesn't take advantage of people."

"Your husband thinks very highly of Sam."

"Very highly indeed. As do all the businessmen. Sam made this town thrive, but he didn't do it by stepping on anyone. But enough praise for Sam, I just wanted to assure you that people were not thinking the worst of your father."

"Thank you, Althea. I appreciate that." And she appreciated the information about Sam, too. If she'd known all that earlier, she might have treated him differently. Realizing that now made her seem like the shallow person.

After saying goodbye, she hurried back out into the cold and made her way to the restaurant.

Rosalyne washed the last supper dish and dried her hands on a length of toweling. She had scooted Mrs. O'Hearn and the children away after the customers had left. The three of them had gone to Mrs. O'Hearn's to pull taffy and give Rosalyne some time alone. She appreciated the respite, mindlessly performing her comforting tasks and enjoying her kitchen and her craft.

In no time, she had four trays of cinnamon rolls rising on the long table.

A knock sounded on the door behind her, startling her. "Who is it?"

"Sam."

Throwing open the door, she stood back as he entered with a rush of frosty air. "The trial will start tomorrow," he told her.

"A jury?" she asked.

"All elected this evening. Robert Billings is the judge this term."

"Maybe he'll be prejudiced because his daughter had her sights on you and they all think you're my fiancé," she worried aloud, remembering Trudy's wistful glances at Sam.

"Any decision is up to the jury," Sam told her. "The judge just keeps the proceedings in order. Charles Grady is the prosecutor, and I'm the defender."

"Althea's husband will prosecute?"

Sam nodded.

Althea had just told Rosalyne how much her husband thought of Sam. Already she felt better about how things would turn out. "I appreciate your help."

He nodded and glanced at the rows of baking sheets on the table. "Are you staying?"

"Yes, I'm doing the baking for tomorrow."

"Everyone's likely to be in court," he said.

She frowned at his logical reasoning, biting the tip

of her finger. "Maybe I'd better take the rolls to court, then."

Sam chuckled. "And bribe the jury?"

"Think it will work?"

"Yes."

They laughed together and Sam helped her brush melted butter over the tops of the pastries before she placed them into the hot oven. He kept her company and later joined her to gather the children and take them home.

"Everything's going to be fine," he told her at the door. "Get some sleep."

"Thank you, Sam."

She locked the door and readied the children for bed. She would send them to school as usual in the morning, and then she'd go talk to her father before the trial. She had long resented his foolishness and his greed. He'd never placed her first or seen to her comfort or education, but she didn't hate him for it, and she didn't want him to come to harm. It was time to let some things go. The bitterness had not solved anything. It was time to be honest with herself and make a fresh start.

The following morning, an enormous basket in tow, Rosalyne gave Sheriff Parker a roll she'd set aside for him and spoke to her father.

Wes stood when he saw her enter the hallway that held the cells, and approached the iron bars. "Rosie? I didn't think you'd come back."

She unwrapped a cinnamon roll and passed it through the bars. "I'm back, Pa."

He took her offering and tears came to his eyes. "I never did right by ya, I know that. Or by your ma, neither. I always wanted to. I always planned to buy us a big fancy house and a buggy and take you on trips."

She'd heard enough pipe dreams for a lifetime, but she listened.

"Don't seem fair a man can work rivers and streams his whole life and never pan more'n a few dollars here and there. And then there's them lucky sons o' bitches like that Calhoun feller who just fall into a gold mine without a minute's thought." He used his thumb to scratch several day's worth of stubble.

"What do you mean?"

"Some drunks was talkin' in here last night and they said Sam Calhoun found his gold mine by *accident*. By accident! Seems he was chasin' a horse what got scared off up the mountain and stumbled across a mother lode. Don't seem fair the bastard didn't do more'n mine enough to hire a crew and buy equipment and never panned a stream in his life. And the rest of us break our backs for chicken feed."

Rosalyne absorbed another shocking revelation about the man she'd imposed so many unredeeming qualities upon without ever knowing him. Sam had told her once that he wasn't a miner, that he just owned a couple of mines and she hadn't paid attention to the semantics.

"There isn't anything fair or logical about gambling," she said. "And mining is gambling. That's something you never could see."

"What do you think they'll do to me, Rosie?" he asked, not hearing her, as usual. "I don't have proof I bought Old Walt's claim."

"I believe that Sam Calhoun, the man you think of so poorly, is going to defend you and plead your case and get you off the hook. And that will be the most luck you've ever known." She turned toward the doorway to the office. "Sheriff, if you've finished your roll, will you please bring soap and water and a razor?"

"Prisoners can't have a razor, Miz Emery."

"I'll shave him myself."

"Right away, Miz Emery."

The Red Dolly had been transformed into a courtroom. Rows of chairs faced three tables arranged for the judge, defender and prosecutor.

Sam glanced at the bullet holes in the tin ceiling. Needle Creek should have a real courthouse; he'd been thinking on that for a while.

The citizens chosen for the jury began to arrive and take their seats, nodding to him as they sat. He glanced from man to man, remembering their names, their wives' names. Ranchers mostly, a businessman here and there. A few months ago, he couldn't have named as many townspeople as he could this morning. He had seen Needle Creek as "the town" he was determined to see grow. Now, through Rosalyne's eyes and because of her influence, he recognized Needle Creek as made up of individuals.

He'd been caught up in the politics of advancing the community, and somehow along the way he'd made friends and started to care. He'd aimed to place Needle Creek on the map, see her prosper and grow, and with the help of these good people, he'd done that. They'd done it together.

For the last year or so, he'd doubled his efforts, because something more important drew him. He wanted to go back to his ranch, live there, work there, get back to his horses and his real life. He'd worked at turning over more and more of the responsibilities and had recently found a partner he trusted to help. He probably would have moved back to the ranch by now if Rosalyne Emery hadn't made things here so alluring.

She entered the saloon ahead of her father and the sheriff, and she glanced around, as though seeing the interior for the first time. It probably was her first time; he didn't remember her ever coming to court for anything in the past. Come to think of it, few of the ladies ever came. Needle Creek definitely needed a respectable court building.

Rosalyne spotted him and gave him a shy smile. He nodded what he hoped was assurance and moved forward to take a seat at a table beside where Seth Parker had seated Wes Emery. Rosalyne sat close behind them.

Robert Billings made himself comfortable at the judge's table and read the charges. Charles Grady halfheartedly told old Walt's version of the story. When Sam's turn came, he stood and spoke directly to the jury members. "I'm not going to say anything bad about Old Walt," he began. "Wes Emery admits he didn't get five witnesses for the sale, and that was a big mistake.''

Rosalyne's father nodded gravely.

"But days and nights are hard up there in the mountains. It's cold enough to freeze to death in your sleep. Food supplies get short. Life being what it is, men don't always think ahead and sometimes they make mistakes. This mistake wasn't malicious. Wes Emery didn't hurt anyone. He traded some food for a deed to a mine.'' Sam grinned at the jurors. "Sounds like a story from the Bible, doesn't it? Cain selling his birthright for a bowl of his mama's stew. The boy was hungry and not looking past the moment."

Several of them nodded and grinned. Attention turned in a wave to Walt Wright, who shamefacedly looked at his hands in his lap and shook his shaggy gray head.

"Maybe two people made mistakes." Sam glanced pointedly from one miner to the other. "But since Wes had no witnesses, his ownership of the claim is not legal. In the spirit of the Christmas season, I suggest he is guilty of an illegal deed, but not of intentionally stealing it. If he's convicted, I highly recommend banishment from Needle Creek."

From her position, Rosalyne watched the faces of the citizens on the jury, all men who'd eaten in her establishment, sat beside her in church. They nodded and their expressions showed regret that they had to be here today.

Banishment was an extremely lax punishment for claim jumping in a mining community. Had Sam convinced them that her father hadn't truly jumped a claim? She folded her hands in her lap and dearly hoped so.

The jurors moved into a huddle, their boots loud on the wooden floor, their voices low as they discussed their decision.

Within moments, they returned to their chairs.

"Has the jury decided?" Robert Billings asked.

Mr. David from the livery stood. "We have."

"And what's your decision?" the judge asked.

Chapter Eight

Mr. David glanced at Rosalyne's father, then at Sam. "We find Wes Emery guilty of holding an illegal deed and we banish him from Needle Creek for five years."

Murmurs flooded the courtroom. Robert Billings nodded, glanced around and, when he didn't find a gavel, smacked the table with his fist. "So be it."

Five years? Rosalyne was astounded. The community hadn't chosen to hang her father or even mutilate him, and they'd miraculously set a time for when he would be able to return. Did their decision have anything to do with the fact that they respected her, as well as Sam? The suggestions had all been Sam's and the jurors had obviously taken his opinion seriously.

Ahead of her, Sam turned and their eyes met.

People had begun to stand and mill about and talk. She moved around a tall man to reach him.

"I think it was your cinnamon rolls," he said, his mustache quirking up.

"I haven't served them yet."

He shrugged.

"It was you, Sam. You did this, and you did it for me." There weren't words to express her feelings. "Thank you."

"It was the only fair solution, but you're welcome."

Rosalyne was surprised to find that several of the women had attended and were making their way toward her. Althea hugged her and Trudy gushed with praise for Sam's efforts.

It was noon by the time she found her father and Sheriff Parker beside the jailhouse. A sturdy bay, laden with a bedroll, supplies and a rifle, stood in the hard-packed snow. Rosalyne looked at the unfamiliar mount with surprise. "Whose horse?"

"Mine," her father replied.

"Sam outfitted him," the sheriff said. He gave Wes a strong warning about returning before his sentence was up and closed himself inside the jail.

Rosalyne looked over the horse and saddle.

"He's not such a bad fella," her father said.

"The sheriff?"

"No, your Sam."

"My—" Uh-oh, he'd heard rumors about their engagement and she hadn't thought to warn him that they weren't true. "He's not my..." Rosalyne's denial ran out of steam and her heart ached with having to state the facts. "We pretended to be engaged," she said. "It's a long silly story, but I was impulsive and rude and Sam made me eat my words. He challenged my thinking, and he...well, he changed the way I see things. A lot of things."

She looked at her father. "I have a good life," she

told him. "I'm happy here. I want you to be happy, too. I hope you find what you're looking for."

"I'm glad you're happy," he said. "You're a good girl, always have been." He squinted into the sun. "I'm thinking I'll head somewhere warmer for a while."

Remembering her intention, Rosalyne reached into her pocket.

Her father held up his hand. "You keep it, Rosie. And I'll send you money to pay you back for the other times."

"I don't want your money," she said.

"You'll get it," he promised. "And Sam will get his, too."

"Did Sam—er—grubstake you again?"

"Yep. He called it a Christmas present, but I said I'd pay 'im back. You wouldn't do so bad to *really* get yerself engaged to that fella, Rosie." Wes checked the saddle and harness and clumsily reached to shake her hand. "You take care o' yerself, girl."

Rosalyne leaned forward and gave him a hug. "You, too, Pa."

He climbed into the saddle. "If I find somebody to write for me, I'll let you know where I am."

"I'll write back," she promised.

Wes urged the bay forward and Rosalyne waved at his back.

She turned and trudged down Home Street to her restaurant.

She didn't see Sam for two days. Matt and Zandy had practice at church each evening, and Rosalyne stayed busy finishing their new clothing and wrapping the items in colorful paper and ribbon.

On Christmas Eve, Sam showed up as promised, greeted surprised parishioners and seated himself on the pew beside Rosalyne. The fragrant scents of evergreen and cinnamon were heavy in the air.

"Here I am, and the walls are still standing," he whispered.

"Don't put on so," she said smugly. "I happen to know that you paid for every board and nail and songbook in this building."

His lean cheeks actually darkened with embarrassment. He shrugged. "It was just dumb luck that I found a rich strike. I shared some of the good fortune."

"Are you sure it was luck?" she asked.

"I wasn't looking for ore," he said. "I was looking for a mountain lion and my horse spooked. I found him beside a glittering hillside."

Rosalyne glanced around the building. "And how many miners—how many people here, for that matter, do you think would have used their gold to build a church?"

He raised a brow as if to say he didn't know.

"But *you* did. So maybe finding the ore wasn't an accident at all."

"Divine intervention?" he asked with a skeptical grin.

"Perhaps."

"Think what you will," he told her.

"I always do."

"I know."

They exchanged a look before the pipe organ bellowed, making the pews vibrate beneath them. The lamps were extinguished in the rear of the building and the makeshift curtains up front parted to reveal children dressed as shepherds. The entire crowd hushed. "There's Matt," she whispered.

Sam showed his appreciation for every scene. He clapped and laughed and pointed and shared the evening with Rosalyne in a way that made her feel like they were part of a family. When refreshments were served, Sam joined the men while she poured mulled cider and coffee and doled out decorated gingerbread men.

The children made their way into the throng, and Sam bent to hug and congratulate Matt and Zandy, careful of her wings and halo. Both latched on to him and proudly held his hands or occupied his lap the rest of the evening.

"We're nearly out of coffee," Sylvie Anne Carter said to Rosalyne and Trudy. The schoolteacher's voice revealed near panic.

"It's a cold night," Rosalyne said. "Everyone's warming up. I'll just run to my place and make more. Won't take but a few minutes."

She gathered her coat and scarf and pulled on her gloves.

"Where are you going?" Sam asked, finding her ready to leave.

She explained the coffee situation. "I'll join you," he said.

They made their way through the lightly falling snow to the restaurant, where Rosalyne used her key to let them in.

Sam stoked the fire in the stove while she poured water into her big coffeepot and measured grounds.

They stood near the heat of the stove, waiting for the water to boil. Rosalyne turned up her face and found Sam watching her.

Light from the flame flickered across the features she'd come to love.

"I wanted to be sure that Needle Creek would be here after the ore was gone," he said to her.

She studied him with interest.

"Building the church and all," he explained. "So many mining towns flourish and then become ghost towns after the ore is mined out. I figured if we had businesses, tradesmen and even a nearby railway that Needle Creek wouldn't be one of those that disappears."

"Well," she said softly. "I think you did it."

"Not alone," he assured her. "Mine was sort of a selfish goal. I liked having a town near my ranch. I didn't want to see it gone in a few years."

"What about your ranch?" she asked. "Did you just leave it behind?"

"My intention all along was to get back to the ranch as soon as I could. I've been working toward that. The day of the party at my place—the one you came to—"

"Barged into," she corrected.

"That day I signed a partnership agreement. Now there's someone to take over most of the town business, so I can go back to my horses."

"Oh." Disappointment stole the warmth from the stove she'd begun to feel. A cold sadness settled in her bones. Once Sam returned to his ranch, she wouldn't see much of him anymore. "Well, I—I'm happy for you."

"You changed how I see things," Sam told her. "This isn't just a town to me anymore. It's a community of people."

"You saw the people all along," Rosalyne said. "If you hadn't, you wouldn't have shared so much with them."

Sam took her hand and held it between both of his, rubbing her palm. "You pointed things out that I hadn't seen," he said.

She shook her head in denial. "You're the one who helped me look at things differently," she finally managed to admit. "I jumped to conclusions about you, and I was all wrong. You have never deliberately set out to take advantage of anyone. If you grubstaked miners, it was because you had the money and they had the need."

"And maybe I'd get richer in return," he offered.

"I don't believe that was your motive. I was blind to everything but the hurt I thought I'd suffered because of my father's gold fever. I thought you were like him, but you're not. He never paid as much attention to me or to my needs as you do to the Baxter children's and they're *not* your responsibility. You're a kind man by nature." She gazed into his black eyes. "I'm sorry for accusing you of anything different."

Sam carried her hand to his mouth, and Rosalyne anticipated the touch of his lips and mustache against her skin. He did not disappoint her. Her eyes drifted closed with the pleasure of sheer sensation.

At her cuff, he slid the fabric upward and pressed his mouth to her sensitive wrist. A battalion of butterflies took up a cadence in her belly. His lips were more scorching than the heat of the stove.

"I made you play along with the engagement farce because I wanted to be near you," Sam confessed.

Rosalyne opened her eyes. "I was a shrew."

He uncurled her loose fingers and placed her palm against his cheek. "You were fire and ice," he whispered. "You were adamant and righteous and full of life and energy. You were beautiful."

She denied that with another shake of her head, but she couldn't tear her gaze from his.

"You *are* beautiful," he assured her. "I love to watch you pour coffee and stir gravy and just walk across a room. I love to watch you touch Matt or Zandy's hair. When you reach to tuck up a loose strand of your own hair, your breast rises just so, and I imagine it beneath your clothing."

Intense heat diffused Rosalyne's body. Her hand on his cheek trembled.

"When I close my eyes," he said, "I still see you, the heat and passion in your blue, blue eyes—eyes like no one else's on this earth. The curve of your cheek and the way your lashes rest against your cheek so delicately...the rosy blush of your skin when I say something shocking."

He leaned forward and pressed a kiss beneath her ear. A shiver turned to a tingle from her neck to her arms and breasts.

"I love you, Rosalyne."

The aroma of boiling coffee surrounded them. His words mingled with the warmth and the smell and the sensation of his mouth against her neck.

He leaned back ever so slightly to gauge her re-action.

Rosalyne opened her eyes and looked into his. Intense. Serious. Questioning.

"I love you," he said again.

The reality of his confession locked into her heart and overtook her with emotion. "And you thought you were the lucky one," she said softly, her trembling voice giving away her feelings.

Raising her hand from his face to his hair, she threaded her fingers against his scalp and pulled him toward her.

The kiss was tender and seeking, a mix of discovery and abounding joy. She had no misgivings, no doubts, no hesitation in her heart, and she showed him how she felt with newly awakened passion and fervency.

"I'm the lucky one," she told him, separating them only enough to frame his face and assure him. Tears smarted behind her lids with a confession that welled up and spilled out. "I love you, Sam. I love you so much it hurts."

Sam pulled her to his chest and hugged her so tightly, she lost her breath for a moment. He loosened the hold to spread dozens of kisses over her face, her eyes, upon her lips. "Marry me, Rosie. Please say you'll be my wife. I want to be with you for the rest of my life."

Nothing sounded better to Rosalyne. The rest of her years in the arms and in the life of this generous earnest man. She wanted nothing more than to say yes. But at that moment, his lips were against hers, his tongue seeking the warmth of her mouth. Minutes later, when they finally moved apart for breath, she gave him her reply. "Only if you kiss me like that forever."

"I will," he promised.

The coffee made hissing noises as it sloshed over into the flames, but they'd been oblivious until that moment. Rosalyne glanced at the spitting pot on the stove and they laughingly pulled apart to clean it up and grab hot pads.

They arrived at the church building out of breath, smiling ear to ear, their faces flushed.

"We're going to get married!" Sam shouted to the crowd.

Only a couple of heads turned their way. A few bystanders replied:

"We know that, Sam."

"Can't surprise us with that news again."

The only people in complete surprise were Matt, Zandy and Mrs. O'Hearn. The little troupe joined them and Sam handed the coffeepot off to Althea.

"You're going to marry Rosie?" Matt asked Sam. "For real and for true?"

"For real and for true," Sam told him.

Mrs. O'Hearn smiled and dabbed at her watering eyes with a handkerchief.

Zandy took Matt's shoulder protectively and pulled him away. "Let's go sit over there, Matt. The grown-ups prob'ly need to talk."

Immediately, Rosalyne understood Zandy's withdrawal. Still holding Sam's hand, she squeezed it until he met her eyes.

"Do you want to start our life together with a family?" he asked gently.

She nodded.

He smiled broadly. "Me, too. The state will grant us the adoption once we're married. We can be married as soon as possible. Or we can wait to plan a wedding and a honeymoon if you like. What's your pleasure?"

"I want to be married as soon as possible," she said. "We can always take a trip later."

Sam smiled into her eyes. "Let's ask them."

In a tiny coatroom that smelled of wet wool and leather, Sam and Rosalyne knelt and looked at the sweet faces of the children they'd come to love.

"Rosie and I would like to ask you something," Sam said.

"Okay." Zandy hadn't let go of Matt's hand for a second. He pulled it away now and rubbed his knuckles.

"I asked Rosie to marry me," Sam explained. "She had free will to say yes or no."

"I love Sam, so I said yes," she told the siblings.

"Just like I asked Rosie to be my wife, Rosie and I are asking you to be our children. We love you and we'd like to be a family."

"Live at your ranch, Sam?" Matt asked, his eyes alight with excitement.

Sam looked at Rosalyne. She nodded. "I'd love to live on your ranch."

"Yes," Sam told Matt.

The boy jumped up and down excitedly. "And the dog? Can the dog sleep with me?"

"We'll see," Rosalyne replied.

Zandy glanced from Matt's delighted face to the adults. "What if you get tired of us or we're lazy or naughty?'' she asked. ''Would you send us to the orphanage then?''

''No, Zandy,'' Rosalyne assured the girl. ''You don't have to ever think about an orphanage again for as long as you live. You'll be our children. We'll be a real true family. Sam and I will adopt you and we'll have papers that make it legal.''

''What if you and Sam have babies of your own?'' she asked, still obviously too skeptical to accept the good fortune without reassurance. ''You might love them and not want us no more.''

Rosalyne met Sam's ebony gaze, so filled with compassion. Believing he'd have the right words, she held her silence.

''Zandy,'' Sam said, taking the little girl's hand. ''Rosalyne and I will surely have babies. Babies are natural, a blessing that comes from loving. And we will love them very much. You will love them, too. But we won't love you any less. The more years people are together, the deeper their love grows. So *our* love will be deeper because it will have been around longer.

''And you can always remember that we *picked* you for our family,'' he added. ''We didn't just get you by chance.''

Zandy smiled then, the first completely uninhibited joyful expression Rosalyne had ever seen on her young face. Love and appreciation shone from her eyes and in her smile. She hugged Sam, and then Rosalyne, pausing to daintily kiss her cheek. ''I love you, Rosie.''

Rosalyne hugged the girl to her breast, Zandy's wire-and-fabric wings taking a bruising. Matt nudged his way into the embrace and Sam wrapped his strong arms around all of them. Voices from the outer room raised in a familiar carol. The sound, the smells, the love wrapped Rosalyne and her new family in a warm cocoon of peace.

When a loud commotion alerted them to the excitement in the other room, Sam straightened. "We'd better go see what that's all about."

Near the front of the church, children crowded around a stocky fellow in a red suit with fur trim. His snowy white cotton beard contrasted with his ruddy skin and dark brows. Something familiar about him nagged at Rosalyne.

"It's Saint Nicholas!" Matt shouted. Zandy took his hand and the two of them raced to where the well-padded fellow was jovially passing out gaily wrapped gifts.

Rosalyne followed at a slower pace, interested to see who was wearing the costume. A pair of dark eyes flashed at her and Sam. Sam chuckled.

"It's Stoney," Rosalyne whispered, and Sam nodded. The jolly man in the costume was indeed the man who worked for Sam.

Sam nodded at Stoney, and Stoney produced a small package from a hidden pocket and presented it to Rosalyne.

"What is it?" she asked, staring at the foil paper and ribbon.

"Open it and find out," Sam suggested.

Excitement making her clumsy, Rosalyne tore away the paper to discover a red velvet box.

Sam nudged her to open it. "Go on."

Inside the box, nestled on a bed of ivory satin, lay

a ring: a deep-red garnet with a row of diamonds circling the stone.

"Oh, Sam, it's beautiful," she breathed.

Enjoying the sapphire light in her lovely eyes, Sam stuffed the box and wrapping in his pocket then slid the ring on her finger. "Merry Christmas, Rosie."

"Thank you, Sam. Merry Christmas." They shared a brief kiss...a promise. Rosalyne Emery loved him. She was going to be his wife.

His heart swelled with joy.

Behind them the townspeople celebrated and sang carols. The children opened gifts and exclaimed over their treasures. Saint Nicholas improvised a remarkably good belly laugh.

Sam's vision for the town had been hollow without the love and companionship he'd found with this woman. Along with Matt and Zandy, she'd shown him what life was all about. Never had a Christmas season held as much meaning or given him such hope as this one had. He truly had much to celebrate, and much to give thanks for—especially thankful for this woman who would soon be his Colorado bride.

* * * * *

ELIZABETH LANE

Elizabeth Lane has traveled extensively in Latin America, Europe and China, and enjoys bringing these exotic locales to life on the printed page, but she also finds her home state of Utah and other areas of the American West to be fascinating sources for historical romance. Elizabeth loves such diverse activities as hiking and playing the piano, not to mention her latest hobby—belly dancing.

You can learn more about Elizabeth by visiting her Web site at www.elizabethlaneauthor.com.

Please address questions and book requests to:
Harlequin Reader Service
U.S.: 3010 Walden Ave., P.O. Box 1325, Buffalo, NY 14269
Canadian: P.O. Box 609, Fort Erie, Ont. L2A 5X3

JUBAL'S GIFT
Elizabeth Lane

For Pat

Chapter One

Arizona Territory
December 23, 1873

Jubal Trask paused at the top of the last ridge. Blinking the desert grit from his eyes, he scanned the wind-scoured flatland below.

The trading post was right where the storekeeper had marked it on the map. It lay like a scar against the scrub-dotted skin of the desert, a cluster of low rambling structures built of adobes that were the same rusty hue as the earth from which they'd been formed. Jubal could see the rutted wagon road that passed along one side of it, the L-shaped house and the jumble of sheds and corrals that lay beyond.

Rage tightened its grip on his innards as he stared down at the godforsaken spot. This was where Tom Curry had brought Lorena. And this was where, just four months ago, Lorena had died.

Nudging his tired horse to a walk, Jubal headed down the ridgeline trail. Now that she was gone, it was time to keep the vow he had made ten long years ago, on the day he'd lost his gangrenous arm to a surgeon's saw in that damnable Yankee prison hospital.

Could he really do it? Jubal forced his mind to dismiss the question. He had killed in battle and in self-defense. But this time would be different. This time he would be challenging a man to a duel and shooting him down in cold blood.

The very thought of such an act left a bad taste in his mouth. But this was no time to back down. He had sworn to see justice done. And if there was one person on earth he was capable of shooting, it was Thomas Curry—the man who had once been his best friend.

"Aunt Tess! Somebody's comin' down the trail!" Five-year-old Beau burst into the kitchen, letting the screen door slam shut behind him.

"Is it your father?" Tess Curry glanced up from the raisin pies she was taking out of the oven. Her brother Thomas had taken the wagon to Fort Defiance for supplies ten days ago. He had promised to be back within the week, but there had been no sign of him, and tomorrow would be Christmas Eve.

"It ain't Pa, and it ain't no Injuns neither! Just a white man on a horse."

"*Isn't*, Beau, not *ain't*." Tess wiped her floured hands on her apron, brushed a lock of dark-brown hair out of her face and followed her towheaded nephew toward the front door. Pausing, she stretched on tiptoe and lifted Thomas's long black powder shotgun from the rack above the door frame. A mounted stranger could mean trouble, and she had two children to protect.

"Where's Lucy?" She checked the double barrels to make sure the gun was loaded.

"Lucy's out by the coop watching the baby chickens."

"Get her and take her inside through the kitchen. Now."

"Yes'm." Young Beau knew better than to argue. The brightly patched seat of his denim overalls flashed as he raced off to fetch his four-year-old sister.

Tess kept her eyes on the approaching stranger as he wound his way down the rocky hillside—a big man, mounted on a long-legged blue roan. His face was shadowed by a low-brimmed hat, but even at a distance she could see the way his broad-shouldered frame filled the long canvas duster he wore. One sleeve of the coat hung loose and empty, flapping in the desert wind.

Tess felt the chill of that same wind as she stepped out into the yard. From the rear of the house, she could hear the bang of the screen door as the children scampered into the house. She gripped the gun tightly, remembering how to aim and fire it as Thomas had shown her. She had shot only at cans and bottles, missing them more often than not. Even so, she had no doubt that, at close range, she could blow a hole in anything that threatened Beau and little Lucy.

The breeze whipped at her drab gingham skirts and tugged locks of dark-brown hair from the spinsterly bun she wore at the nape of her neck. She was thirty years old and had led a quiet life since the end of the war, teaching history and grammar at Miss Fanshaw's School For Girls in Lexington, Kentucky. But everything had changed with Thomas's sudden bereavement and his desperate plea for her help—a plea Tess could not refuse.

Three months ago her days had been calm, safe and ordered. Now, in this desolate land where every living thing seemed to bite, sting or jab, danger was a constant presence; fear, its grim companion.

The lone rider was nearing the open gate. At close range he looked even bigger and meaner than he had from a distance. Tess could see the thick stubble of beard that darkened his jaw and hear the subtle flapping sound where the wind blew his empty coat sleeve against his body. As he entered the yard she could sense the dark aura that emanated from his presence, as if the Grim Reaper himself had just passed between the gateposts.

Trembling, Tess raised the shotgun to her shoulder and sighted down the barrels. "That's far enough," she called out. "I've got a bead on your chest, mister, and unless you want a big hole blasted through your rib cage, you'll stop right there."

At the sound of her voice the man halted a scant twenty paces from where she stood. Only his horse moved, snorting as it shook its massive head.

"Hands in the air," Tess ordered, bracing the weight of the heavy gun. "Then you can tell me your name and state your business."

The stranger did not stir, and Tess suddenly realized his eyes were staring at her intently from beneath the drooping brim of his hat.

"Tess?" His voice was that of a ghost, deep, hoarse, resonant, echoing from the shadows of her past. "Good Lord, what are you doing here?"

Tess was barely aware of her arms lowering the gun. Her entire body had gone numb. Even her heart felt as if it had ceased to beat. She stood paralyzed by shock as the stranger reached up and removed his dust-coated hat.

Time had weathered his features like the cover of a well-used book, etching furrows at the corners of his eyes, burnishing his skin to the hue of polished walnut and leaving flecks of silver in his tawny hair. But his eyes were even bluer than she remembered. There could be no mistake. She would have known him anywhere. His image was etched in her heart.

"Jubal…" Her quivering legs could barely support her. "Dear heaven, it's really you!"

A wry smile tightened the corners of his mouth. "What's the matter, Tess?" he asked. "You're as white as an undertaker's sheet."

"As well I should be." She gazed up at him, still reeling. "Thomas told me—told everyone—that he saw you fall at Sharpsburg. He told us all you were…dead."

In the silence that followed, Jubal studied her pale, earnest face, realizing that in the past ten years he had scarcely given a thought to Tom Curry's shy younger sister. The images that drifted back to him now were blurred by time. Tess, curled in a chair with a calico kitten in her lap and an open book in her hands. Tess, watching from behind a veil of spring willows as the boys wrestled and chased on the open lawn. Tess, glancing up at him from her needlework, her cheeks flushing at the accidental contact of their eyes...

In later years, at parties and balls, he had danced with her once or twice. But by then he had fallen in love with Lorena and had eyes for no one else. He had given little thought to the slim, quiet girl in his arms—the same girl, now a woman, who was staring up at him, her hands gripping the stock of the heavy gun.

"Dead?" Jubal forced a bitter laugh. "Do I look like a dead man to you, Tess?"

She shook her head, still visibly stunned. Her features were sharp in the slanting light, softened by the fullness of her mouth and the tendrils of dark hair that framed the pale oval of her face. What had happened to her in the years they'd been apart? Jubal found himself wondering. Had she married? Loved? Had children?

But what was he thinking? He had come here for just one purpose, and the longer he delayed the more difficult his mission would be.

"Thomas isn't here," she said, as if reading his mind. "He went to Fort Defiance for supplies. But we're expecting him back anytime. After all, tomorrow is Christmas Eve."

She lowered her gaze, her graceful throat moving as she swallowed. When she looked up at him again, her eyes were moist. "Oh, Jubal, he'll be so happy to see you, so surprised—" A tremulous smile lit her face. "But where are my manners, Jubal Trask? Put your horse in the corral—there's plenty of hay and water there. Then come inside for a bite of supper. After you've eaten, you can tell me everything that's happened to you.''

Cursing under his breath, Jubal steeled himself against her warmth. None of this was working out as he'd planned. He'd expected to confront Tom Curry, force a showdown and ride away—assuming he didn't die in the shoot-out. The last bloody thing he'd counted on was finding Tess here.

''My business is with your brother,'' he said gruffly. ''I'd best ride on and come back when he's here.''

''Ride on *where?*'' she countered. ''For heaven's sake, Jubal, look at your poor horse. He's nearly spent. Besides, I just took some raisin pies out of the oven, and I'm not letting you ride out of here without a hot meal and a good night's rest!''

Jubal struggled to ignore the tantalizing aromas that wafted from the direction of the low adobe house. He had not come here to be welcomed as an old friend. He had come here to settle a score with the man whose betrayal had destroyed his life. The smart thing would be to head out of the gate, ride up the road until he met Tom Curry and confront the yellow-bellied traitor before he had a chance to reach home.

But Tess was right about the horse—the big roan was too worn out to go another mile. As for himself, he hadn't eaten since dawn, and the mingling odors of fruit, cinnamon and fresh-baked crust were already making his mouth water.

''If it's propriety you're concerned about, there's a

spare room off the storage shed,'' Tess was saying.
''There's a bunk with clean sheets on it and there'll
be—''

She broke off, a sudden shadow clouding her face.
''Jubal, why are you looking like that? Something's
wrong! What is it?''

''Nothing,'' Jubal lied, mentally cursing her ability
to trap him in her innocent web. ''It's…been a long
time, that's all. I'll just unsaddle my horse, toss my
bedroll in your shed and wash up. Then I'll be hon-
ored to join you for supper.''

Tess's tightly drawn features relaxed in a radiant
smile. She was beautiful when she smiled, Jubal realized. But she was Tom Curry's sister; and Tom
Curry was a sneaking, lily-livered coward who deserved everything Jubal planned to give him.

He was wondering what to say next when the front
door of the house inched partway open to reveal two
small faces peering out at him from the shadows.

Jubal stifled a groan. He hadn't counted on children
being here. Cliff McBride, Lorena's cousin and one
of the few people Jubal had kept in touch with since
the war, had written him about his Lorena's death. In
the same letter, Cliff had mentioned that her small
son and daughter were being brought to Virginia, to
be raised by Cliff and his wife on the old family farm.
Jubal had assumed the children would be long gone
by now, and Tom Curry would be here alone.

Could these two youngsters be Tess's and not Lorena's at all? Jubal's spirit lightened, then abruptly
sank as Tess motioned the little boy and girl out onto
the porch. Emerging shyly, they stood side by side.

The boy's fair hair showed signs of darkening. He would look like the Currys when he was grown. But the little girl...

Jubal's heart ached as she stared up at him with the violet eyes he remembered so well—eyes set in a heart-shaped face and framed by a fairy veil of silver blond hair.

Tess's words confirmed what he already knew.

"Beau, Lucy, say hello to Mr. Trask. He's an old friend of your father's and he'll be staying the night with us, perhaps...." She glanced up at him, her dark eyes shining. "Perhaps even a bit longer."

Tess studied Jubal as he greeted the children curtly, almost brusquely. She could imagine what he was thinking. These were Lorena's children. If he'd come home after the war, Lorena would have married him instead of Thomas, and this beautiful girl and boy might have been his.

Why hadn't Jubal come home? And what was he doing here now? Did he know how Lorena had died, or even that she was gone?

So many questions. And so many tragic answers.

She stood with the children, noticing the proud set of his shoulders as he turned the horse and rode toward the corral. Even as a boy, Jubal Trask had been slow to forgive shortcomings in others—and even slower to forgive them in himself. The horror of the war and the harshness of the intervening years were written all over him. Had he lost the arm at Sharpsburg? Was that why he hadn't come home after the war? Was that why he had continued to let everyone believe he was dead—even his own sweetheart?

"Aunt Tess?" Beau tugged at her apron, his hazel eyes big and solemn. "What happened to that man's arm? Did the Indians cut it off?"

"Of course not!" Tess look sternly at both children. "Mr. Trask may tell us about his arm if he chooses, but you're not to ask him about it, do you understand, Beau?"

"Yes'm."

"And you're not to stare at him, either of you. Is that clear, Lucy?"

The four-year-old nodded gravely. She seldom spoke—a silence that had fallen on her when her mother died. Tess's heart ached for the little girl, but her efforts to cheer Lucy with toys, treats and affection had come to nothing.

As she shooed her niece and nephew into the house, Tess turned to see Jubal by the corral gate. He had dismounted and was unsaddling the tall roan, his strong right arm doing the work of two.

For all her admonitions to the children, she could not tear her eyes from his powerful figure. He moved with an awkward grace, unbuckling and lifting the heavy saddle with an ease that amazed and touched her. Dear, proud, wounded Jubal. She had worshipped him since she was no bigger than Lucy. He had always been first among her brother's friends—the strongest, the swiftest, the handsomest, the wisest and the kindest. Tess had loved him with all the passion of her innocent young soul. But Jubal had scarcely given her a glance. His eyes had been drawn to dainty, laughing, honey-haired girls; and when Lorena

McBride had come from Richmond to live with her uncle, Jubal had given her his heart.

Why had he come here? How much did he know?

Placing the saddle on the top rail of the fence, he slipped off the horse's bridle and moved around to open the corral gate. Only then did Tess notice the stiffened left knee that caused him to move with a pronounced limp. *Oh, Jubal...* Her lips parted in a small, silent cry of dismay.

By chance, Jubal chose that very instant to turn and look directly at her. His eyes flashed blue lightning across the distance, and Tess felt her heart drop. She had been staring at him—at the way he used his arm, at the way he walked. Jubal's pride would not suffer her curiosity, let alone her pity.

Once, in that long-ago world, she would have dropped her gaze and darted, crimson-faced, into the house. But Tess Curry was no longer the tongue-tied girl she'd been before the war. Her mind was bursting with questions that demanded answers—answers she might never get if she waited for Jubal to volunteer them.

By now, he had let his horse into the corral and was struggling to fasten the gate. The latch was a tricky one that could be worked only by lifting the sagging boards with one hand and sliding the bolt with the other. She could see the frustration etched across his face, but she knew Jubal would not welcome her help.

Never mind. She was going to offer it anyway.

Taking a deep breath, Tess squared her shoulders and strode across the yard.

Chapter Two

As she came up behind him, Tess heard Jubal cursing under his breath. He shot her a sharp sidelong glance, his eyes darkly dangerous, his mouth set in the stubborn scowl she remembered so well.

Resolving not to be intimidated, she moved closer, seized a low rail of the sagging gate and raised it to bring the two halves of the latch into line.

Jubal did not move. Tess could feel the tension in him, the electric contact where their bodies touched. She could feel his seething pride, his anger—not so much with her, as with his own limitations. That anger, she realized, had been his constant companion for long and bitter years. It had walked in his footsteps, slept in his bed and seeped like slow poison through every nerve, vein and fiber of his being.

Oh, Jubal.

Tess's mouth had gone dry. She held the gate level, her heart battering her ribs as she waited for him to slip the bolt into place. Her senses swam with his nearness—the low, taut sound of his breathing, the subtle aroma of mesquite smoke that clung to his canvas coat.

For the past ten years she had believed Jubal Trask was dead. She had mourned in lonely silence, holding his image in the most secret part of her heart. Now he stood beside her—the same proud bearing, the same riveting cobalt eyes, but a far cry from the Jubal she remembered. Had she not been gripping the gate, Tess would have been tempted to reach out and stroke the back of his hand, just to convince herself he was flesh and blood.

What would it be like to touch him—to feel him quiver beneath her fingertips like a wild animal poised for flight? But Tess sensed he would not want to be touched. Nor would he welcome anything that smacked of curiosity or compassion, let alone pity.

An eternity seemed to pass before he jammed the iron bolt into place, lowered his arm and stepped away from the fence. "It's been a long time, Tess," he said.

"Too long," she replied, grateful that he had broken the awkward silence. "Where have you been keeping yourself, Jubal?"

"Mexico." He squinted into the sunset that was painting the desert with brush strokes of mauve and flame. "After the war, I went partners with some friends on a silver mine. Last year I sold out for enough to buy myself a ranch north of Santa Fe. I just finished building the main house."

"Do you have family there? A wife? Children?" Tess could have bitten her tongue for asking so bluntly.

He gazed at the deepening hue of the sky, then shook his head, turned and began to walk. "What about you?" he asked. "A pretty woman like you wouldn't have stayed single for long, even with the war."

She pushed aside his compliment, knowing it was just a pleasantry. "Remember how Thomas used to say that if I didn't get my nose out of my books, I'd end up an old maid schoolteacher? Well, his prediction came true."

"You're joking."

"Not at all. I was in Lexington, teaching young ladies to use proper verbs, until...until Thomas's letter arrived three months ago."

Jubal did not respond this time. Faced with unsettling silence, Tess plunged ahead. "You're a long way from home, Jubal. How did you ever find us?"

"It wasn't hard. I just asked along the way until I found a storekeeper who'd been to the trading post."

"That doesn't answer my question," Tess said.

"I've kept in touch with Cliff McBride since the end of the war. He wrote to me now and again, when there was news."

Tess's throat tightened. "Then you know..."

"Yes. I know about Lorena."

He moved with surprising quickness, keeping pace with her despite his limp. Tess stared down at his dust-coated boots, her mind spinning.

If Jubal had kept in touch with Cliff, he would have known all along that Thomas and Lorena were here. Why hadn't he come to see them while Lorena was alive?

But she already knew the answer to that question. Proud Jubal would not have wanted Lorena to see him as he was now. And he would not have wanted to see the love of his life married to another man.

"The leg's all mine," he said, his eyes following the direction of Tess's gaze. "The Yankee doctor was able to save that, at least. But by the time they got me to the surgeon's tent, the arm was so far gone there was only one thing to be done."

Tess suppressed a horrified shudder. "What happened to you after that? Where did you go?"

"I spent the rest of the war locked up in Camp Douglas. That's where I met my mining partners. We spent our time making plans, and when the Yankees finally let us go, we lit out for Mexico. You know the rest of the story."

"Yes, I do," Tess lied, thinking how little she did know. The military prisons on both sides of the Mason-Dixon line had been living hells where men froze, starved and died by the hundreds. Even so, the prisoners had been allowed to write to their loved ones and to receive letters and small packages. If Jubal had sent word that he was alive, Lorena would surely have waited for him. Clearly it had been his choice to break off all contact with home.

Why? Had it been for the sake of his ridiculous pride? If so, that pride had cost Jubal dearly.

"The shed's right over there," she said, indicating a solid adobe outbuilding on their right. "It's something of a mess, I'm afraid, but at least it's cleared out around the bed."

"Where did you say the pump was?" He was making small talk now, filling the moments until he could break away.

"The pump's out back, just off the kitchen. And the outhouse is behind that clump of—" She broke off, realizing she had just spoken in a manner that would have horrified Miss Fanshaw and her girls back in Lexington. "I'll be in the house if you need anything. Supper will be ready in the time it takes to heat the stew, set the table and slice the bread."

His mouth tightened in what might have passed as a smile if his eyes had not been as cold as a January sky.

Tess had taken a half-dozen steps back toward the house when, struck by a sudden sense of foreboding, she swung around to face him again.

"Why did you come here, Jubal?" she demanded. "Why now, after all this time?"

His gaze narrowed, transforming his face into an unreadable mask. "It's too soon to explain, Tess," he said in a flat voice. "Or maybe it's too late. Either way, this is no time to talk about it."

Tess recoiled, stung by his bluntness. "Very well, I won't press you," she replied, hiding the hurt. "You're Thomas's oldest friend, and whatever your business, you're welcome here."

"Thank you." He spoke the words mechanically, giving her no comfort. As he turned away, Tess saw the wind catch his long canvas coat, lifting the front flap. Her heart stopped as the fading light glinted bloodred on the heavy-caliber revolver that hung at his hip.

* * *

The evening meal was simple but inviting—hot mutton stew with onions, carrots and potatoes and thick slices of crusty bread. Tess had insisted that Jubal sit at the head of the small table, in Thomas's place. She sat across from him now, with the children on either side. Lamplight gleamed on the sleek, dark wings of her hair.

Jubal bowed his head, staring down at the chipped, unmatched plate and bowl as the boy mumbled a few words of grace. Hell's bells, what was he doing in this house? Why hadn't he taken the trouble to make sure Tom Curry would be here alone? Cliff's letter, describing how Lorena had died in this miserable spot without a doctor, or even a midwife to attend her, had set him off like a fuse to dynamite. He'd flung a saddle on his horse and ridden west with just one thought in his head—to destroy the spineless bastard who'd ruined Lorena's life as well as his own. Now look at the mess he'd gotten himself into!

Glancing up as the prayer ended, he found himself looking directly into Tess's eyes. It struck him suddenly that she had beautiful eyes—flecked with copper, framed by thick, silky lashes and shining with an intelligence that seemed to pierce the depths of his black, wounded soul.

How could a man lie to such eyes?

Strange, he had never noticed her eyes in those early years. But then, there were many things he hadn't noticed about Tess until now. Her fragile shyness was gone, replaced by a womanly warmth that kindled an ache in his vitals—a yearning for all the sweet and tender things he would never have.

Under different circumstances he might have been interested in getting to know her better. But sparking Tom Curry's sister wasn't in the cards. He would be wise to keep his eyes, his thoughts and his hands where they belonged. He was going to hurt her enough as it was.

The children, too, were watching him—the boy with open curiosity, the girl shyly, giving him dazzling glimpses of her mother's periwinkle gaze. Resolving to ignore them, Jubal picked up his knife and began to butter a slice of bread. Getting entangled with Tom Curry's children would be just as foolish as dallying with his sister.

"Were you in the war?" The boy's question shattered the awkward silence in the kitchen.

"Yes. But it was a long time ago." Jubal took a bite of bread, hoping that would be the end of the questions.

"My pa was in the war, too," the boy said. "He was the bravest man in the whole army. That's what Ma told me."

Jubal dipped a spoonful of stew from his bowl, filled his mouth and forced his knotted throat to swallow. The stew was so hot it made his eyes water. Mentally he cursed.

Tess's eyes flickered knowingly. "Maybe Mr. Trask doesn't want to talk about the war, Beau," she said. "Why don't you ask him about something else?"

"Like what?"

Jubal felt her hesitate before she spoke again.

"Well, Mr. Trask has lived in Mexico. Why don't you ask him something about Mexico?"

"Like what?" the boy repeated maddeningly.

"Well…" She glanced hurriedly around the drab kitchen as if searching for some inspiration. At last her eyes fixed on an object that was just visible through the open doorway that led to the parlor. Following her gaze, Jubal saw that it was a raggedy-looking mesquite bush with its base stuck into a rusty bucket. Its dying branches were draped with strung popcorn and festooned with paper chains that looked as if they'd been cut from the pages of old magazines. At its top, carefully fashioned from wheat straw, was a single handmade star. Tess had clearly done her best with what she had. But even she was no miracle worker. It was the most pathetic-looking Christmas tree Jubal had ever seen.

"Perhaps—" Her face brightened desperately. "Perhaps Mr. Trask could tell us how people in Mexico celebrate Christmas!"

Jubal sighed, feeling cornered. Tess had rescued him from having to talk about the war but she was not letting him off without payment.

"Do they have Christmas trees in Mexico?" the boy asked, dutifully following her lead.

"No," Jubal said. "But they have a custom that's just as fine in its own way. It's called *posadas*."

"That's a funny name," the boy mumbled between bites of stew. "What does it mean?"

"Remember the story of Mary and Joseph and how they went from one *posada*—one inn—to the next, looking for a place to stay?" Jubal asked.

"Uh-huh. There was no room."

"In Mexico, every night for the nine days before Christmas, groups of neighbors walk from house to house, carrying lighted candles and little statues of Joseph and Mary. At each house, when the door is opened, they sing a song, asking for a place to stay."

Jubal paused, remembering. He had long since given up Christmas. But even he had enjoyed the haunting beauty of the *posadas* in the mountain village where he and his mining partners had rented a house. A fleeting sense of peace crept over him as he recalled the candlelit processions moving through the darkness of the winter night, and the echo of singing voices from the street below his window.

"At the first and second house they're always turned away," he said. "But in the third house they're welcomed with more singing. They go inside, and there's a celebration waiting for them, with a *piñata* for the children and hot punch for the grown-ups."

"All this is planned, I take it," Tess said with a soft smile. "Nine nights, you say?"

"Nine." Jubal nodded, warmed by her interest. "With nine different families hosting the party. But the last night—Christmas Eve—is different. After the *posadas*, everyone lights their candles and walks to the church for a midnight service to welcome the baby Jesus."

"Church in the middle of the night?" The boy's hazel eyes were incredulous. "I wouldn't like that much."

"You'd like it if you were there," Jubal said. "All those candles moving in the darkness like a river of stars. And every few feet, on both sides of the road, there are little bonfires to light the way to the church. *Luminarias,* they call them. The whole night is alive with light.''

"How beautiful that must be," Tess murmured, and Jubal noticed that, beside her, the little girl's eyes were shining with wonder.

"What about presents?" the boy asked impatiently. "You have to get presents for Christmas."

"Not in Mexico," Jubal said. "If you lived in Mexico you'd have to wait until January 6, the Day of the Three Kings, to get your presents."

"No tree and no presents!" The boy flashed Jubal a look of pure disdain. "Jehosephat! That's what my Pa would say. *Jehosephat!*"

He bent over his bowl and began sopping up the last of the stew with the crust of his bread. The little girl, who'd eaten only a few bites, continued to stare at Jubal with luminous, wondering eyes, as if he'd fallen from a star.

"Well, now." Tess spoke into the awkward silence. "I'd say it's about time for some nice warm raisin pie!" Her chair made a scraping sound as she slid back from the table, rose and bustled to the counter where the pies had been set out to cool. Jubal's gaze followed her deft, sure movements, thinking what a pity it was she hadn't had a family of her own. She would have made a wonderful mother, as well as a loving wife for some fortunate man.

What would it be like to love her? To kiss that ripe, serious mouth and bury his face in the soft, dark cloud of her hair? To nuzzle the silken sweetness of

*her breasts and hear her little cries of need as he
plunged into her tight moist, enfolding heat...*

But that kind of thinking was pure poison, Jubal
reminded himself harshly. He had come here seeking
retribution for the wrong that had robbed him of happiness and condemned the woman he'd loved to poverty, isolation and death. He had waited too long to
be dissuaded by this tender woman and these beautiful children. Lorena's children.

His gaze moved deliberately around the drab
kitchen, taking in the rickety table, the unmatched
chairs, the sunbleached gingham curtains at the window. If Tom Curry had provided Lorena with a good
life, Jubal might have forgiven him all the rest. But
he had brought her to this miserable spot, with no
friends, no neighbors, no one to help her in her time
of desperate need. In his bumbling, ineffectual way,
Tom Curry had killed his wife. For that, there could
be no forgiveness.

Not ever.

While Tess was clearing away the dishes, Jubal had
vanished into the night, muttering something about
seeing to his horse. After the awkwardness of the evening meal, she had not expected to see him again until
morning. But an hour later, when she returned from
tucking the children into bed, she found him waiting
for her at the kitchen table.

"I do believe there's a piece of that raisin pie left,"
she said, forcing a smile. "If you don't mind waiting
a few minutes, I'll make you some coffee to go
with it."

He shook his head. "I was going to use the pie as an excuse if I needed one. But the truth is, you've been far too good to me already." He shifted his weight on the creaking chair. "I was just hoping we could talk."

Tess felt her heart lurch. Years ago she would have bargained away her girlish soul to hear Jubal Trask say those words. Now they only made her uneasy. Jubal was hiding something, she sensed. Something dark and secret and frightening.

Something with the power to break all their hearts.

Chapter Three

"Why don't we go into the parlor?" Tess studied his face, reading nothing. "I have some sewing to finish before Christmas, and we can visit while I work on it. We'll be less likely to disturb the children in there."

He nodded, rising slowly from his place at the table. Tess reached up and lifted the lamp from its long metal hook, aware of his eyes following her every move. She could feel her heart battering her rib cage as she walked ahead of him into the shadowed room.

Oh, Jubal...

Turning away from him, she placed the lamp on a high shelf, letting its light fall on the rocker where she sat to do her sewing. Jubal settled himself opposite her in Thomas's sagging leather armchair, his stiffened leg thrust awkwardly toward one side. His eyes inspected the room, taking in the Navajo rugs on the floor, the mismatched furniture and faded cushions, the photograph of Lorena's parents, with its cracked glass that had been broken in the move from Virginia and never replaced.

The makeshift Christmas tree sat drooping in the middle of the room, a silent mockery of the grand holidays she and Jubal had known when they were young, in the years before the world changed.

Tess sat down in the rocker and took a handkerchief-size doll's dress from her sewing basket. She knew what he was thinking; and she chose to answer his question before it was asked.

"Lorena didn't have an easy life here," she said, looking directly at him. "But Thomas was good to her. He loved her. He did everything in his power to make her happy."

"And *was* she happy?"

Tess took her time threading her needle, lining up the ends of the thread and pulling the knot tight. "Do you want to know the truth? Lorena tried to be happy for the sake of her children. But I think she mourned you every day of her life. After you were reported dead, she waited a full year without allowing any man to court her, even Thomas, your best friend."

He made an odd little sound that seemed to be half growl, half cry. Tess continued to press him, driven by a perverse need to return some of the hurt he'd caused.

"Why didn't you come back, Jubal? Lorena would have taken you without your arm! She would have taken you without your legs if need be! As it was, we all had to pick up the pieces you left behind. We had to make do with whatever was there. Lorena married Thomas. I…" She shrugged, biting back the impulse to reveal too much. "Never mind," she said. "It's over and done with. We can't go back and change anything, can we?''

Jubal had not moved. He sat frozen in the chair as if her outburst had turned him to stone. In the stillness Tess could hear the rattle of a loose shutter, plucked by the night wind. She plied her needle into the delicate fabric, waiting for him to respond.

''Where are your war wounds, Tess?'' he asked, fixing her with a steady gaze. ''Did you love someone? Lose someone? Is that why you never married?''

Tess flinched as the needle pricked her finger. She lifted it to her mouth to keep the crimson bead of blood from staining the tiny dress.

''Tess?''

She forced herself to look at him, aching inside. ''Yes, I loved someone. And I lost him…in the war.'' *Not that he was ever mine to lose,* she added silently.

''I'm sorry,'' he said.

''In my case, it wouldn't have made much difference.'' She gulped back the surge of emotion that threatened to creep into her voice. Her fingers plied the needle furiously, creating a line of jagged stitches along the dress's ruffled hem.

''That strikes me as a lot of work,'' he mused, shifting the conversation to safer ground.

''It's for Petunia, Lucy's doll,'' Tess said, forcing a little smile. ''The children won't have much of a Christmas this year. I'm doing my best to make it special, and I'm hoping Thomas will bring a few little gifts back from Fort Defiance, but…''

Her voice trailed off as she thought of her brother, so distracted by grief that he could barely run the trading post, let alone provide Christmas for his children. And now he was fearfully late. What if something had happened to him on the long ride back from Fort Defiance? What would Beau and little Lucy do if he didn't return at all?

"Cliff wrote me that the children were going to come and live with him," Jubal said. "Don't you think they'd be better off in Virginia?"

"Perhaps. But Thomas wouldn't hear of it. He wrote me a heartbreaking letter, begging me to come here, so that he wouldn't be forced to send them away." She sighed, thinking of poor Thomas and the string of business failures he'd suffered after the war. This isolated trading post, in the middle of the Navajo reservation, had been his last chance. It had provided his family with a measure of stability, but little more.

"I don't see much evidence of business around here." Jubal spoke as if he had read her thoughts.

"It comes and goes. The Navajos seem to know when Thomas is low on supplies, and they don't come around. But when he returns from Fort Defiance they'll wander in to see what he's brought back. They're good people who appreciate honest treatment. Thomas gets along well with them."

"And the children? Are they safe here?" Jubal asked a bit sharply.

"As safe as they'd be in Virginia, judging from what I've seen. The Navajos appear to love children. And once you learn to watch out for snakes and scorpions, the desert can be a fascinating playground."

She glanced down at the tiny dress, which she'd pieced together from the hem of Lorena's worn-out petticoat. "Right now all I want is to get the children through this holiday with a few good memories. Last night we decorated the tree. I know it doesn't look like much, but they had a good time making the paper chains and stringing the popcorn. There won't be much in the way of presents, I fear. But if they can see that life continues, and that happiness can return even when you've lost someone you love…" She glanced up at him, her voice catching. "Maybe then they'll be all right."

"I take it they're not doing as well as they appear to be."

Tess shook her head. "Lucy's barely spoken a dozen words since her mother died. And Beau—he puts on a brave face, but when I feel his damp pillow in the morning, I know he's cried himself to sleep."

"And your brother?" The edge in his voice made Tess glance up, startled; but she saw that Jubal's expression had not changed.

"I worry almost as much about him as I do the children," she said. "He seems lost without Lorena. It's all he can do to get through each day. Oh, he'll be so happy to see you, Jubal! It will be so good for him to have you here. I do hope—"

She broke off as something flashed in Jubal's eyes—a torment so dark and so intense that it almost made her gasp. She gazed at him in the shadowy lamplight, struggling to see past the walled expression on his face.

"Why are you here, Jubal?" she whispered. "What happened to you back there at Sharpsburg? Did you lose your soul as well as your arm?"

He flinched as if she had struck him. For the space of a breath, Tess battled the impulse to fling herself across the gulf that separated them and enfold his tired head in her arms—to press his face between her breasts, bury her lips in the silvered tangle of his hair and caress away the pain.

But that would only make things worse, she admonished herself. She had loved Jubal Trask for most of her life, even after being told he was dead. But this new Jubal, this wounded ghost from her past, was a dangerous, wary stranger. She could not risk exposing her heart to this man.

She lowered her gaze to the sewing in her lap, forcing herself to think about Thomas's children and how much they needed her. When she looked up again her own serene mask was firmly in place.

"Lorena and her baby are buried on the knoll west of the house," she said. "It's a peaceful spot and not a far distance to walk. You may want to visit the grave while you're here."

Nodding, he stirred in the chair and shifted his legs in a prelude to leaving. Not that Tess could blame him. After the way she'd confronted him, any man would walk away from her.

"You must be tired," she said, offering him an easy excuse. "You've ridden a long way."

"Yes, I suppose I have." He rose awkwardly, pushing off with his arm and his good leg. Tess suppressed the urge to steady him. Images from the old days flashed through her mind—Jubal racing, climbing, swimming with the other boys, always first, always best. How cruel the years had been to him.

"Thomas is bound to get here tomorrow," she said, putting the dress aside and rising from the rocker. "He promised he'd be back before Christmas."

"Does your brother always keep his promises?" The edge in his voice startled Tess, causing her to glance up.

"Of course he does," she declared. "Unless something goes wrong—something he can't help. I'm praying everything's all right. Christmas will be hard enough on the children without their mother. To have their father gone as well—" She shook her head, the very prospect too awful to put into words.

"I'd like to earn my keep while I'm waiting," Jubal said. "You'll find I've learned to make one arm do the work of two."

"Oh, but that's not—"

Tess bit back the rest of her words. Jubal would want to be occupied with something useful. Refusing his help would only heighten the tension between them.

"I noticed some loose boards on the back of the coop," he said. "It would be easy for a snake or weasel to slip through one of the cracks and kill the chickens. A couple of your fences could use mending, as well. If you've got a hammer and some nails—"

"You'll find a tool bench at the far end of the shed where you're sleeping. Everything you need should be there."

"Fine. I'll get started with the work at first light."

"If you need it, there should be a candle on the table next to your bed," she added, moving back toward the kitchen. "Thomas keeps the matches on the ledge above the door, where the children can't reach them."

"I've no reason to need a candle. I'll be fine, Tess." He moved behind her into the shadowy kitchen. Moonlight gleamed through the windowpanes, casting a pattern of pale squares on the far wall. She was acutely conscious of his large, male presence behind her, the sound of his breathing, the clean, smoky aroma of his skin. His nearness triggered hot, shimmering sensations in her loins. For the barest instant she was tempted to turn and fling herself at him like a wanton little fool. What, after all, did she have to lose? She had long since abandoned any hope that she would ever love anyone else.

But what was she thinking? Jubal had loved Lorena, not her. And even now, it was Lorena's lovely golden-haired ghost who stood between them.

"I—should go and check on the children," she stammered, the heat rising in her face. "They go to bed nicely, but sometimes they have trouble falling asleep without a lullaby or a bit of extra snuggling. I know I'll never replace their mother, but I do the best I can."

"Sometimes I have trouble falling asleep myself," Jubal said with mock innocence. "Do your lullaby and snuggling services extend to guests?"

Tess willed herself to ignore the sudden leap of her heart. "Oh, stop it!" she exclaimed. "You were always such a tease, Jubal Trask! At least it's good to know you haven't lost your touch!"

The moment would have passed lightly if she had

not stepped on a miniature wheeled cart one of the children had left near the shadowed base of the kitchen cupboard. Tess gasped as her foot slipped on the rolling toy, throwing her off balance. She pitched sideways, and would have gone crashing to the floor if a powerful hand had not reached out and caught her waist. She felt the iron pressure of Jubal's fingers through her corset stays as he wrenched her upright. Still reeling, she stumbled the other way and fell hard against his chest.

In the grip of his arm, she struggled for a footing. His body was big and solid, his stubbled jaw rough against the tender skin of her forehead. The wood smoke aroma of his clothes surrounded her, cradling her senses in masculine warmth. For the space of a breath she closed her eyes. His nearness dizzied her, assaulting her reason with the ache of needs too long suppressed. It was all she could do to keep from wrapping him in her arms and holding him with all her strength.

Jubal, my dearest love…

"Are you all right?" His husky whisper jerked her back to reality. She looked up into eyes that were dark pits of shadow. His hand gripped the small of her back, pressing her tightly against him. With each ragged breath, his chest rose and fell against her breasts.

With effort Tess found her voice. "Yes—I'm fine," she stammered. "You saved me from a nasty fall. Those children and their toys—"

His hand moved against her back, drawing her upward. Her breath stopped as his head bent lower…lower…

"Aunt Tess."

They broke apart as the plaintive voice echoed down the hallway. Beau's flannel nightshirt and blond hair were just visible in the darkness.

"Aunt Tess, Lucy's havin' a bad dream. She's cryin' and I can't wake her up."

"Oh, dear—I'll be right there." Cheeks flaming, Tess spun away from Jubal and rushed down the hall. Beau's pale form floated ahead of her like a small ghost, leading the way to the children's bedroom.

Jubal watched her vanish into the shadows. For a long moment he stood in the darkness, listening to the rustle of her petticoats and the anxious murmur of her voice. His mind pictured her bending over the bed to gather the distraught little girl into her arms. Tess—warm and loving, strong and tender, with a quiet beauty that drew his eyes and stirred longings he had sworn to forget.

Jubal cursed under his breath. What in hell's name was he doing here? From the moment he'd ridden through the gate, nothing had gone according to plan. He had come here seeking satisfaction for a terrible wrong. Instead he had found these needy children and this long-forgotten woman.

She had felt so damnably good in the brief instant she'd fallen against him—the yielding softness of her breasts, the tiny span of her waist beneath his hand. Her hair had smelled of spring violets, and her husky little gasp of surprise had triggered a jolt of erotic desire. For the space of a breath, her nearness had overpowered his judgment. If that boy hadn't appeared...

Jubal sighed raggedly. Common sense told him that kissing Tess would have been a disaster. But even now, his body burned with the need to hold her again, to taste her satiny mouth, to feel her arms around his neck, her ripe, womanly curves pressing against him, molding to his heat.

Tom Curry's sister.

It was going to be a long night.

Muttering a curse, he turned and strode out the kitchen door, closing it softly behind him. The night was cold and crystal clear, the stars a spill of silver across an obsidian sky. Above the desert hills, the newly risen moon hung like a glowing *farolito*—the paper lantern that led every procession on the nights of the *posadas*.

In Santa Fe, where he had passed a winter, the people had put lighted candles inside small paper bags and placed them along the roads and sidewalks, leading the way to mass on Christmas Eve. Jubal paused as the memory crept over him—the black December night, softly glowing with a thousand lights, and, everywhere, the songs of wandering Christmas pilgrims….

The night wind stung Jubal's eyes. Its chilly fingers raked his hair, sweeping it back from his face. Tomorrow would be Christmas Eve. And Tom Curry had promised to return by the end of that day. What would happen when the backstabbing coward rode in through the gate to be welcomed by his sister and his children?

Jubal kicked a loose stone into the darkness, his emotions churning. Honor demanded retribution for

Tom Curry's despicable act—demanded it now. Christmas was a time of peace, but what did that matter? Jubal had not kept Christmas in more than a dozen years. The day meant nothing to him.

But it meant something to Tom Curry's children. And it meant something to Tess.

The shed was dark inside, its thick adobe walls muffling the sound of the wind. Jubal's saddlebags and bedroll lay on the narrow bunk where he had tossed them earlier. The slight bulge in the mattress beneath assured him that the heavy Peacemaker he'd brought was still there, safely hidden. Restlessly, he drew it out and checked the loaded cylinder. Even with one arm, Jubal was a superb marksman. Tom Curry, as he remembered, couldn't hit a two-gallon jug at fifteen paces. There was only one way their duel would end, and it would give him no peace. Nothing would.

Hiding the weapon again, he stood beside the bunk, scowling into the darkness. The day had been long and tiring, and he knew he could use some rest. But he was too uneasy to lie down, let alone sleep.

Behind him, through the open doorway, he could see the faint glow of lamplight through the parlor window. Tess would be at her sewing again. She would probably work late into the night, preparing Christmas for Beau and little Lucy. He imagined her there in the rocker, her graceful hands plying the needle along the ruffled hem of the tiny white dress, her copper-flecked eyes catching soft glints of lamplight. Loneliness hung like a black weight in Jubal's soul, and for a moment he toyed with the idea of wandering back to the house, just to sit with her, to watch her work and share the silence of the bleak winter night.

But no, that would not do. Either they would end up arguing again, or he would be unable to keep his hands off her. Either way, he was better off out here. Alone.

Something rustled in the shadows at the far end of the shed. A pack rat, Jubal surmised. If he didn't chase it outside, it could keep him awake all night.

Finding the matches, he lit the candle Tess had left on the table. Flickering light danced off the rough adobe walls, casting the jumbled crates, boxes and barrels into crazy-quilt patterns of shadow. Jubal sighed. The mess was typical of the scatterbrained Tom Curry he remembered. A pack rat could play hide-and-seek all night in this place.

As he moved toward the cluttered tool bench at the far end of the shed, his glance passed over a keg of rusted nails, some coils of dusty rope, a box of half-burned candles. Here was a pile of old harness leather, there a wooden crate half-filled with empty tin cans.

The hammer Tess had mentioned lay on the tool bench, next to an awl and a sturdy iron vise that was bolted to the battered surface. At least he had the tools for the work he'd promised to do. But Jubal found himself burning to do more. Something for her, for the children.

Something for Christmas, heaven help him.

His gaze wandered from the awl to the vise and from there to the tin cans and the box of candle stubs. The idea that had burst into his mind made no sense at all. He had come here to fight a duel, not to create a surprise for two children—a surprise they might never see if Tom Curry rode in through that gate tomorrow and things went as planned.

How could he do it? How could he carry out his grim justice at the price of three innocent hearts?

And how could he *not* do it, when his whole being cried out against the man whose betrayal had shattered his body and his future?

Did you lose your soul as well as your arm?

Tess's question lingered in the stillness as Jubal placed the candle on the workbench, selected an empty tin can and positioned it carefully in the vise.

Chapter Four

A chilly dawn crept across the desert, brushing the ragged gray clouds with flecks of rose and amber. As the sun rose, retreating shadows flowed across the stark landscape, leaving pools of night in rock-sheltered hollows. From the top of a glistening prickly pear, a solitary kestrel stretched its wings and soared into the sky.

It was the morning of December 24. Christmas Eve. And there was still no sign of Tom Curry.

Jubal stood on the knoll above the trading post, his long shadow falling across Lorena's grave. The spot was desolate but beautiful in its own wild way, with a sweeping view of the desert and a scattering of dried stems that would be wildflowers in the spring. Someone had made an effort to protect the grave's precious contents. Heavy stones had been carried up the slope to make a long, flat cairn as high as Jubal's knees. Thrust into the far end of it was a wooden cross fashioned from scrap lumber and bearing the clumsily carved letters of Lorena's name, along with the dates of her birth and death.

It was a sad resting place for a young woman who, by rights, should still be laughing, loving and caring for her family.

Why didn't you come back, Jubal? Lorena would have taken you without your arm! She would have taken you without your legs if need be! As it was, we all had to pick up the pieces you left behind. We had to make do with whatever was there.

Tess's words returned to haunt Jubal now. Lorena had waited for him. Even after hearing the news that he was dead, she had waited. And he had not returned. He had let her down as surely as the poor, inept fool who had become her husband.

But what else could he have done for her? He'd emerged from Camp Douglas a one-armed cripple without a penny to his name. He had stayed away in the hope Lorena would find a better life than he could give her. Instead she had found Tom Curry.

The cold morning wind stung Jubal's bloodshot eyes. He had not slept—could not have slept even if he'd tried. The task he'd begun last night had taken long hours to finish. While he labored with the vise and awl, the dilemma of what to do about Tom Curry had kept his conscience in turmoil. Not until the coldest, darkest hour before dawn had Jubal come to a decision.

Only a monster would shoot a man on Christmas Eve, in the presence of his family. The duel would have to wait, perhaps a few days, perhaps longer. But it would take place. Honor demanded that much.

When Tom Curry arrived, Jubal would give him time to greet Tess and the children. Then he would take his former friend aside, confront him and demand satisfaction. Once the time, place and weapons were agreed upon, he would leave the Curry family to their holiday and ride off to wait for the appointed hour.

In the old days, before the war, there would have been seconds for both men, and perhaps a doctor. There would have been matched pistols in a velvet-lined box, or even sabers. But this was now, and this was the West. It would be enough for two men to face each other, draw and shoot.

Jubal heard the sound of a footstep and turned to see Tess emerging onto the top of the knoll. She was slightly winded from the steep climb, and her words came in breathy little gasps. Until this moment he had wanted nothing more than to be alone. But the sight of her pink-flushed face and wind-disheveled skirts flooded his heart with sunlight. Under different circumstances he might have reached out and pulled her beneath the flap of his canvas coat to shelter her from the chill. Even now, the thought of holding her triggered an ache in a place so deep it had no name.

"I like to walk in the morning, while the children are still asleep." Her voice, still breathless, blended with the musical chorus of morning birds. "Am I intruding?"

Jubal shook his head. "I was getting gloomy up here. You've come to my rescue."

She moved toward him, swathed to the chin in a dove-gray shawl. Her wide fawn eyes studied his face, reading every weary line. "Oh, dear, you really didn't sleep, did you? I saw the light flickering under the door of the shed until all hours and—" Color rose in her face as she realized what she had just told him—she had been awake, too, and watching.

"Maybe a lullaby and a bit of snuggling would have helped," he said lightly.

Her cheeks deepened from pink to plum. "Jubal, you're incorrigible!" she declared with a nervous little laugh.

"And you haven't lost your blush," he said. "I used to enjoy teasing you just to watch your face go beet red."

"You didn't have to tease me to do that. All you had to do was look at me." She turned away from him, toward the brightening sky. Her skin glowed in the soft mauve light.

Jubal battled the urge to catch her waist, spin her against him and devour her with kisses. His throat ached as he moved forward to stand beside her. It was the dawn of Christmas Eve, and the weight of all the lonely years lay on his spirit, crushing him with despair. He needed this strong, tender woman as he had never needed anyone in his life. But he knew he had no right to touch her.

Tess willed herself not to tremble as Jubal's nearness enfolded her senses. It had taken all the courage she possessed to climb the path up the knoll, knowing he would come here to visit the grave of the woman he had loved. Even now, her heart fluttered against her ribs like a caged bird, threatening to take wing and desert her.

She had wrestled all night with the question of Jubal Trask and why he had come. At first glance, the reason was obvious—Jubal was Thomas's oldest friend. He had heard about Lorena's death and come to pay his respects. But no, she sensed, there had to be more. She had watched Jubal grow from boy to man, and she recognized every nuance of expression that flickered across his face. All Tess's instincts told her that something was terribly wrong.

Last night, in the bleak hours before dawn, she had made up her mind to find out what it was.

But how should she approach him? Confrontation had already failed. A more confident woman might use her wiles to lure secrets from a man. But when it came to playing such a game, Tess did not trust her heart. Not when the game involved Jubal.

There was no recourse left but simple friendship and honesty—put him at ease, win his trust and hope he would confide in her. With this purpose in mind, she had climbed the knoll this morning. But she had almost lost heart as she gained the top and caught sight of him, standing beside Lorena's grave. That was when the fearful truth had struck her—if she wanted honesty from Jubal, she would have to be honest in return.

Now, as he stood beside her in the morning wind, Tess took a deep breath and plunged ahead.

"You were always my hero, Jubal," she said. "You were the handsome prince in every fairy tale I ever read. Surely you knew that—why else would I have blushed every time you looked at me?" She swallowed, feeling as if she had just leaped off a precipice. "Not that I ever had any serious hopes. I knew that one day the prince would find his beautiful princess—and you did. I'm only sorry you lost the chance to live happily ever after.''

He made a low, wounded sound. ''I'm no prince, Tess,'' he said. ''In the past ten years I've lied, cheated, stolen, even killed—whatever it took to survive from one day to the next. The life I've led has turned me into someone you wouldn't even like, let alone admire.''

Tess gazed up into his bitter blue eyes, forcing herself to see the anguish that lay beneath their cold anger, wishing she could simply take him in her arms, kiss the proud, hard line of his mouth and love that pain into oblivion. Stinging tears welled in her eyes, tears she knew she must not let him see.

''It doesn't matter anymore,'' she said, turning away to stare out over the desert. ''Nothing matters except that, after all this time, you're alive. My hero—my friend—is alive.''

She heard him swallow in the stillness, but he did not move or speak. Tess let the chilling wind dry the wetness on her cheeks, not trusting herself to turn and look at him. Seconds ticked past, measured by the beating of her heart. She had revealed too much, she chided herself. Instead of opening up, Jubal had retreated into embarrassed silence.

Unable to bear the tension, she shifted to safer ground. ''Tell me about your ranch in New Mexico,'' she said. ''How large is it?''

He exhaled as if in relief, turned and began moving back toward the downward trail. ''Seventeen thou-

sand acres, with an option on five thousand more. Not
all that big as ranches go, but it's choice spot, at the
foot of the Sangre de Cristo Mountains, where the
springs run out of the hills. I plan to run a couple
thousand head of beef cattle on the land, and breed
some horses—Spanish barbs, if I can buy the right
stallion and some good mares." He shrugged, punc-
tuating the gesture with a rough little laugh. "Dreams.
I guess we all need them to get us through the bad
spells. Over the past dozen years, I've spent a lot of
time dreaming about the ranch I'd have one day. Now
that dream's come true. It's a good feeling."

He paused on a level spot, allowing her to catch
up with his uneven strides. "What about *your* dreams,
Tess? Grant you, there are worse things than teaching
school and caring for your brother's children. But that
can't be all you ever expected from life. You deserve
something more, something of your own."

"Something of my own?" Tess glanced up at him,
forcing herself to smile. "Could any of us have
planned what the war would do to our lives, Jubal?
You've managed to pick up the pieces and rebuild a
part your dreams. Some of us haven't been so lucky."

"You have to make your own luck." His voice
carried an edge. "Life isn't going to hand you anything without demanding payment—that's the one
thing I've learned."

His profile was dark and craggy against the sunlit
sky. Tess eased ahead of him and lowered her gaze
to the rocky trail, the way being treacherous and too
narrow for them to walk side by side. Her mind sifted

through every word he had spoken, seizing on a phrase here, a gesture there.

Life isn't going to hand you anything without demanding payment.

Was that why Jubal had come—to demand some kind of payment? Or was her imagination grasping at straws?

Never mind, she admonished herself. She had more pressing concerns than trying to figure out Jubal Trask. Today was December 24, and she desperately needed a bit of Christmas magic for two lonely, anxious little children whose father had not come home.

What would they do if Thomas didn't arrive in time for Christmas? Dear heaven, what if something had happened to him?

What if he didn't come home at all?

Tess stood at the corner of the house, wiping her hands on her damp apron. Her gaze followed the deep-rutted wagon road, eyes straining to see the point where it disappeared behind the distant mesa. The sun blazed high in the cloudless heavens, its harsh light glittering on sandstone ledges and silvery clumps of cholla.

It was well past midday, and still there was no sign of Thomas.

From the far end of the yard, the sound of Jubal's hammering echoed in her ears. He worked with an efficiency that amazed her, pushing each nail point into the wood with his strong thumb, so that the nail stood in place, ready for the blow of the hammer—a blow that never missed.

Over the course of the morning, he had mended the coop and fashioned a brace for the corral gate to stop it from sagging. Then he had started on the neglected fence, working as if driven by some demon that would not let him rest. It had been all she could do to get him inside the house for the midday meal—a tense and hurried affair that had lasted only long enough for him to bolt down a sandwich and a cup of coffee. Then, with scarcely a glance in her direction, he had returned to the refuge of his task.

She had said too much up there on the knoll, Tess berated herself. She had wanted to win Jubal's confidence, but she should have known better. Her clumsy attempt at honesty had only made him uncomfortable.

What was he thinking? That she loved him? That she wanted him? Oh, why hadn't she held her tongue? No wonder he was taking such pains to avoid her!

Try as he might, however, he could not avoid the children. They had tagged him around the yard for most of the day. Not that Jubal had made any effort to charm them—on the contrary, he had been as gruff and distant as a rogue bear, ignoring Lucy's violet-eyed gaze and fielding Beau's stream of questions with shrugs and monosyllables. All to no avail. The two youngsters could not seem to get enough of him.

Under different circumstances Tess might have called them back to the house. But she'd been immersed in the flurry of last-minute baking and wrapping, and had welcomed the chance to work alone. Even with her best efforts, it wouldn't be much of a Christmas. But for the children's sake they would make a fine day of it, she and Thomas—and, yes, Jubal. Whatever dark forces drove the man, his presence here was a Christmas miracle in itself. Jubal, so long dead and lost, was alive again—and even amid the strain and worry she could not stop the singing of her heart.

Tess's gaze strayed across the distance to where his tall figure was bent over a section of broken fence. Her eyes lingered on the broad expanse of his shoulders and skimmed the tangle of his wind-rumpled hair. For a long moment she held his image, etching every detail in her memory. Then, turning with a sigh, she shifted her attention toward the empty road.

Jubal watched her walk back to the house, stealing a tug of pleasure from the sight of her flying hair and billowing skirts. She moved with unaffected grace, striding strong and tall across the empty expanse of yard, beautiful against the blazing sky.

You were always my hero, Jubal...the handsome prince in every fairy tale I ever read.

The memory of her words quickened his pulse. Tess was not a woman given to flirtation. But she had told him, in her quiet, forthright manner, that if he reached out to her she would not turn away. Her love would be warm, sweet and healing—everything he had needed for so long. He imagined her in his arms, in his bed, and the ache that filled him was soul deep.

Jubal had watched her again and again that morning as she walked out of the house to stare up the road, one hand shading her eyes, the other twisting the hem of her apron. He had burned with the urge to go to her and take up the conversation where it had died that morning. But that would be a bad idea, he'd reminded himself. In the end, reaching out to Tess would only make things worse. She was Tom Curry's sister, and the aftermath of her brother's return would tear them apart forever.

By suppertime the sky was already deep indigo, with a bright sprinkle of evening stars. When Jubal entered the kitchen he saw that Tess had taken extra pains with their Christmas Eve meal. A faded crimson cloth had been laid on the table and decorated with a centerpiece of carefully arranged juniper sprigs, piñon cones and dried berries. The cracked dishes shone in the flickering lamplight, and the aromas of fresh meat pie, baked apples and mulled cider filled the air with mouthwatering promise.

Tess glanced up from slicing bread as he came inside. Her heat-flushed face, framed by tendrils of damp, dark hair, was radiant in the lamplight. Only the shadows in her eyes betrayed her worry. It was Christmas Eve, and her beloved brother was still missing.

Jubal's heart gathered weight as he paused to pull out her chair, then seated himself in Tom Curry's place. The children were already at the table, their freshly scrubbed faces damp and pink and shining.

Beautiful children, who had stormed his defenses all day like miniature Visigoths, defying all his efforts to keep them at a distance. Even now he was at the mercy of those elfin features and heart-melting eyes. Jubal had told himself he never wanted children of his own. But now...

Tess bowed her head and, when Jubal and the little ones had followed her example, she began a heartfelt grace. The words blurred in Jubal's mind as he lost himself in the husky sweetness of her voice.

"We thank thee, Lord, for the bounty of this food, and for the friend who has come to sit at our table and share this meal with us...."

What if things could be this way forever? he found himself wondering. What if Tom Curry had gotten his just desserts at someone else's hands, silencing, once and for all, the terrible cry for vengeance and honor?

What if he, Jubal, were free to take this woman and these children home with him to the ranch, to cherish and protect as his own? By heaven, he would do right by them all. He would see that none of them ever wanted for anything again.

"...and please bless Thomas, Lord, wherever he might be this night. Comfort and deliver him, and bring him safely home to us...."

Her words stung Jubal out of his reverie like a slap, and he cursed his own secret yearnings. These people were someone else's family. No matter what happened tomorrow, he had no claim on them. Not now. Not ever. He had come here to satisfy a long-owed debt. And even if someone else were to cancel that debt for him, the blackness would remain in the depths of his spirit.

He would despise Tom Curry to his dying day.

"...and help us to keep Christmas in our hearts forever, Lord. Amen."

Tess raised her glowing eyes to his—eyes made even more beautiful by the concern that flickered in their depths. Looking into those eyes every night would be heaven, Jubal thought. But why torment himself with things he could never have? Tomorrow he would stay long enough to find out what had happened to Tom Curry. If the man had been murdered or met with some grisly accident, he would make sure Tess and the children had the means to travel back East. Then he would ride away and never set eyes on this miserable place again.

And if Tom Curry arrived safely...

"When do you think Pa will get here?" Beau's piping voice broke into his thoughts. "He promised he'd be home by Christmas, and it's almost Christmas now."

Tess's gaze flickered cautiously in Jubal's direction, then back toward the boy. "I'm sure your father's doing everything he can to get here," she said. "But in the meantime, he wouldn't want us to be sad and worried, would he? He'd want us to go right ahead and celebrate Christmas as if he were here!" She scooped a midsize portion of meat pie onto his plate and a smaller one onto Lucy's, then passed the pie to Jubal. The rich aromas of roast mutton, onions, vegetables and fresh-baked crust wafted into his nostrils as he helped himself to a generous slice.

"It's been a long time since I sat down to a meal this appetizing," he said, playing along with Tess's effort to be cheerful. "It smells like Christmas."

"Can we sing?" Beau asked. "Mama—" He swallowed, blinking hard. "Mama always sang with us on Christmas Eve."

Once again, Tess's eyes met Jubal's across the table, their expression sad and knowing. "Of course we can sing, if you like," she said brightly. "We'll do it after supper is cleared away. I happen to know Mr. Trask has a fine singing voice."

Jubal groaned. "That was a long time ago. I haven't sung in years. Probably don't even remember how."

"It's Christmas Eve," Tess said firmly. "Anyone can sing on Christmas Eve."

"Maybe," Jubal said, thinking of the gift he'd labored on all last night and wondering, now, whether the whole thing had been a foolish idea. "I've got a surprise for you after supper," he said, taking the plunge. "You'll have to stay in the house, all of you, while I get it ready. No peeking outside until I tell you it's time. Promise?" He glanced around the table.

"I promise!" Beau almost shouted. "I like surprises!"

"Promise?" Jubal looked at the little girl. She gave him only a silent nod, but her violet eyes were shining.

"And you?" He looked straight at Tess. "You'll

keep everyone in the house and make sure they don't look outside?''

''Yes.'' She smiled, her eyes sparkling like dark burgundy wine. Jubal felt his heart swell as he looked at her, thinking how damnably difficult it was not to love the woman.

''And you're not to look, either,'' he said. ''The surprise is for you, too. Promise?''

Her radiant gaze softened. ''No looking,'' she vowed. ''I promise.''

Chapter Five

Tess glanced anxiously toward the kitchen window, reminding herself once more that she'd promised not to look outside. Jubal had been gone no longer than ten or fifteen minutes, but the time had already begun to crawl. What could he be doing out there? And when could he have found the time to prepare a surprise? He had spent the whole day working within sight of the children.

Beau and Lucy sat at the table, squirming with excitement. The fact that they were too short to see over the sill lessened their temptation to peek, but for Tess, the urge to fly to the kitchen window and peer into the darkness beyond was almost more than she could contain.

"Let's sing some Christmas songs while we're waiting!" she exclaimed. "Beau, do you and Lucy have a favorite?"

The small, freckled forehead creased. "Can we sing 'Silent Night'?"

"Of course we can." She sat down across from the children, took a deep breath and began the song.

"'Silent night, holy night...'"

The children's mother had been gifted with an exquisite voice, but Tess was an average singer at best. Beau, who'd inherited his father's tone deafness, joined in with loud enthusiasm. The sound was far from angelic, but it filled every corner of the kitchen. Lucy clutched Petunia in her arms and watched them in saucer-eyed silence.

They had just reached the end of the first verse when a light rap on the door galvanized them into silence. Jubal slipped in from the darkness, his cobalt eyes sparkling with mystery.

Tess stared at him, almost forgetting to breathe. It was as if the Jubal she remembered—her impulsive and mischievous prince—had appeared from beneath the bitter shell of the man who'd ridden in the gate yesterday. The magic was fleeting, she knew. But even if it could not last, she would treasure this small, private miracle to the end of her days.

"Blow out the lamp," he said, glancing at Tess. "Then everyone come over here by the door, where I can guide you outside with your eyes closed. Don't look until I tell you."

"What is it?" Beau groped his way around the table, his eyes already squeezed shut. "Is it an elephant?"

"An elephant!" Jubal laughed gruffly, the sound warming Tess all the way to the soles of her feet. "Now, where in blazes would I hide an elephant around here? You've got too much imagination for your own good, boy!"

Tess snuffed out the lantern that hung above the

kitchen table. Anticipation tingled in the darkness as she shepherded Beau and Lucy toward the kitchen door. She felt like a child herself, giddy with the magic of Christmas Eve—a night when anything was possible.

"Eyes closed, all three of you." Jubal guided them over the threshold until they stood clustered on the back porch.

"All right," he declared. "Go ahead and look."

Slowly they opened their eyes. For the space of a long breath none of them spoke. They could only gaze, awestruck, at the splendor of Jubal's gift.

The entire yard glittered with light from a myriad of small, flickering lanterns. Everywhere—along the fences and walkways, around the well and the windmill and across the open spaces, they spilled their golden magic into the night.

Only when she looked at one of them closely did Tess realize what she was seeing. Each lantern was nothing more than an old tin can, its sides pierced and slashed to make a filigree through which light from a candle stub flickered in lacy patterns. The workmanship was rough, but the effect was glorious, as if handfuls of stars had been flung from the sky to settle here, in this dark and lonely spot.

Luminarias. Was that what Jubal would call them?

Tess glanced up at Jubal where he stood beside her. He must have created them last night—that would explain why she'd seen candlelight beneath his door at such a late hour.

But *why* had he done it? Had it been it a simple impulse, an act of compassion or an act of love?

The question was just one more mystery on this magical Christmas Eve.

"'Silent night...Holy night...All is calm...All is bright....'"

The small singing voice that rose from within their midst was as clear as the night and as pure as the stars. Hearing it for the very first time, Tess felt a lump rise in her throat. Even Beau stayed quiet as his little sister sang, stumbling over words, but keeping true to every note of the old melody.

"'Sleep in heavenly peace....'"

Overcome, Tess fumbled for Jubal's hand in the darkness. Her fingertips brushed the hollow of his palm. She heard the sharp intake of his breath, and then his long, hard fingers closed around hers, holding them tightly as Lucy's song faded into starlit silence.

Jubal sat alone on the back porch, watching as the candles guttered and burned low. Tess had taken the children inside to tuck them into bed. Now he could hear her moving softly in the kitchen—the faint clink of porcelain; the light scrape of chair legs sliding across the tiles. She seemed to be taking her time. Maybe she was waiting for him to leave the back porch and go to bed.

If he had any sense, that's exactly what he would do, Jubal lectured himself. But then, nothing about tonight had made any sense—least of all the dizzying surge of sweetness when Tess's fingers had curled into his palm. That simple act of trust had almost undone him. He had clung to her slim, warm hand as a drowning man would cling to a life preserver, dreading the moment when he would have to let her go.

That moment had come all too soon as the children tugged her away to explore the wonderland he'd created for them. Jubal had remained on the porch, watching with pleasure as they darted from one side of the yard to the other, clasping hands and laughing as they ran. His eyes had feasted on Tess's wild beauty—the apricot glow of her candlelit skin, the lithe, joyful grace of her body, the tempestuous mane of her hair, which had tumbled loose to blow like a dark banner in the soft night breeze.

He had wanted her with an ache that reached every cold and lonely part of him.

Afterward the four of them had clustered on the back steps and sung every Christmas song they could think of. Tess and the children had even persuaded Jubal to sing as much as he knew of the *Posadas* song. They had listened raptly, even though the words were in Spanish and he had to stop between verses and translate. When they had sung themselves out, Tess had herded them back into the kitchen for hot cider and oatmeal cookies.

It had been a wonderful night, Jubal reflected. Maybe that was the reason he hadn't retired to his bunk—though Lord knows he was weary enough for sleep. Like a reluctant child at bedtime, he clung to the magic of this Christmas Eve, knowing that when he awakened in the morning it would be gone forever.

"I think they've finally fallen asleep." Tess's voice startled him as she tiptoed out onto the porch, closing the door softly behind her. Jubal's pulse quickened as she sank down beside him on the top step, her skirts brushing his knee. Her hair fluttered around her shoulders like windblown silk. He was glad she hadn't taken the time to pin it up again.

For a long quiet moment she gazed around the yard, one hand rubbing the stiffness from the small of her back. He would give ten years of his life to have her reach out and touch him again, Jubal thought. But it would not happen. The next move, if it came, would have to be his.

He would be a fool, of course to make that move. Loving Tess would be pure heaven, but when it was over and she learned the truth, she would hate him for deceiving her. He should walk away now, excuse himself and retreat to the shed. That would be the sensible thing to do.

She stretched, arching her back like a wild, lovely cat. Her breasts strained against the thin fabric of her dress, nipples cast into sharp relief by the candlelight. One hand reached up to clear the tousled hair from her face, the gesture so erotic that Jubal felt a sudden, sharp tightening in his loins. It was all in innocence, he knew. Tess was not an accomplished seductress. She might not even be aware that she was playing with fire. But even now he found himself blazing with need, wanting her in every way a man could want a woman. All the good ways. All the bad ways.

Turning, she rested a featherlight hand on his shoulder. ''Thank you, Jubal,'' she whispered. ''Your gift was…perfect. It made Christmas Eve happen for all of us.''

''Tess—'' Her name emerged as a twisted groan.

He heard the sharp catch of her breath as his arm hooked her waist and pulled her against his side. She strained upward. Her fingers cupped the back of his neck as her moist, seeking lips closed on his.

Their first kiss was tentative, almost fragile, as Jubal held back, letting her taste and feel him, gentling her to his touch the way he might gentle a wild mustang mare. But he should have known the effort would prove too much for him. As the tip of her tongue brushed his lower lip, his self-control snapped. With a half-muttered curse, he caught her against his chest. His hard, hungry mouth captured hers. The dying candles spun and burst like rockets in Jubal's head as he drank in her sweetness, devouring her, wanting more of her. Wanting all of her.

Tess had gone molten against him. She whimpered like a small, lost animal, her fingers furrowing his hair as she pulled him down to her, fierce with need. Her torso arched against him, eager for his touch, open to all he could give her.

Jubal thought of the dark shed, the waiting bunk, his touch on every warm, silken part of her body....

"Jubal, my dearest love..." Her lips brushed his mouth with frantic little nibbling kisses. "I've loved you so long, for years, ever since we were children. There's never been anyone else...not ever..."

Her words stunned him like a slap across the face. He had ached to hear them, Jubal realized. But now that she'd spoken, the awareness of what he was about to do triggered a spasm of self-loathing.

Tess's love was living flame—pure, bright and infinitely precious. It made him yearn to be the man he once was, young and strong, his head full of high-minded ideals—courage, hope, compassion and honesty. Ideals that had been starved, kicked and beaten out of him in the hell of Camp Douglas and the raw years that followed.

Was it too late for him? Could Tess's love, and the love he ached to give her in return, free him from the prison of hate and self-pity he'd built around his own heart?

"Jubal, what is it?" She had pulled back and was gazing up at him with hurt, puzzled eyes. "Did I say too much? Do you want me to go away and leave you alone?"

In answer he gathered her close again, cradling her head in the hollow of his shoulder. "Lord, no," he murmured, his lips brushing her tangled hair. "I don't think I could stand it if you were to go away and leave me alone."

"Then what's the matter?" She pushed away once more to face him, her eyes deep pools of concern. "The whole time you've been here, I've sensed that something was wrong—something you weren't telling me. I love you Jubal, but if—" She hesitated, as if gathering her resolve. "If there's to be anything of value between us, we can't hide secrets from each other. I've been honest with you. Now it's your turn to be honest with me. Otherwise I'm not staying out here another minute!"

Jubal felt the resistance tightening like a clenched fist inside him. Tess was right. If he wanted her love, there could be no secrets between them. But it had been there for so long—the black rage that had seeped like snake venom through every fiber of his being. That rage had fed him, driven him, kept him alive and fighting when there was nothing else left. But it had kept him solitary. It had not allowed him to trust another living soul.

It had not, would not, allow him to love.

Could he open himself to Tess now? Even the idea of showing her that dark and ugly presence triggered a cold dampness along Jubal's hairline. Would she understand and continue to love him? Or would she recoil in horror and snatch her golden gift away?

He had been a gambler all his life, Jubal reminded himself. The Mexican silver mine had been a gamble. Buying the ranch had been a gamble. But he had never played for higher stakes than these—his own heart, his own soul and Tess's love.

He was about to risk them all.

Tess felt the weight of Jubal's silence beside her in the darkness. Aching with love, she slipped her arms around him, binding his sinewy body to hers. His muscles strained beneath her touch as if he were fighting some hidden battle. Where her head lay against his chest, she could hear the violent pounding of his heart.

What ugly secrets could he be holding back from her? Tess's arms tightened around him as she steeled herself for what she might learn. Jubal was the only man she had ever loved. That love, she sensed, was about to be tested.

"I'm ready to listen, Jubal," she said. "Tell me everything."

He exhaled raggedly. "The war," he said, his voice strangely hollow against her ear. "It started with the war."

"Sharpsburg." It was not a question.

"You had to be there to know how it was," he said, the words coming slowly at first, then spilling out of him. "Those high-minded sentiments about marching off to defend the noble South—they were blown to kingdom come by the first mortar blast that hit our company. Lord, it was our first battle, and we were so green we were puking up our grits on all sides. I saw men getting hit all around me. One man on my left…" He paused, shuddering in her arms, unable to finish. "It was hell. The worst hell you can imagine."

She pressed her cheek against his quivering chest. "I know," she whispered. "Thomas told me."

His breath jerked sharply. "What did your brother tell you, Tess?"

"Thomas told me the two of you were going through the woods with you a dozen yards ahead of him. He said he saw a grenade explode, and when it cleared, you were…dead." She choked on the last word, her arms tightening around him. "But you weren't dead, Jubal. You survived. You came back. That's all that matters now."

Jubal did not reply, and Tess realized she'd spoken empty words. Even now, everything that had happened mattered greatly. Before the war, Jubal's future had been secure—a good income running the freight business he'd inherited from his father, an imposing family home, and marriage to the prettiest girl in three counties. Neither the house nor the business had survived the war. And as for Lorena McBride...

"Thomas wrote to Lorena himself to tell her what had happened," she said. "They both grieved for you—I think it must have been the grieving that brought them together. Oh, Jubal, if you'd written—if you'd let anyone know you were alive—"

She fell into awkward silence, holding him tightly, knowing there was nothing she could say to erase the past or bring back what Jubal had lost. Around them in the darkness, the last of the *luminarias* glimmered like dying stars.

"It wasn't that easy," Jubal replied. "For months after the Yankees carted me off to that miserable camp hospital, I was too weak and fevered to sit up, let alone write a letter. Later on, when I was stronger, I took a good, hard look at what was left of me and decided Lorena deserved better than a one-armed cripple. Since she had every reason to believe I was dead..." His shoulders rose slightly, then sagged as if pressed by an invisible weight. "I thought it might be best to leave things that way. No, I didn't write. Not to her, not to anyone. Not until after the war."

Tess's arms tightened hard around him. *Oh, Jubal, you dear, proud, blind fool!* she wanted to shout at him. *Don't you know what it would have meant to me to learn you were alive? I would have come to you, no matter what the cost! I would have camped outside the gates of that foul prison until they let you go— even if it meant bringing you home to marry another woman.*

"So, after the war you got in touch with Cliff—

swearing him to secrecy, I take it,'' she prompted, filling in what she knew of the story.

''I figured Cliff was most likely to stay put through the war. His family would have needed him to run the farm, and with that club foot of his he couldn't have gone off with the army, even if he'd wanted to. It took a few weeks for his reply to catch up with me—one of my partners had a sister in Texas, and I'd given Cliff her address. When I read the news in his letter—that my house and business were gone and Lorena had married your brother—I knew I'd never come home again. Nothing in my past was worth coming home to.''

''*I* was part of your past, Jubal,'' Tess whispered into the soft, thick wool of his shirt. ''You could have come home to *me*.''

She had not meant for Jubal to hear her, but the sudden intake of his breath told her she had spoken too distinctly. His fingers caught and cupped her chin, lifting her face, forcing her to gaze up into his tormented eyes.

''Maybe it's not too late, darling Tess,'' he murmured huskily. ''Maybe I can still come home to you.''

His searching mouth closed tenderly and hungrily on hers, seeking all that she yearned to give him. Tess arched upward to meet his kiss, wanting him, all of him; wanting to take him into her pulsing warmth and heal his pain, to fill his life with love and laughter and children. A heavy, liquid heat curled upward from the depths of her body. With frantic fingers, she fumbled with the buttons of her high-necked dress, needing his touch on her skin, on every part of her. He was the love of her life, and she had spent too many long, cold nights alone.

But no. Her fingers paused as she realized something was wrong—something Jubal had not told her. She felt it in his tense, quivering body, as if he were pushing against a black door, fighting to contain the horror that lurked on the other side.

Knowing she must, she ended the kiss and nestled her head against his shoulder. "There's more, isn't there?" she said, feeling the convulsive ripple of his throat against her forehead. "Something happened at Sharpsburg—something that changed things forever. I need to know what it was."

He sighed raggedly. "It will hurt you to hear it, Tess. And, Lord knows, the last thing you deserve from me is more hurt."

Straining upward, she brushed a forgiving kiss along his stubbled jaw. "Nothing you could say would make me stop loving you, Jubal," she said. "But I can't—won't—spend the rest of my life wondering what terrible secrets you've kept hidden from me."

Jubal was silent for a long moment. When he began to speak his voice was a low rasp, haunted and hollow.

"It was just after dawn when the fighting started," he said. "General Hood called for a scouting party to report on enemy positions. We were to circle north of the Miller Farm and come out above the East Wood, behind Yankee lines. There were six of us— me, Tom and four others, all new recruits. The mission went fine until we were on our way back and hit the wood again. That's when all hell broke loose.''

''Artillery fire.'' Tess had heard that much of the story from her brother.

''It was all around us—our sergeant got blown to bits a dozen feet away. The rest of us scattered for cover. Tom and I stayed together, and when the shells stopped falling, we decided to make a run back to our own lines. We'd reached the edge of the wood and were diving into the cornfield when a stray minié ball caught me in the leg. I went down with a shattered kneecap.''

Tess groped for his hand and squeezed it, imagining what he must have felt, the agony, the terror. His fingers gripped hers as he relived the nightmare.

''Looking back through the trees, we could see flashes of blue—Yankee soldiers, moving in our direction. I...raised up on one elbow and held out my arm to Tom. 'Help me up,' I said. 'They're not coming fast. If I lean on you, we can still make it.'''

Tess's fingers had turned ice-cold in the hollow of his hand. She knew, even before he said it, what must have taken place. Thomas had returned from the war without a scratch. Jubal had not.

''Tom just stood there looking down at me, with a face as white as death. I tried to reach out to him, but suddenly he spun around and bolted into the cornfield, running as fast as his legs would carry him. I never saw him again.''

Tess stared up at Jubal in the darkness, her throat knotted, her stomach clenching. *Liar!* she wanted to scream at him. *My brother is a brave man, an hon-*

orable man! He would never have run off and left his best friend in danger!

"It's not true," she whispered, too stunned for tears. "It can't be." But she knew it was. Jubal had no reason to invent such a heartbreaking story.

"The Yankees were coming closer," he said in a flat voice. "I tried to drag myself into the underbrush, where they wouldn't see me. But one of them lobbed a Ketchum grenade to clear the way ahead. The thing exploded a dozen paces from where I lay—"

"Your arm—"

He nodded grimly. "The Yanks were retreating. They threw me onto a cart with their own wounded. The arm didn't seem that bad at first, but prisoners were last to be seen by the surgeons, and it was days before they got to me. By that time gangrene had set in. You've heard the rest of the story."

"Yes." Tess felt as if the sky had caved in on her, crushing her with its weight. All that Jubal had suffered, all that he had lost, was because of Thomas. Thomas, who had lied to her, lied to Lorena, lied to everyone.

"Why did you come here?" She stared up at Jubal, shivering as the nighttime chill penetrated to her bones. "Why now, after so many years?"

"I think you know, Tess." He spoke gently, giving her time to answer her own questions.

Why had Jubal been so surprised to find her and the children here when he arrived? And why had he seemed so much at a loss when he discovered Thomas was away?

Was it because he'd planned to confront his former friend alone, man to man?

A little cry broke from Tess's throat as the full impact of the truth struck her. She'd told herself she could forgive him anything. But this? The color drained from her face as she edged away from him. "You didn't come here to visit Thomas, did you, Jubal?" she said in a strangled voice. "Lorena was dead and couldn't hate you for it any longer, so you came to kill him."

Jubal did not reply, did not even move. His eyes were granite chips, catching glints of moonlight but otherwise lifeless.

"What in heaven's name were you expecting me to do?" Tess scrambled to her feet, snatching up her skirts. "I know Thomas did a terrible thing! But if you think I'd stand here and let you gun down my own brother and make orphans of those two precious children—"

She stood over him, dizzy with rage. Jubal gazed up at her, proud and impassive, refusing to deny a single word she'd said.

"And what about me?" Tess flung the words at him. "You never cared a fig for me, did you? Kill Thomas Curry and ruin his sister in the bargain! That was your plan as soon as you saw me, wasn't it?" She staggered back toward the door, her legs threatening to give way with every step.

"I want you gone by sunup tomorrow!" She groped behind her back for the doorknob. "And if you ever try to come back here...if you ever lay a hand on my brother, so help me, Jubal, I'll kill you myself!''

Somehow Tess got the door open. Stumbling into the kitchen, she jerked it shut behind her and slapped the bolt into place. Then, as her self-control gave way, she slid to the floor and burst into racking sobs.

Chapter Six

On Christmas morning the rising sun seemed to bleed like a raw wound, flooding the eastern sky with crimson. The air was so cold that Jubal could see his own white breath as he bent to tighten the cinch on the big roan's saddle. His gaze flickered back toward the house, searching for a movement at the window, wisp of smoke from the chimney, anything that would tell him Tess was up and about and had repented of last night's scalding tirade.

He saw no sign of welcome—and that was just as well, he lectured himself as he thrust a boot in the stirrup and swung into the saddle. He should have known that once she learned the truth, Tess would never want to see him again. Now it was time to ride out of her life and give her some peace.

It was the most loving thing he could do for her.

With a last glance at the silent house, he turned the horse toward the gate. If Tom Curry was dead, Cliff would learn of it sooner or later and let him know. If the cowardly bastard was alive...

Jubal sighed, feeling bleak and hollow. Much as he

hated the man, he could not wreak suffering on Tess and the children. Someday, he vowed, there would be a full reckoning. But not now. Not on Christmas Day.

He was bending to unfasten the gate when a movement up the road caught his eye. Jerking himself erect, he saw a lone figure staggering around the bend, hair and skirts whipping in the wind.

A woman.

Jubal's pulse lurched. For one blind instant he thought it might be Tess—but no, Tess would be taller, more slender. The woman stumbling along the rutted road, clutching a thickly wrapped bundle in her arms, was a stranger, and she was clearly in trouble.

As he swung the gate open to ride through, he glimpsed Tess coming out onto the front porch, fully dressed, clasping her shawl around her shoulders. Her eyes stared past him, toward the approaching figure. As Jubal spurred the roan forward she bounded off the porch and broke into a tearing run.

Jubal reached the woman first. She was young, no more than thirty, her flaxen hair loose and tangled. Her plain, broad face was scratched and dirty, as were her clothes. The watery eyes she cast up at him were stark with terror.

"My husband—" She gasped out the words, clutching the blanket-swathed bundle against her chest. "Bandits—his wagon's trapped in a box canyon—about three miles up the road. He's holding them off with his rifle, but he's hurt—can't last much longer. He's—"

A plaintive wail interrupted her words as the bundle began to squirm. The blanket parted to reveal a fretful baby, perhaps nine or ten months old, with drowsy blue eyes and matted blond curls. The woman cradled him, rocking him in her arms, crooning under her breath. Jubal imagined her crawling through the brush in the winter darkness, then running three miles with a child in her arms. His respect for the woman's courage grew.

"Please," she begged. "You've got to help my husband! There are three of them—horrible, filthy men—and now that it's light they'll be—"

She broke off as a windblown, breathless Tess, who'd been hidden from her view by Jubal's horse, burst into sight.

"Good heavens, you must be frozen!" Tess flung off her shawl and wrapped it around the woman's trembling shoulders. "We need to get you to the house—get you warmed up and fed! Here, let me carry your baby."

She held out her arms for the child, but at that moment the woman's eyes brightened in sudden recognition.

"Why, you must be Tess!" she exclaimed. "Thomas told me all about you and the children!"

Jubal felt his stomach contract as if he'd been punched in the gut. Tess was staring at the woman, her dark eyes wide, her lips parted.

"Oh, dear, I'm so sorry." The woman glanced from one to the other, seeing the confusion her words had caused. "I certainly didn't plan for us to meet like this. My name is Sarah. Thomas and I..." She inhaled jerkily, gulping back a sob. "We were married at Fort Defiance, four days ago." She swung toward Jubal again. "Oh, sir, whoever you are, he's such a good man! Please, you've got to save him before it's too late!"

Tess's gaze flashed upward to Jubal's impassive face. She had overheard enough to know that Thomas was in desperate need of his help. But Jubal's eyes had narrowed to icy granite slits, revealing no trace of emotion.

Please. Tess's lips moved in a silent plea. *Please, Jubal.*

But Jubal's flat expression did not change. What was he thinking? Tess wondered frantically. That this was the perfect opportunity to take his vengeance? That he had only to choose between killing Thomas himself and letting the outlaws do it for him?

His stony gaze flickered toward her. Then, without a word, he swung the tall roan toward the road and kneed the horse to a gallop.

Jubal!

Tess swallowed her own scream as he vanished around the bend. She would not risk alarming her new sister-in-law. Poor Sarah had been through enough already.

Gathering the fretful toddler into her arms, she turned back toward the house. Soon Beau and Lucy would be waking to the wonder of Christmas morning. Whatever happened, Tess vowed, she would protect these precious hours for as long as she was able.

"Your friend strikes me as a hard man, but a good man," Sarah said with forced cheerfulness. "All my instincts tell me that Thomas's fate couldn't be in better hands."

Tess glanced at the woman's dirt-stained profile, thinking that, for all the suddenness of this marriage, her brother had chosen well. "Your instincts are right, Sarah," she murmured, praying the words would prove true. "I would trust Jubal Trask with my life."

The sound of gunfire reached Jubal's ears as he neared the box canyon—the boom of heavy caliber pistol fire and, less often, the sharper bark of a rifle. Bullets whined as they ricocheted off the sides of the canyon. Tom Curry had never been much of a marksman. Judging from the sound of things, neither were the bandits. But there were three of them against one injured man, and if they persisted long enough, there was only one way this standoff would end.

All he had to do was ride away.

But that would make him no better than Tom Curry, Jubal reminded himself harshly. Honor demanded that he settle this affair in person.

Reining in the horse, he paused to size up the situation. On the near side of the box canyon, the land sloped upward to crest in a jagged sandstone escarpment. If he could get above the canyon he could look down on the fight and decide what to do next.

His empty stomach churned as he guided the horse partway up the slope, dismounted and tethered the animal behind a clump of creosote. From the moment he'd left Tess and Sarah standing in the road, he had warred with his own emotions. Now, as he climbed toward the rocks, the battle raged on. *What about honor?* the wounded, angry part of him raged. *What about justice? What about satisfaction?*

There is honor in compassion, a gentler voice whispered. *There is justice in forgiveness and satisfaction in friendship....*

The pale oval of Tess's face, as he had last seen it, seemed to float before him, her sleepless, haunted eyes burning into his soul. *Please, Jubal...* Her lips moved in a silent whisper.

Jubal forced the vision from his mind. He had lost Tess for good last night. There was no use thinking of her, nor of anything else that had happened in the past two days. Nothing mattered now except settling the score with the miserable coward who had destroyed his life.

The climb was not a long one. Within minutes Jubal had reached the top of the escarpment and found his way to a sheltered cleft between the boulders. From here he could look down into the box canyon with little danger of being hit by gunfire.

Twenty feet below, he could see the wagon. It had been pulled around a narrow bend in the canyon, where one of its wheels had dropped into a deep crevice between the rocks, leaving the whole conveyance tilting crazily to the right. The two mules stood in the tangle of their traces, protected by the wagon and half-concealed by a thicket of scrub oak.

In the open wagon bed, surrounded by a jumble of boxes, crates and barrels, Tom Curry lay with his rifle propped on the tailgate. His aim was fixed on the rocks at the bend of the canyon, where the bandits would have to pass to reach him. A dirty, bloodied rag was knotted around his left thigh.

How long had he been here? Jubal wondered. Why

hadn't the bandits rushed him in the night or circled in above him, as Jubal himself had done? Either Tom was damned lucky or the bandits weren't very bright—that, or they'd started drinking when it got dark. That would explain a lot, including how Sarah had managed to get away.

"Trust you to get yourself into a fool mess like this one, Tom," Jubal said in a calm, clear voice. "You never could handle mules worth a hang."

Tom jumped, glancing from side to side in a frantic attempt to locate the source of the voice. Jubal kept an alert eye on the rocks that shielded the bandits to make sure they didn't catch him off guard.

"Who is it? Where are you?" Tom glanced up, blinking. The expression on his face was the same lost, sad look Jubal remembered so well.

"I'm up here, right above you." Jubal waved cautiously and saw Tom's face turn the color of pig tallow.

"Jubal?" The name emerged as a gasp. "Jehosephat, you're alive!"

"No thanks to you, you lily-livered skunk!" Jubal had been waiting a long time to say those words. So why did they sound so foolish now, like a line from a bad melodrama? "You sentenced me to hell, Tom Curry," he growled. "I lost an arm, two years of my life and my girl in the bargain."

"Lord, Jubal, I thought you'd died. We all did. I tried to do right by Lorena. Heaven knows I loved her." Tom was staring up at him now, unmindful of the danger. "But it was so hard after the war, hard for everybody. I—"

He ducked his head as the roar of Jubal's .45 Peacemaker echoed down the canyon. There was a yelp of agony as one of the bandits staggered back behind the rocks.

"You always were the best shot in the county," Tom said as the sound died away. "For most of my life, I wanted to be like you, Jubal, but I could never measure up. That day at Sharpsburg…" His Adam's apple bobbed as he swallowed. "Lord, I wish I could say it was some mistake, but the truth was, I was scared to death. I panicked. Couldn't think of anything except getting out of there, not even when it meant leaving my best friend. And I never got over it. The bad times, the nightmares…always told myself that when I got through the Pearly Gates, the first thing I'd do was find you, fall on my knees and beg you to forgive me."

"I don't see any Pearly Gates around here, do you?" Jubal's eyes focused on a flicker of movement down the canyon.

"You could leave me now," Tom said. "You could do just what I did to you, ride away and let those bandits kill me. It would serve me right."

Jubal sighed wearily as he cocked the Peacemaker and sighted down into the rocks. "If you don't stop yapping, we'll be stuck here all day!" he growled. "It's Christmas. Your wife and kids and sister are waiting for you at home. So shut the blazes up and start shooting!"

For Tess, every minute of the morning had been slow torture. But she'd tried not to show how worried she was. Settling Sarah and the baby by the warm fire, she'd whipped up a hearty breakfast of scrambled eggs and flapjacks. When everyone had eaten she'd put on her work coat and ushered the children outside to feed the animals.

"No opening presents until the chores are done," she said as she filled their small pails with wheat for the chickens. "But I think it would be all right to sing a few Christmas carols, don't you?"

"It doesn't feel like Christmas without Pa," Beau complained. "He promised he'd be here, and he never breaks promises."

"And where's Mr. Trask?" Lucy piped, as if she'd never been silent. "I don't see him anywhere."

"Something strange is going on," Beau observed with a wisdom beyond his years. "But I like having Miss Sarah here. She's nice."

"She let me hold her baby," Lucy said. "His name is William. He smiled at me."

Hearing them, Tess kept her silence. She and Sarah had agreed it would be best not to introduce her as the children's new mother. Thomas could explain everything to Beau and Lucy when he came home.

If he came home.

But what if Thomas didn't come home at all? The question tore at Tess as she finished feeding the horses and hurried into the shed to milk the cow. What if Jubal had already taken his terrible vengeance?

What would they do?

What would *she* do?

Sinking down onto the three-legged stool, she began filling the bucket with twin streams of warm, creamy milk. A single tear trickled down her cheek as she remembered the heaven of Jubal's kisses. What if she'd given him everything he wanted last night— all the things she had yearned to give him? Would that have changed his mind?

Would things be different now if she hadn't insisted on knowing the truth?

If only she could go back....

"Aunt Tess!" Beau burst into the shed, flushed and grinning. "The wagon's comin' down the road! It's Pa! He kept his promise!"

Tess stumbled to her feet, knocking over the stool and spilling the milk in her haste. "Is anyone with him? Anyone riding behind?"

Beau shook his head. "Don't look like it. Just Pa. Come on!"

He raced out of the shed with Tess close behind him. In the yard, Lucy was hopping up and down, fluttering like an elated little bird. Sarah had come out onto the porch, holding her baby.

The wagon was nearing the gate. Thomas was alone on the seat, driving the two mules. There was no sign of Jubal.

"Pa! Merry Christmas, Pa!" Beau tugged against Tess's restraining hand as the wagon rumbled through the gate and pulled up outside the corral. Thomas looked pale and shaken as he climbed down from the wagon seat. His clothes were torn and rumpled, his leg freshly bandaged. Tess stared at him, her mind spilling over with questions she was afraid to ask.

Still clasping her baby, Sarah hurtled across the

yard and flung herself into his waiting arms. The children, too, exploded into action, throwing themselves against Thomas's legs, hugging any part of him they could reach.

They looked like a family, Tess thought. A family who no longer needed a spinsterly aunt to look after them.

Thomas's eyes met hers above the melee of embraces. "It was Jubal who came to my rescue," he said. "We drove off the bandits—wounded two of them. Then he helped me pull the rig out of the canyon. I owe him my life. More than my life."

"More?" Tess's ribs ached from holding her breath.

"Someday, when I can find the courage, I'll explain it all—" Thomas's voice choked, and she realized his cheeks were wet with tears. "For now, let's just say that Jubal forgave me for the worst thing I've ever done. He gave me back my soul, Tess. For the first time in years, I feel as if—" He swallowed hard, unable to continue.

Tess stared at him, seized by a sudden dread.

"Where *is* Jubal?" she demanded, forcing her mouth to form the words. "Has something happened? Thomas, is he—?"

"Lord, no!" Thomas shook his head. "Jubal's fine. I wanted him to spend Christmas day with us. But he said he needed to get back to Santa Fe. He took the mountain trail, where it branches off the road."

Tess felt the relief take her in a joyful, dizzying sweep. She was barely conscious of her feet touching the ground as she raced to the corral, singled out a sturdy mustang, slipped the bridle over its head and flung a blanket and saddle across its back. Minutes later she was mounted and galloping out the gate.

"Where do you think you're going?" Thomas's voice carried a teasing note as he shouted after her.

"I think you know! Merry Christmas!" She leaned forward in the saddle and gave the horse its head. The wind caught her hair, unfurling it into wild streamers as she rounded the bend and made for the mountain trail.

Jubal's long-legged roan was stronger than the peppery little mustang. The gouging hoof marks she followed told Tess that Jubal was pushing the animal hard, moving fast to put distance between himself and everything that had happened in the past two days.

As the winter sun crested the sky, Tess began to lose heart. She had planned to catch up with Jubal quickly and, by whatever means, bring him back to the trading post. But she'd been riding for hours, with no sign that she was gaining on him. By now she was getting cold and hungry. She had taken the time to fill a canteen, but had brought along no food and no bedroll. If she did not turn back now, she could find herself stranded on the rugged trail in the dark.

Pausing on a ridge, she weighed her risks. The physical danger was daunting. More fearful even was the chance of discovering that Jubal did not want her, that he had never truly wanted her.

Perhaps this adventure was no more than a fool's errand. After all, he had not proposed marriage. He had never said he loved her, nor spoken any of the pretty words that came easily to most men. She could be throwing away her heart, even her life, for nothing.

She thought of safety—of turning back to a place where she was welcome but no longer needed, of the years ahead, teaching school or looking after someone else's children, the empty days, the solitary nights.

Squaring her shoulders, she pushed on.

Darkness had fallen by the time she rounded a bend and spotted the flicker of a small campfire beneath a sheltering ledge. Dismounting, she dropped the reins and moved cautiously through the shadows. It would be foolhardy, she knew, to burst into the camp before she'd made certain it was Jubal's.

A hulking, dark shape moved against the firelight. Tess gasped, then began to breathe again as she recognized Jubal's roan, grazing in a thicket. Beyond the horse she could see the ledge with Jubal's saddle and bedroll laid out on the ground near the fire. But there was no sign of Jubal anywhere. Her heart crept into her throat as she edged forward.

"Stop right there, whoever you are."

Tess froze as Jubal materialized out of the darkness behind her, his pistol drawn and cocked. She heard the sharp intake of his breath as he recognized her.

"What the devil are you doing here?" he demanded gruffly.

"That's a fine way to welcome a friend." Tess kept her voice light, struggling to mask the stark fear that she'd come all this way for nothing.

"Friend, is it?" He released the hammer and dropped the Peacemaker back into its holster. "Well, I'll tell you right now, friend, if you've come to weep and flutter and make a fuss over me, you can climb on your horse and go right back the way you came.''

Tess forced herself to laugh. ''Now why would I want to do that, Jubal Trask? I came to keep you company, that's all. No man should be alone on Christmas night.''

The firelight glinted in his narrowed eyes. When he spoke his voice was rough and husky. ''I take it you brought along your own bedroll.''

''No.'' Tess's heart slammed against her ribs.

''Well, then, you'll have to understand that I only have one blanket. And it's a cold night. I'm not about to give it up.''

''I'm not asking you to,'' Tess whispered.

''I'm willing to share,'' he said, ''but only on two conditions.''

''Name them.'' Tess's legs had gone watery beneath her.

''First—'' he paused, scowling down at her ''—if I have trouble sleeping you have to promise me a lullaby and a bit of snuggling.''

Only then did she see the twinkle in his eyes. ''Oh!'' She gasped, leaping at him, her fists pummeling his chest in mock fury. ''You're terrible! It's a hard bargain you drive, Jubal Trask, but I agree!''

He caught her close, the steel strength of his arm pinioning her against his big, solid body. His eyes drilled into hers, piercing the darkness. Tess felt the simmering heat between them, felt the molten weight of desire pulsing inside her, and she knew that she would give anything to have this man—here, now, always.

Both of them were breathing hard. "Don't you want to hear my second condition?" he murmured, his voice a velvety rasp.

"Tell me." Tess's lips brushed the stubble on his chin.

He eased her away from him, so that he could look down into her face. "Santa Fe's a long ride from here. If you come with me, we'll be spending a good many nights under that blanket, and I'm not a patient man, Tess." His gaze was hot and tender. "But if you come with me, you'll have to understand that as soon as we run into a preacher, I intend to make an honest woman of you. Agreed?"

Tess's reply was a lost murmur as she kissed him with all the passion of her bursting heart. Jubal's was not the most elegant proposal, but it was all she needed. All she would ever need.

As they held each other close, the stars above them glowed like ten thousand *luminarias* and suddenly, for the first time that bleak day, it was Christmas.

Epilogue

New Mexico Territory
December 23, 1874

Jubal stood with Tess on the portico of their ranch house, sheltered by the long eave of the roof. Behind them, through the open doorway, firelight danced on gaily festooned walls and dangling *piñatas*. The everyday furniture had been moved aside to accommodate long tables laden with platters of tamales, meats, breads, and pitchers of festive *ponche de piquete*. Everything was ready.

It had been Tess's idea to host the eighth night of the *posadas* for the families of their Mexican ranch hands. She had spent weeks planning and preparing for this night. Now she sagged against him in weary contentment, soft and fragrant within the circle of his arm.

"It's beautiful, isn't it?" She gazed out at the glittering yard, where a hundred *luminarias* lined the long walkway leading from the gate to the house.

"You've done us proud, Mrs. Trask." Jubal pulled her closer, bursting with love. "But I've worried about you these past few weeks. This is no time to wear yourself out." His hand moved lower to cradle the growing bulge below her waistline. His heart stopped as he felt the flutter of life beneath his palm.

"Oh, I've had plenty of help," she said, laughing. "Juanita and Pilar—and you, of course. Besides, the doctor says I'm as strong and healthy as one of your broodmares. I'll—we'll—be just fine."

"All the same, I want you in bed as soon as the party ends," he said. "Leave the cleanup to the hired hands."

"And do you promise to join me in bed?" Her hand crept playfully up his chest, then paused as the sound of chanting voices reached their ears. "Listen!" she whispered. "They're coming!"

From beyond the gate, the lanterns appeared, bobbing like suspended moons as the procession wound its way toward the house. Men, women and children, friends and neighbors, lighting the darkness of this magical night.

"Oh, Jubal, I almost forgot," she said glancing up at him. "A letter came from Sarah today. Business is good at the trading post. Thomas and the children are well, and she's expecting another baby."

"Another?" Jubal raised an eyebrow. "That little house will soon be bursting at the corners."

"You're a fine one to talk!" She nuzzled him adoringly, then took his hand as the procession approached the steps, singing the simple chant whose words she had taken such pains to learn. Candlelight glowed around them as her voice joined Jubal's in the last joyful stanza of the song.

* * * * * *

MARY BURTON

Mary Burton calls Richmond, Virginia, home, where she lives with her husband and two children. Her story in *Christmas Gold* is her fourth historical romance.

Please address questions and book requests to:
Harlequin Reader Service
U.S.: 3010 Walden Ave., P.O. Box 1325, Buffalo, NY 14269
Canadian: P.O. Box 609, Fort Erie, Ont. L2A 5X3

UNTIL CHRISTMAS
Mary Burton

P.O. Box 969 Park Stn, Ont. L4A 1A5

For Julia and Natalie

Prologue

Timberline, Colorado
October, 1882

"May the Almighty have mercy on their souls and may He watch over those who now grieve for their departed loved ones." Sadness choked Reverend Bower's normally clear voice, forcing him to pause, head bent. He stood at the entrance to the Butler's Folly mine, in front of six bodies, now lined shoulder to shoulder under bloodstained sheets.

The soft cries of the dead miners' wives squeezed Laura Butler's heart, making it difficult for her to breathe. Since the alarm bell had first screeched its warning just after supper, she and the other women had huddled close to the mine entrance waiting for news of their loved ones. Less than an hour ago, the first of the dead had been brought to the surface.

Laura had known each of the miners: she'd sewed with their wives in the quilting guild and had taught their children in her school. She'd miss them all.

Hugging her arms around her chest, she turned from the women and started to move away. Her emotions swung between grief and hope. As much as she ached for the families who'd lost a loved one, she guiltily gave thanks that her grandfather hadn't been among the dead. He'd been working near the cave-in site and remained among the missing. She clung to the hope that he'd come through alive.

Zachary Butler, her grandfather and only family, was a tall burly man, who claimed a large handlebar mustache and a booming laugh. He was so tough, so unbreakable. He just couldn't be dead.

Shouts and the grinding gears of the winch sliced through her thoughts. She faced the mine entrance in time to see Roman Maddox, her grandfather's mine manager, stride out of the black entrance. His gaze locked on hers.

As the miner moved toward her, he pulled off his hat and shoved his long fingers through his hair. Grief etched deep lines in his proud face streaked with grime and blood.

Any hope Laura had harbored for her grandfather, vanished at the look in Mr. Maddox's weary, gray eyes. A wave of nausea slammed through her. The taste of raw metal coated the inside of her mouth. "Where is my grandfather?"

Dark stubble sharpened the angles of Mr. Maddox's face. "Gone."

"Oh, God." Boneless, Laura's knees buckled and she crumpled.

Mr. Maddox grabbed her shoulders and steadied

her. "I'm so damn sorry, Laura. He was a good man."

Unshed tears burned her eyes as her fingers bit into his steady arms. "Are you sure it was him?"

His fingers tightened around her shoulders. "Yes."

Laura tried to pull free. Mr. Maddox was mistaken. He had to be. "I need to see him."

He swallowed as if his throat was raw, but he held her steady. "You wouldn't recognize him."

She squeezed her eyes shut and leaned her head against Mr. Maddox's chest. He wrapped his arms around her, drawing her against him.

"Did he suffer?" she whispered.

"It was quick, painless."

Her hazy mind processed the information. Obligation had been bred into her and she shifted her mind from her own pain to the other missing miners. "What of the other two men?"

"Injured, but alive."

Laura whispered her thanks. "Good."

"Laura, let me take you home." Mr. Maddox's deep voice seemed to drift far above her.

She prayed for strength. "My grandfather would want me to speak to the women who lost their husbands. The responsibility falls to me now." She barely recognized her hollow voice.

Mr. Maddox made no effort to release her. "There'll be time enough for all of that."

She choked back the tears, refusing to acknowledge them. If she didn't cry, then perhaps all this wouldn't seem so real. "I have to do *something*."

He stroked her hair. "I'll take care of everything, Laura."

There was so much to think about. So much to do. But she didn't know where to begin. So she simply nodded, too numb to argue. The steady beat of Roman's heart tapped against her cheek and the heat of his body swirled around her.

Nothing would ever be the same again. But for these precious moments cocooned in Roman's embrace, she could almost believe that everything would be fine.

Chapter One

Timberline, Colorado
December, 1882

Roman Maddox burst into the book-lined study, shattering the morning calm. His eyes were wild with fury as he strode across the Indian carpet toward Laura. "Wilbur Hollis tells me you're leaving Timberline!"

Guilt rolled over Laura. She had avoided Roman these last couple of days, dreading his reaction to her departure. "Yes, I'm leaving."

His palms pressed flat against the desk, he leaned toward her. "Why didn't you say something to me?"

Laura laid her pen down. The dangerous tone in his voice had her easing back from the massive rosewood desk that had belonged to her grandfather. "I was afraid you'd try to talk me out of it."

Grinding his teeth, he struggled with anger. "You're damn right I would."

Wilbur Hollis appeared at the library threshold. He

was trying to catch his breath as he waved a crumpled paper in his hand. "Roman, what the devil got into you? You didn't sign the contract and ran out of my office like somebody was chasing you."

Roman had had a meeting scheduled with Mr. Hollis, Timberline's title officer, this morning. The miner was to have signed the contract that would transfer ownership of Butler's Folly from Laura to him.

Ignoring Hollis, Roman's gaze didn't waver from Laura. "Timberline is your home. Why are you leaving?" He'd been in America since he was a boy, but when angered the cadence of his ancestors, miners who'd earned their living in the coal pits of Cornwall crept into his voice.

Nervous, Laura drummed her fingers on the desk's polished wood. "Once you take over the mine, I'll have no real purpose in Timberline."

He flexed his fingers. "That's not true."

Laura looked to Mr. Hollis, silently pleading for support.

Mr. Hollis tugged his vest over his round belly, then slid his hand over his thinning hair slicked back with bear grease. "Roman, I ain't happy about Laura leaving, either, but you got to look on the bright side."

"Bright side?" Roman thundered.

"She's selling you the mine for one dollar. You'll be richer than Midas."

"I don't care about the money," Roman growled.

"Then think about the three hundred jobs that'll be saved if you buy the mine. The other buyers wanted to gut the crews. With you as owner, Laura can move back to Virginia knowing her grandfather's company and employees will be well taken care of. It's a fine deal for everyone.'' The title officer edged toward the desk and, careful not to get too close to Roman, smoothed the crumpled contract flat.

''It's time that we both move forward with our lives,'' Laura added.

Roman muttered an oath under his breath and though she didn't quite catch what he'd said, she'd spent enough time with him these last few months sorting through her grandfather's cluttered papers to know that it was best not to ask him to repeat it.

Seven months ago, her grandfather had hired the seasoned miner to turn the failing Butler silver operation into a profit maker. The mine's balance sheets shifted from red to black during his first three months on the job. And during those months, he'd not only learned the name of each miner, but he'd handled explosives when others refused. He had also ignored unstable timbers and wielded the first pickax after the October cave-in. That night Roman had saved dozens of lives before the shaft had finally given way and claimed seven lives, including her grandfather's.

Laura picked up the pen and dipped it in the inkwell. ''All it needs is your signature, Mr. Maddox.''

Roman made no move to take the pen. ''Why are you doing this, Laura?''

She blinked, taken aback by the emotion in his voice. ''We've discussed this. You want Butler's Folly and we both agree that no one knows the mine better than you.''

Frustration darkened his deep-set eyes. ''I'm not

talking about the bloody mine. Why are you leaving Timberline?''

She ignored his harsh tone, reminding herself that he had been a good friend to her and out of respect she did owe him an explanation. ''An old friend has invited me to come stay with him at his parents' plantation. I'm leaving right after Christmas.''

Roman's right hand curled into a fist. ''That's only four days.''

Mr. Hollis tapped his meaty finger on the contract. ''Roman, you best stop worrying over Miss Laura's future plans and think about yourself. Men like you don't get chances at ownership like this.''

Roman shoved out a harsh breath. ''I'll survive with or without my name on the title.''

Mr. Hollis's cheeks reddened. ''Then think of the miners. Don't you care about the men?''

Roman stared at Hollis like a predator until the man visibly flinched.

Laura rose, ready to head off a confrontation between the men. ''No one cares about those men more than Mr. Maddox. We all know that.''

Mr. Hollis bristled. ''Well, he sure ain't acting like it right now.''

''He'll see that it runs for years to come.''

Mr. Hollis glanced nervously at Roman. ''He's got to sign the paper first.''

Roman shook his head. ''I want a word in private with Laura first.''

Laura's nerves tingled with dread. She'd hoped he'd let her leave Timberline without a fuss, but as she'd feared, he wasn't going to let the matter drop so easily.

"Have I overlooked something in the contract?" she said hopefully.

"When we're alone," he said with an earthiness that jolted her nerves.

Mr. Hollis snapped open his pocket watch. "Roman, I don't have time for this. I should have opened the office fifteen minutes ago. Just sign the blasted paper and be done with it."

Gray eyes darkened with resolve. "Not until I talk to Laura."

There was a new calmness in Roman's voice that made her worry more than the anger. He was mentally entrenching, readying for siege.

The older man opened his mouth as if to argue, then taking in Roman's rigid features seemed to think better of it. Everyone who'd met him knew blasting through granite was easier than changing his mind. "Don't mess this up, Roman."

Laura managed a bright smile. "I'm sure this won't take long, Mr. Hollis. I promise that once Mr. Maddox signs the papers, I'll bring them by your office."

"Fine," he grumbled.

Mr. Hollis stalked out of the library into the foyer tiled with black-and-white marble. A chandelier, decorated with scented evergreens and red bows, glistened above a polished round mahogany pedestal table that sported a blue porcelain bowl brimming with pinecones and sprigs of holly.

Laura's black woolen skirts rustled as she followed

Mr. Hollis. "Thank you for coming. And don't worry, everything is going to be fine."

He paused, his door on the front doorknob. "Talk some sense into him."

"I will."

He shoved out a sigh. "Almost forgot, Mrs. Hollis said to say she's fixing to bring her rum cake to the Christmas party."

Roman had moved to the doorway dividing the study and foyer. He stood on the threshold, his silent presence setting her nerves on edge.

Laura managed a grin. "It wouldn't be the perfect party without her cakes and I want everything to be just right for my last party in Timberline."

Mr. Hollis shook his head. "Christmas won't be the same without the Butlers. You're first-class, just like your grandfather. We miss him and we'll miss you."

Emotion banded her chest. "Perhaps Mr. Maddox will continue the tradition after I'm gone."

Mr. Hollis yanked open the door. "I ain't counting on it," he grumbled as he hurried down the stone stairs.

Cold winds rustled the garlands draped around the front porch's tall white columns and cut through Laura's gown as she closed the heavy door.

When she faced Roman, she had to resist the urge to step back. The intensity of his stare shrank the distance between them.

Laura smoothed damp palms over her skirt. The last two months had drained her of emotion and she didn't have the reserves to argue with Roman. "I suppose you have more questions regarding book-keeping?''

''No.''

''Payroll? Or perhaps you would like a tour of the house?'' she said, trying to shift the conversation away from the inevitable. ''It all belongs to you as soon as you sign.''

He crossed the distance between them in quick purposeful strides. Pride kept her from taking another step back.

Cupping her elbow in his hand, he escorted her back into the library. ''Have a seat.''

Laura remained standing as she studied his granite features. ''I know you're anxious to move into the house. And I promise to be out right after the Christmas party.''

The etched lines in his face deepened. ''Who's this *friend* in Virginia?''

She reminded herself again that leaving was best for everyone. ''His name is Michael. Why do you ask?''

Roman's jaw pulsed. ''He must be special for you to uproot your life for him.''

''We grew up together and have corresponded for years. I am looking forward to seeing him again.''

He started to pace then stopped. ''Is there any kind of formal agreement between you two?''

She released a heavy sigh. ''Not yet.''

His shoulders relaxed a fraction. ''Then there's no rush to get back to Virginia. You can at least stay until spring.''

''I can't.''

"Why not?"

Suddenly, she felt so weary. "There are too many sad memories in Timberline since the accident and Grandfather's death."

"Memories fade," he said softly.

For a moment, she remembered the procession of wagons, filled with seven coffins, traveling from the church to the mountain cemetery on a gray, snowy October day. She shook her head, willing the image to vanish. "I want a normal life. Marriage. Children."

An unnamed emotion crossed his smoky eyes. "This Michael fellow isn't the only man who can give you that. There are plenty of good men in Timberline."

"The only marriageable men in Timberline are miners."

"What's wrong with miners?"

"Nothing," she rushed to say, remembering Roman was a fifth-generation miner. "They are good, proud men. But I don't want a husband who works under such dangerous conditions. I watched seven women bury their husbands. It devastated them. I couldn't bear that kind of pain, not after losing Grandfather in the cave-in."

His eyes didn't leave hers. "There are no guarantees in life, Laura."

A sob filled her throat. The conversation poked at emotions she didn't want to feel. "Maybe not, but I'm going to hedge my bets by marrying a gentleman farmer, a banker or a lawyer. I want a man with a safe, steady job who will live to see our children grow."

"Like Michael," he growled.

"Yes." Feeling shaky, she walked toward the desk and picked up the contract. Nothing was going as she'd expected. "Mr. Maddox, I'm sorry. I'm not sure how our conversation strayed so far from business." She held out the paper and pen. "Sign this and we can both build new lives for ourselves."

His gaze fixed on her, he moved toward her until he stood inches away. His masculine scent and power enveloped her. "I've changed my mind."

"About what?" A drop of ink dripped from the nib and splashed onto the contract.

"The contract. I'm not signing."

Chapter Two

Laura stared at Roman, stunned. She opened her mouth to speak, closed it, then squeaked, "What do you mean you don't want to sign?"

He shrugged. "I don't want Butler's Folly anymore."

She shoved the pen in the inkwell. "But, just yesterday you said you wanted the company. You agreed it's a wonderful opportunity for you."

Roman picked up a crystal paperweight, inspected it, then set it back on the table. "I'll get by without it."

Laura's plans were unraveling before her eyes. Panicking, she snatched up the contact and held it in her fisted hand. "No one else knows that mine better than you. You have to buy it."

"Anyone can learn the business." His calm voice grated her nerves.

"But I don't trust anyone else." She started to pace. "If you don't buy the mine, I can't leave Timberline."

"Oh, well."

She stopped pacing. "*Oh, well!* How can you say that? You know I want to return to Virginia."

"You belong in Timberline."

"I do not!" She shook her head. "Everything was set perfectly. You wanted to buy the mine. You wanted to see that the miners kept their jobs. What changed?"

His dark penetrating stare pinned her. "If I sign, you leave Timberline forever. I want you to stay."

She rocked back. "Staying or leaving is my choice to make!"

He studied her face, as if weighing what he was about to say. "Can I be honest with you?"

"Why hold back now?" she said tartly.

The courage and confidence that were his trademark faltered. For the first time, she glimpsed a man uncertain—a man standing on the edge of a cliff overlooking a deep gorge, trying to decide if it were safe to jump or not. "I've wanted you."

"For what?" she said confused.

"For myself."

All the blood drained from Laura's face as she grasped his meaning. "I see."

Roman let out a deep breath. "Every day for the last seven months, I've thought about you." He shoved his hands in his pockets. "At first I kept silent because I thought you were no more than a passing fancy—a bit of society fluff, pretty but worthless."

She stared, unsure if she should be insulted or complimented.

The barest hint of a grin tugged at the corner of his mouth. "Then I saw how involved you were—the schoolhouse, the trips into the mountains to visit the sick. I realized you were a woman I wanted not only in my bed but my life.''

Laura pressed trembling hands to her temples. Before the accident, there had been something between them, but the mine disaster had obliterated all that. The falling beams and rocks had shattered her confidence and courage just as surely as they had crushed the life from her grandfather and his men. She was simply too damaged and too afraid to love anymore. ''Why wait until now to say all these things?''

His gaze didn't waver. ''I'd planned to approach you but the accident changed things. You needed time to grieve for your grandfather, but I was determined to start courting you right after the holidays. Your offer to sell me the mine bolstered my courage. It told me there was respect between us.''

Her throat tightened. ''Of course. That's always been there.''

A wry smile touched his lips. ''We can build on that.''

Laura's emotions scattered inside her. ''I-I'm flattered, but this doesn't change anything. I am leaving. I can't stay—it's just too painful.''

He flexed his fingers. His voice was even, eerily calm. ''I know you better than you think, Laura. You won't leave the people of Timberline in trouble. You'll stay until the mine is sold.''

''What if I don't? What if I'm selfish and put myself first for once?''

''You won't.''

She waved the contract in the air like a battle flag. "I will!"

He folded his arms over his chest, so confident and sure. "Then go ahead."

She wanted to call his bluff and get on the next stage east, but of course he was right. She wouldn't leave until he signed. Frustration ate at her. "Why are you doing this?"

He took a step toward her. "Because I want time to find out if we have a chance."

She backed into the desk. "We don't."

He braced his feet, trapping her between the desk and his body. "How do you know?"

"I belong in Virginia. It's where I grew up. I've friends, family."

Jaw set, he added, "And Michael."

She heard the savagery in his voice. "He's a good, dependable man."

"He won't make you happy."

Fire sparked her temper. "And when did you become such an expert on me?"

He stood inches from her, his presence curling around her. "A woman doesn't move west unless she's got spirit and a taste for adventure. It takes strength to take that kind of chance. Virginia and society teas will bore you to tears now."

She shook her head, willing back unwanted tears. "The accident, the death of Grandfather cured me of any taste for adventure. Frankly, boredom sounds wonderful right now."

He laid his hands on her shoulders. "Let me be

strong for you while you heal and regain your footing.''

The warmth of his hands seeped into her body, beckoning her. Surrendering to Roman appealed more than she'd dare admit. ''Oh, no! I've already depended too much on you lately.''

''I haven't minded at all.''

It had been natural to share the mining responsibilities with him. They'd worked well together, but a business relationship was all she'd dare share with him. If she opened the door to loving Roman, there'd be no turning back. ''You are exactly the kind of man I could never lean on.'' She crushed the contract in her hand, and tried to sidestep him on the left.

He blocked her escape with his muscled arm. ''Because I'm a miner.''

''Not just any miner,'' she said louder than she'd intended. She edged right, desperately needing to put distance between them. She never could think when he was too close. ''Roman, you take more chances than any man. Fate is going to catch up with you one day.''

''I've no plans to die until I'm a very old man, but I won't cower, stop living my life, hoping fate leaves me be.''

Tears glistened in her eyes. ''No, it's not in your makeup to cower, even from danger or death.''

A devilish glint glistened in his gray eyes. ''Would it bother you if something happened to me?''

Her heart tumbled. ''Yes!''

He grinned, his masculine pride evident. ''You care about me,'' he said.

A rush of heat colored her cheeks. "You're a good man, Roman. I'd never say otherwise, but if I gave my heart to you, I'd spend my days worrying if you'd make it home safely each night."

He traced circles on her shoulder. "If you're waiting for me, I'd get home *every* night."

Roman's husky tone hinted at an intimacy that left her breathless. Excitement fluttered inside her before she ruthlessly shoved it aside.

"I have to get to the schoolhouse!" She blurted the words out, grateful she had good reason to leave. "The children will be waiting."

He captured her arm. "Can you look at me and tell me you've never thought about me—us together?"

She moistened her lips. Yes, she had. "I've got to go."

"The children can wait a few more minutes. Answer the bloody question."

He stared down at her with such intensity that her insides jumped. In truth, she'd first really noticed him this past Fourth of July picnic when he had challenged two other men to a stake-driving contest. He'd tugged off his shirt in the hot summer afternoon and not a woman around, including Granny Davis, hadn't noticed the way the sweat had glistened on his bare, muscled chest.

Since that picnic she had wondered what it would be like to kiss him, to feel his bare skin against hers. He wasn't handsome in the conventional sense, but his very maleness made him the kind of man that made her senses tingle.

Shocked by her thoughts, she straightened, her face

warmed with embarrassment. "This discussion is academic. I'm leaving Timberline."

As if he'd read her thoughts, he grinned. "You do think about me."

Her pulse quickened. "I—I really do have to go to school—the children are waiting."

He studied her an extra second, then stepped back. "I'll drive you."

She moved away from the desk and him. "That's not necessary."

"It's too cold for you to walk today." He cradled her elbow in his palm and escorted her into the foyer where her coat lay draped across a side chair next to a large basket of freshly baked cookies. He picked up her coat and held it out for her.

Warily, she studied her gray woolen overcoat like a rabbit a snare.

He dangled the coat. "I don't bite."

Challenged, she moved closer and slid her arms into the coat. Before she could step clear of him, he wrapped his arms around her and engulfed her. His hold was gentle, but unbreakable. "I'm not giving up on you."

His warmth tantalized, excited and scared the devil out of her. "I'm not available." She held up the paper still fisted in her hand. "Just sign the contract and be done with this foolishness."

He turned her around and tilted her head back with his finger under her chin. His hot breath warmed her face. "We are meant to be and I am going to prove it to you."

"You sound as if you've got it all figured out."

He shrugged on his coat. "I do."

Laura jammed the contract in her pocket. "My life plans do not include you."

The glint in his eyes turned to steel as he slowly fastened the buttons on his coat. "Life's made me tough and stubborn, Laura. I learned long ago not to listen to others. I do what feels right in my gut."

"Maybe you just ate something this morning that didn't agree with you," she said hearing the hint of desperation in her voice.

He grinned, flashing white teeth. "I want you, Laura. And deep in your heart you want me. Now, I'm going to prove it."

Chapter Three

Roman knew Zachary Butler's death had been a terrible blow to Laura and though she'd never cried in public or asked for help, he'd seen the pain etched in her proud features. There'd been nights after the accident that he'd been unable to sleep. During most of his midnight walks, he'd seen the lights burning in her house and watched her pacing in front of the windows. He knew she'd been suffering and he'd hated that there wasn't a damn thing he could do about it.

But now there was something he could do for her. He could stop her from making the worst mistake of her life. Returning to Virginia wasn't about any great desire to see family and friends or to rekindle old feelings for Michael. She was running scared from memories that would follow her to the ends of the earth and torment her until she faced them.

Hell, he'd wanted to walk away and start life anew anywhere else after the accident. But he'd stayed because leaving Timberline would have meant leaving her. So, he'd forced himself back into the shafts to prove to himself and his men that the past would not haunt him.

Most of his men had regained their courage and followed his lead. Now, it was Laura's turn.

They had a future together—he had felt it in his bones the first time he'd seen her—and at times, he wanted her so much he ached. So, he'd do anything in the next four days to convince her to stay.

The grandfather clock in the alcove by the stairs chimed. Startled, Laura shoved trembling hands into her gray gloves.

She reached for her basket. "This is not the time to talk about this. I am really late for school."

Roman glared at the clock, cursing its intrusion, but as always, he accepted what life offered and adapted. He brushed her hand aside and picked up her basket. "I heard about what the children have planned. I'll drive you."

On the last school day before the holiday, he'd heard it was tradition for the children to demand a "toll" of her—a cookie for each child—before they'd let her pass into the schoolhouse. Many parents lingered near the schoolhouse to watch the exchange, which he'd heard Laura enjoyed as much as everyone.

Today of all days, she'd not want to be tardy.

Laura chewed her bottom lip. Her stubborn nature would view his offer of a ride as a surrender of sorts and she'd have refused if the children hadn't been waiting. "I'm only agreeing to a ride, nothing else."

He pressed his hand into the small of her back, guiding her to the door. "One step at a time."

Minutes later, as his wagon crunched through the

packed snow on Main Street, Roman stared at Laura's long, straight nose, creamy skin and golden curls. She sat so straight he'd have bet her spine would have snapped if he'd said "boo."

As if sensing his gaze, she glanced up at him. A spray of curls peeked out from her bonnet rimming her clear, bright face. "I think I've figured out what's wrong with you."

He liked the Southern lilt in her voice. "Wrong with me? I'm not sure I like the sound of that."

"Stress." She shook her head gravely. "And I'm afraid I'm to blame."

He almost smiled. She always worried about someone other than herself. "How's that?"

"I shouldn't have tried to sell you the company. It's too much for you. Not only did you have the cave-in to deal with, but during the last few months you've been doing Grandfather's work on top of your own. I also know you've taken time to visit the families who lost men in the accident." She shook her head. "And what do I do? I dump more responsibility on you."

He straightened his shoulders. "I can handle whatever you throw my way."

She shook her head. "You're not the type who'd admit he's got too much on his plate. I know that, and I should have been looking out for you instead of losing myself in sorrow." She laid her hand on his arm. "Tell me what I can do?"

He leaned closer to her, savoring the scent of her rose perfume and the softness of her body close to his. "Stay in Timberline."

She pulled away. ''I was thinking more along the lines of hiring a manager for you. Grandfather spoke of a man in Leadville—''

''I want you, not a manager.''

She pressed her fingers to her temples. ''You're just confused.''

''My mind's never been clearer.''

She reached in her pocket and pulled out the crumpled contract. ''Just sign it.''

''Nope.''

She raised her finger, ready to make another point when children's laughter tumbled down the snowy street toward them. She turned toward the clapboard building dusted with snow that sat just beyond the edge of town. In the distance, white-capped mountains scraped toward the azure sky and rimmed their small valley.

In front of the building, two dozen children stood shoulder to shoulder. Dressed in gray and black overcoats with sprigs of holly pinned to their lapels, their ages ranged from six to sixteen. The little ones jumped around as if standing in one place required too much discipline. The older girls giggled while the taller boys stood straight, pretending an aloofness they likely didn't feel.

Claire Brown, one of the smallest children, spotted their wagon first. She squealed as she waved her gloved hands. ''She's coming! She's coming!''

The other children immediately tightened their ranks. The older ones struggled to keep a straight face. The younger ones grinned.

Roman had lived in mining towns all his life. Many

didn't have schools and the ones that did were as lifeless as the teachers. Thanks to Laura, neither was true of Timberline.

He pulled the wagon to a stop at the edge of the boardwalk where dozens of parents crowded to witness the holiday ritual.

Laura scanned the faces of the smiling townsfolk. She let the contract drop into his lap. "I've never seen so many parents turn out for this."

"You're the ray of sunshine they all need."

She frowned. "The holidays always brighten everyone's mood."

"Not when there's nothing to hope for. You give these parents and their children hope."

She drew away. "I've done nothing that special."

"Look around you, Laura. These people are here today, happy for the first time in months because of you." Her gaze lingered on him and she looked as if she were going to argue. Instead, she turned toward the children. In a voice loud enough for everyone to hear she said, "Time to ring the school bell. We've a full day of work."

Excited laughter rippled through the group of children.

Roman shoved the contract into his coat pocket, tied off the reins and jumped down. He strode around the wagon to Laura's side and stretched out his arms to her. She hesitated only an instant, then leaned into him. His fingers banded around her narrow waist and her hands went to his shoulders as he lifted her to the ground.

He held on to her an extra beat, unwilling to share

her just yet. He wanted Laura all to himself—naked and in his bed. As if she'd read his thoughts, deep crimson colored her cheeks.

With no hint of apology, he stepped back, lifted the basket filled with cookies from the wagon and handed it to her. "Have a good day."

She swallowed, clearly a little thrown off by his touch. "Thanks."

Grinning, Roman folded his arms over his chest and leaned against the wagon as giggles rippled among the children.

"You can't come inside," Claire shouted.

Laura pretended to look upset. "What do you mean, Miss Brown?"

The redheaded child looked up at one of the older girls who winked at her and nudged her forward. Claire planted her hands on her hips. "You have to pay a toll."

Laura lifted her eyebrows. "What kind of a toll?"

Seth Tyler, a nine-year-old boy with thick, black hair and freckles sprinkled on his nose, stepped past Claire. "We want something sweet!"

Laura made a face as if she didn't know what to do. "But what if I don't have anything?"

Claire shook her head. "Then you can't come in."

Laura pretended to think. Then very slowly she lifted the tea cloth draped over her basket and peeked under it. She looked at the children, then back into her basket. Several children squealed from anticipation. "Would a cookie do?"

Two of the littlest children started to rush forward, but Oscar Davis, a strapping boy of thirteen, held them back. Oscar was as big as some men, but he possessed the chubby face of youth. Many boys his age had already started work in the mines, but Zachary Butler had made it a policy not to hire anyone under fifteen to work the shafts. Roman had never questioned the old man's rule. Life had robbed him of his own childhood and he'd be damned before he'd steal a child's youth.

Oscar cleared his throat. "Miss Laura, we can't let you pass less you're willin' to give us each two cookies."

"Two!" Laura shouted. "That's a mighty steep price, Oscar Davis. How about one cookie?"

Oscar wrinkled his nose, forcing away a grin. "No, ma'am, that won't do. Two cookies is the price."

Laura wrinkled her nose. "You drive a hard bargain, Mr. Davis."

"Business is business."

Laura paused as her gaze touched the older boy's, then moved to each child's bright face. Her expression softened, an odd mixture of love and sadness, as she seemed to drink in the scene. Finally, she grinned. "How about three cookies?"

The children shouted their joy and swarmed around her. She held her basket high, promising each their treats as she slowly made her way up the three steps into the schoolhouse.

Roman lingered, stealing an extra peek at Laura through the schoolhouse's clean window. Even from his distance, he could see that she was laughing. It had been too long since he'd seen her happy.

He imagined their own children gathered around

her skirts, the smell of cinnamon in the air, the soft sound of her voice as she read a Christmas story before a crackling fire.

An angular woman with graying hair and pinched features moved away from the other parents on the boardwalk toward Roman. Her name was Fran Warner and with her husband she owned the mercantile. Their sons, Nick and Stuart, were in the third and fourth grades. "What brings you out here this morning? I've never known you to be late for work."

Roman tore his gaze from the schoolhouse. "Just curious. I'd heard about this tradition Laura started and wanted to see it for myself."

Mrs. Warner's brown eyes warmed. "Normally, it takes dynamite to get my son Nick out of the bed on a school day, but today he was dressed and asking for breakfast before I was even out of bed. He couldn't wait to get here." She shook her head. "It'll be a sad day when Miss Laura leaves."

Roman frowned. "You know she plans to leave?"

"She told the church ladies two days ago."

It bothered Roman that she'd not told him. And he began to wonder if she'd ever planned to. Perhaps she'd thought to slip out of town, understanding deep in her heart that he'd move heaven and earth to keep her here.

"I know several ladies in town who are fixing to go by her place this evening and have a talk with her," Mrs. Warner continued. "They're hopeful, but I'm not. I've never seen Laura quite so determined."

Roman pushed away from the wagon. "Tell the women to hold off."

Mrs. Warner's gaze sharpened. "Why, you got something up your sleeve?"

He climbed up onto the wagon and untied the reins. "Maybe."

She edged closer to the buckboard, her interest piqued. "Tell me, what is it?"

"Can't say just now."

She lowered her voice. "You can tell me. I won't tell a single soul."

No, she'd tell a hundred. And maybe that's just what he needed. He wrapped the reins around his hand and leaned toward Mrs. Warner. "I can't say. You know what a private woman Laura is."

She fastened an imaginary lock on her lips. "I'll put it in the vault."

He leaned closer to her and in a low voice asked, "Are you still baking the special occasion cakes? Like the one you did up for the Lancasters?"

Mrs. Warner's mouth dropped open then she clamped it shut. "You mean a *wedding* cake?"

Roman grinned. "That's the kind."

"Is someone getting married?"

"Can't say just yet." He looked toward the schoolhouse, his gaze lingering on Laura.

Mrs. Warner glanced at the schoolhouse then back at Roman. Her feet started to dance with excitement. "I'm still making wedding cakes."

Roman glanced from side to side, and lowered his voice. "I'd like to order one for Laura's Christmas party."

"Are you trying to tell me what I think you're trying to tell me?"

He winked and smiled.

She giggled and pressed her hands to her lips. "Consider it done."

"I knew I could count on you."

As Roman watched Mrs. Warner scurrying toward a circle of women, he realized she'd tell everyone she saw that he and Laura had ordered a wedding cake.

Roman grinned and snapped the reins. The wagon jerked forward toward the mine.

He wasn't fighting fair. But fair and patient had gotten him nowhere.

Chapter Four

"**M**iss Butler!" Natalie Hunter, an eight-year-old with black hair and wide eyes, tugged on Laura's sleeve. "You're not listening again."

Laura forced her gaze from the window and the view of Roman's mine office back to Natalie and the other five children in the reading group. Their desks were arranged in a semicircle around her chair and they were all staring at her. She'd not heard a word the child had read, her thoughts still on what Roman had said earlier.

"I was listening." She coughed and glanced down at *McGuffy's Reader*, forcing her mind to focus on the words. "Now once again, give me three words that start with the letter *L*."

"You're a page behind, Miss Butler," Natalie said.

Laura flipped the page. "*M*, then."

"Mine, money, mother," Natalie said.

Mine, marriage, Maddox.

She conjured images of Roman's tough, angled face, his supple lips pressed against her bare neck. Over and over, her thoughts returned to his broad shoulders, muscular chest and the coarse hair that peeked out the top of his shirt, which she imagined trailed over his hard flat stomach all the way, well, *down there*.

"Miss Laura! Is that right?" Natalie demanded.

The little girl's voice jolted Laura from her thoughts. Blushing, she sat straighter. "Y-yes. That's right." She had to get control of herself and her over-zealous imagination. "Julia, what about the letter *N?*"

The little girl with the curly hair and round face blinked and grinned. "Nuts, nugget…"

Nuptials. There'd been no talk of marriage, but it was the natural ending to courtship.

Laura nearly jumped out of her seat. Marriage to Roman was absolutely out of the question. It challenged her hopes of building a safe predictable life, free of devastating accidents.

She fidgeted in her seat, tapped her foot and glanced at the clock for the hundredth time today— 1:32. When would this day ever end?

"Miss Butler, is that right?"

Laura smiled at the eight-year-old. "Thank you, Julia. That was excellent." She snapped her book closed and rose. "You've all done such a wonderful job today, I'm dismissing school early."

Three boys, who sat in the corner next to a small tree decorated with paper chains, pinecones and strings of cranberries, looked up from their shared copy of *A Christmas Carol.* "You never let us out early, Miss Butler," said Alex, a towheaded boy with bright green eyes.

"Is you sick?" Matthew asked.

Laura started to collect the extra slates. *No, I'm insane.* "I suppose I'm just excited about the party. It's only three days away and I've so much to do. I can't string two thoughts together."

"But you're grown-up," Julia said. "You ain't...aren't supposed to get excited."

Laura laughed. Out of the mouths of babes. The truth was she hadn't felt this excited or alive in years. As frustrated as she'd been with Roman this morning, he'd reignited a fire in her that had been extinguished by the accident.

"Well, I am, so take advantage of it. Besides, the weather is lovely and you should all enjoy it." She clapped her hands. "Everyone. You are dismissed."

Excited whispers swept the classroom as the children hurriedly packed their books. Laura slipped on her coat and opened the door. As the children passed, she said, "Happy Christmas! I hope to see you all at the party."

Laura lingered in the doorway and grinned when little Julia scooped up a handful of snow, packed it into a ball and threw it at Alex. The snowball hit him square in the back. The boy laughed and started to chase the girl who giggled as she darted down the boardwalk.

Smiling, Laura closed the door and set about the task of cleaning the slates as she had every school day for the last three years. Alone in the room, she realigned the desks, shoveled out the stove and swept the place clean. She'd already cleared out her personal items and everything was in place for the new teacher.

Laura slipped on her bonnet and tugged on her gloves. The empty cookie basket in hand, she opened the door and glanced back at the classroom for the last time. Her heartbeat faltered as she looked at the children's pictures of Father Christmas clipped to the wall, the collection of well-worn readers that had cost her a fortune in Denver three years ago and the neat row of desks. Emotion tightened her throat. Lord, but she was going to miss the children.

Tonight, she'd have to write a letter to the new teacher. There were so many things she needed to tell him. Oscar needed help with his numbers. Claire loved to draw. Julia's voice could be loud but she was a good child with a big heart.

An unexpected melancholy settled in her bones as she shut the door behind her and fastened the padlock.

She strode down Main Street past the newspaper office sporting a wreath on its front door and the millinery which showcased a collection of festive red hats in the front window. At the edge of town Garth Jackson, the saloon's owner and bartender, had slung a garland of cedar over the saloon's wide double front doors. The air crackled with excitement and most everyone was smiling. Except Laura.

She nodded to three matrons grouped standing on the boardwalk. Huddled together, they giggled like schoolgirls as she passed. Laura paused and looked at the women over her shoulder. Their smiling expressions immediately sobered.

Fran Warner, who stood in the middle of the trio, waved thin fingers at her. "How are you doing today, Miss Laura?"

"Fine. And you?"

Martha Powell shifted the weight of her parcel wrapped in brown paper to her other hip. "We're just perfect. Plans for the Christmas party coming along?"

Awful. The party was her formal goodbye to Timberline and she'd procrastinated the final chores for days. "Wonderful. I can't wait to have everyone over to the house."

Molly Bamberger pursed her lips, trying to bite back a smile. "Got anything *special* planned for the party this year?"

Laura cocked an eyebrow and wondered what had made the stern matron so giddy. "A few new dishes and more decorations."

The three women erupted in a gale of laughter before she could respond.

Laura edged closer. "Is everything all right, ladies? You haven't had any of Mr. Gunnerson's special nog, have you?"

Eyes filled with laughter, Martha waved away her question. "Oh, no, dear. We're just really looking forward to the party."

"Chocolate cake still your favorite, Miss Laura?" Fran asked.

Laura brushed her gloved hand over her cheek, wondering if she had chalk smudged across it. "Yes."

"Vanilla icing?"

"Yes."

The women started whispering among themselves.

Laura leaned closer. "Is there something I'm missing?"

Fran swallowed another smile. "Just three old women having a bit of fun. Now, you run on."

Laura turned slowly, wondering what had gotten into the women, and headed toward the title office. She prayed Roman had seen reason and had dropped off the signed contract.

Laura pushed open the door to the small title office that smelled of paper and dust. Small bells attached to the top of the door jingled, announcing her arrival.

Afternoon sunlight glowed off the stacks and rows of ledgers arranged from *A* to *Z* on tall shelves located behind a long counter.

"Hello?"

Mr. Hollis rose up from behind the counter. He groaned as he straightened his stiff legs. He wasn't a man who smiled often, his mind always consumed with the thousand details of a boomtown title office. But today the scowl on his face softened at the sight of her.

"Miss Laura! A good afternoon to you."

His good humor suggested Roman had indeed been by and signed the contract. "I'm well. And you?"

"Fit as a fiddle."

"I'm glad to hear it." She moved to the counter. "By your high spirits can I assume you received good news today?"

"I did indeed."

She released the breath she'd been holding. "Then Roman did come by and sign the contract?"

He shook his head. "Well, no, he didn't."

She stilled. "But you're smiling. You never smile...I mean like you are right now."

"I may be smiling but it ain't because of Roman or Butler's Folly."

Laura's eyes narrowed. "Has something changed that I'm not aware of? Roman has to sign that contract before I leave."

Mr. Hollis peered over the rim of his glasses. "Are you really leaving Timberline? Folks believe this talk of yours about moving back east is just smoke and mirrors."

First the women, now Hollis. The Christmas spirit had banished good sense. "Why would anyone say such a thing? Half the folks in town know I have train tickets dated for December 26."

"Tickets can be cashed back in."

"I'm not cashing in mine. And I am leaving whether Mr. Maddox signs that contract or not."

"Right," he said drawing out the word.

Laura suddenly had the feeling she was the only one not privy to a private joke. "Mr. Hollis, what's going on?"

"Now, don't go pretending with me, the cat's out of the bag."

"What cat?"

He adjusted his glasses. "I *know*. We all know."

"Know what?" she said her teeth clenched now.

"About you and Roman."

She raised a thin eyebrow, waiting for him to finish what he now seemed itching to talk about.

"We all noticed that Roman drove you to school."

"I was running late," she challenged.

He hooked his thumbs in his suspenders. "The man

stares at you like he's half-starved. Has since the day he arrived in town.''

Heat rose inside her, coloring her cheeks. There'd been a time this past summer when she'd turned and caught Roman staring at her. They'd been in the mercantile. He'd been buying boots; she'd come in for groceries.

Roman hadn't been a bit taken aback when she'd looked him right in the eyes. Instead, he'd let his gaze trail up and down her body, making her feel as if she'd just been caressed. Rattled, she'd bumped into a stack of flour, barely righting herself before she'd stumbled. She'd forgotten what she'd come to the store for, so with no other recourse, she had mumbled an excuse to Mrs. Warner and fled.

"He does not," she whispered.

"He does. Ask anybody."

"W-what does that have to do with anything?"

"We know he *ordered a cake*." Mr. Hollis lowered his voice. "A cake. Like the one Mrs. Warner made for the Lancasters this past summer."

For an instant she hesitated, her mind searching her memory, then she remembered the three-tiered confection. "That was a wedding cake." Suspicion blossomed. "Why would I need a cake like that?"

He planted his hands on his hips. "Stop pretending, Laura. We all know you and Roman is getting married. He told Fran Warner so this very morning."

She grabbed the counter to steady herself. "He didn't."

He crossed his heart. "Heard it from Martha who heard it direct from Frances not two hours ago."

"I can't believe he'd do this to me!" Laura's hands shook with fury as she whirled on her heel and headed for the door.

Mr. Hollis's expression sobered a fraction. "Where you off to, Miss Laura?"

"To kill Roman Maddox."

Chapter Five

As Laura hurried toward the mine eleven people stopped her to offer their congratulations on her upcoming wedding to Roman. At first she tried to explain that it was a misunderstanding, but the more she tried to deny the rumor the more knowing smiles and grins she received.

By the time she'd reached the mine office, her temper had warmed from a simmer to a boil.

Murder was too good for Roman Maddox.

The roar of the conveyor belts from the nearby ore-processing mill drowned out her entry as she pushed open the office door. Despite the bustle of men and equipment, she spotted Roman immediately. He stood with his back to her in the center of a half-dozen other men. His foot was propped on a chair and he leaned over a large desk scattered with papers. The purely masculine stance drew Roman's shirt tight over his wide shoulders, and despite her simmering temper Laura could only stare.

The energy that flowed from him had her craving a primitive, and certainly most unladylike, kind of loving. The kind that left her breathless in the afternoon, naked and entwined in his arms. This reaction was nothing like the gentle thoughts she had for Michael.

Roman sensed her presence and turned. His eyes darkened seductively and his lips curled upward in a warm welcome. She could feel a flush rising in her cheeks.

He winked at her.

Her heart swelled with a wanting she couldn't define and for an instant she forgot why she'd come to see him.

Roman fired orders at his men then moved toward her in quick, purposeful strides. Her stomach jittered. He stopped inches from her. She swallowed, her mouth as dry as cotton.

Taking her elbow, he led her outside into the cool afternoon air toward a small stand of trees away from the noise. "What brings you here?"

Murder. That's right, she'd come to murder him. Laura cleared her throat, wishing he wasn't standing so close. She thought better when there was more distance between them. "We have to talk."

His gaze narrowed. "Have you come about the contract? Because if you have, I've not changed my mind." His tone possessed a steely resolve that told her he meant what he said.

"It's on my list of things to discuss with you, but right now it's not at the top. We have an emergency on our hands."

He raised a thick eyebrow. "I'm all ears."

She spotted two miners striding up the mountain

path toward the mine and lowered her voice. "When you ordered the cake from Mrs. Warner, you gave her the wrong impression."

He looked mildly surprised. "Something wrong with chocolate cake?"

"Our problem has nothing to do with the flavor of the cake," she said as if speaking to a child. "It's the fact that you ordered a cake at all."

He folded his arms over his chest. "I like cake."

For a smart man, he was acting very stupid right now. "You asked for a cake like the one the Lancasters ordered this last summer."

"Vanilla icing?" he offered.

"Wedding!" she shouted.

The miners looked up. They paused long enough for Laura to catch their devilish grins.

Horrified, her face turned crimson. "It's not what you think," she called out to them. "We are *not* getting married."

One jabbed the other in the ribs, whispered something and they both laughed.

"I'm not kidding," Laura said, more frustrated.

They touched their hats and said, "Yes, ma'am."

Swinging her gaze back to Roman, Laura snapped, "You've got to go speak with Mrs. Warner and tell her that you didn't order a wedding cake."

"Why do you care what other people think?" His tone turned low, rough. "Is the idea of marrying me so bad?"

"No! I'm sure you'll make a wonderful husband. You're just not my type."

"I'm exactly your type." He moved closer, took her hands in his.

Her breath caught in her throat. "I'm not marrying you."

He grinned. "The more I hear the word *no* the more determined I am to turn it into a *yes*."

"You can't have everything you want."

"I don't want everything. Just you."

She was quite certain then that the color drained from her face. "I'm leaving town right after Christmas."

He straightened. Some may have seen the shift in posture as casual. She saw it as a battle stance. "Without the mine sold?"

She yanked her hands free of his. "Why can't you just buy the blasted mine? You are a responsible man, a man who takes care of the men who work for him."

He touched a curl that had escaped her chignon. "For the last seven months, I've put the men first. I've put the mine first. Obligation first. Respect for your grandfather first. Your grief first. Everything came *first* but *us*. Patient, polite, persistent have gotten me nowhere with you." Puffs of cold air caressed her skin. "I want you. I won't apologize for it. And I'm not backing down."

Her head started to pound. She took a step back. "You don't even know me. Not really."

"That's easily fixed," he said huskily. He advanced a step, then traced his finger along her jawbone.

She shook her head, trying to ignore the thread of emotions that pulled her toward him. "What we felt wasn't real. The feelings are leftovers from the cave-in. We both shared losses that day.''

She could feel the heat of his body. "Emotions *we're* feeling?"

"I—I mean you," she stammered. She took a step back and bumped into the trunk of a wide tree.

He planted his hand on the tree just above her head and leaned, trapping her. "You said *we*."

A riot of sensations thrummed through her body. "I-I'm just flustered."

His voice grew husky. "Laura, you been thinking about me in *that way* again?"

She bit her lip wondering how he'd managed to steer her so far off course. "I'll admit, I've been distracted today because of your stubbornness."

He grazed her lips with his fingertips. "You've only been thinking about my stubbornness?"

When had she lost control? "Yes, of course. It would not be proper to think about anything else."

He grinned. "So did you daydream about me all day?"

She raised her chin primly. "Certainly not."

The humor in his gaze dissolved into desire. "I could make some of those dreams come true."

Her mouth went dry. That throbbing sensation she'd felt when she'd first seen him in July returned. "You're driving me crazy."

"It's about time."

She shoved out a sigh. "What is it going to take to make you understand that we're all wrong for each other?"

He traced her jawbone with his callused finger. "I

want you to give us a chance. A fair, honest chance. Spend time with me. If nothing happens between us, then I'll sign the contract.''

In the space of a day, he'd turned her well-ordered emotions into a jumble.

"Four days, Laura," he prompted. "What's it gonna be?''

He was offering her a way out. She should have felt elated. But she didn't. "You really will sign the papers?''

"I never say what I don't mean." He held out a wide, callused hand.

Her fingers tingled at the thought of touching him. "And you'll tell Mrs. Warner the cake is not for our wedding?''

"That's yet to be decided. What are your plans for tomorrow?''

Her mind shifted, trying to keep up. "I've hired a wagon and Mr. Warner is coming with me to cut my Christmas tree.''

"I'll take you.''

His offer surprised her. "But you're working.''

"I can spare the time.''

"Perhaps our first outing shouldn't be as adventurous. Dinner at the hotel would be more respectable.''

Sensing her hesitation, he laughed. "Nothing's more respectable than cutting a Christmas tree. Besides, the outing will be good for you. I'll speak to Warner and tell him I'm taking you into the mountains. I'll pick you up at eight o'clock tomorrow morning.''

His take-charge attitude grated her nerves. "You're mighty sure of yourself."

He brushed a snowflake from her shoulder. "A man has to be when he's in an all-or-nothing game."

Roman wasn't the kind of man she'd ever have bet against, but she had no choice this time. She laid her small gloved hand in his, marveling at the way his fingers gently engulfed hers. "You're going to discover we're not suited."

He tugged her gently toward him, so close that her breasts brushed his chest. His head bent toward her, and she could feel his hot breath on her chilled skin. "Let's see."

Roman cupped his hand behind her head, ensnaring the curling wisps of hair between his fingers. He coaxed her head forward.

His mouth closed over hers and her entire body went still. For an instant, she didn't breathe and was half-convinced that her heart had stopped beating. Then all at once her blood raced and the heat in her body rose. Her rigid limbs relaxed and she rose up on tiptoe, greedy for more.

His strong arm banded around her narrow waist and pulled her against him. He tasted of coffee and the barest hint of tobacco.

The sane corner of her brain, the part where her mother had instilled every value and snippet of common sense chastised her. She'd been raised better than this!

Yet, the dark sensuous side of her, the part that lusted for Roman, savored the moment. Kissing Roman felt better than she'd ever imagined.

Now she understood what the ladies in the quilting guild giggled about when they talked of the private moments they spent with their husbands.

Laura's brain barely registered the crunch of branches, but Roman processed it instantly. Cursing under his breath he pulled away from her, lifting his head as if the separation hurt.

Laura realized, to her great horror, that they had an audience. The two miners had returned—with friends. Immediately, she shoved away from him and brushed a curl from her forehead.

Roman swallowed, but didn't completely release her. He faced his man. "What is it, Simpson?"

"The charges you asked us to set are ready, sir," the tall gangly man replied. "We need you to inspect them."

Roman's body was rigid, tight with desire. "I'll be right there."

The man started to leave then paused. He faced Laura and Roman. "The wife tells me you two are engaged. Me and the men just wanted to offer our congratulations."

Laura opened her mouth. "Oh, no. You don't understand. We—"

"Thank you," Roman said in a clear voice.

Chapter Six

Laura supposed matters could have been worse as she stood in her kitchen hours later. Mother Nature could have dumped seven feet of snow, forcing her to dig a tunnel to the privy one hundred feet from her back door. She could have been lost in the mountains, as she had been her first spring here, staring down a mountain lion.

Instead, thanks to Roman, the entire town was planning their wedding and her emotions, which she'd prided herself on controlling, had as many peaks and valleys as the Sierras.

She'd rather have been digging through a wall of snow.

Laura wiped the flour from her hands onto her apron. In the last few months, baking had calmed her nerves and made her out-of-kilter life feel just a little normal. But as she stared at the dozens of freshly baked gingerbread cookies mounded on the silver tray, she wondered if she'd ever feel normal again.

"If Roman cared about me, he'd let me go." She dumped another pound of butter into a bowl and jabbed the spoon into the thick chunk, breaking it up into smaller pieces.

Her mind conjured the image of Roman's eyes, so piercing they never failed to take her breath away. She thought of his strong hands. His full lips.

Laura muttered an oath as she looked at the half-creamed butter. "I'm not thinking about Roman." She dumped two scoops of sugar into the bowl and started to mix. "I'm not going to think about Roman."

But the faster she stirred and the harder she tried not to think about Roman, the quicker her thoughts circled back to him.

In defense, she focused on Michael. She summoned pale-blond hair and blue—or was it green?—eyes. He was tall, not as tall as Roman but tall. She closed her eyes, trying harder to imagine his face, but nothing came. Disturbed that she'd forgotten so much in the last five years, Laura stood a little straighter, digging into her memory.

"I haven't forgotten anything," she muttered. "I just need to try harder."

Michael was book smart, better read than any man she knew. He could discern Mozart from Chopin in just a few notes. And all agreed he was witty, charming and kind.

However, he didn't possess the street savvy of a man accustomed to surviving alone. He couldn't spot a silver vein even if he was standing on it and he wasn't the kind of man others turned to in crisis.

He wasn't Roman.

Laura mixed the batter with renewed violence.

"I'm not going to love you, Roman Maddox. I'm not."

She resolved then to renege on their outing tomorrow. The attraction between them was too powerful, too compelling, and a day spent alone with him could be her undoing. Until she got on that train for Virginia, she'd stay as far away from Roman as possible and just pray that he signed the contract.

"Who cares if half the people in town think he ordered a wedding cake?"

She spooned the dough into cookies and placed them in the oven. The savory ginger scent evoked memories of last Christmas and reminded her of just how much her life had changed. Last year, she and her grandfather had baked the cookies together, laughing as she tried to sing hymns in her loud, very off-key voice.

Tears burned her throat. She felt so alone.

Pulling in a ragged breath, Laura turned from the platter of cookies on the kitchen table. She'd not wasted her time on tears or self-pity these last two months, and she'd not start now. Hard work got her through the last two months and it would get her through tonight.

Determined to keep a tight rein on her emotions, she pulled her dishes, silver and crystal from the storage closet off the kitchen. There was plenty of polishing and cleaning to be done before the party. And she'd clean each and every piece until they shone.

By two o'clock in the morning, she'd done just that. Freshly washed china, crystal and silver covered her dining room table and glistened in the lantern light. Laura's arms ached with fatigue, but despite her accomplishment, her mind refused to slow.

She turned to the closet under the staircase where her Christmas decorations were stored. Opening the triangular door, she hauled out a large, dusty trunk, unlatched the straps and flipped open the lid. Inside lay dozens of ornaments, a legacy of her German-born grandmother, neatly wrapped in muslin and twine.

The ornaments would make her feel better. Excitement raced through her as it did every year before the holidays. She sat down on the floor and picked up a small bundle.

Gingerly, she unwrapped a glass star. Holding it high, she marveled at the way it bent the lantern light into a rainbow of colors. How many times had she and her grandfather looked at this star and made a wish?

But instead of her spirits rising, the strength began to seep from her limbs as she laid the star down. She missed her grandfather so much: the smell of his pipe tobacco, the sound of his steady clear voice when he read out loud in the evenings, the way he left his shoes scattered about the house.

Slowly, she opened another parcel. A silver bell winked in the lantern light. Gently she shook the bell, allowing its whispery chime to summon memories. She remembered her grandmother's piano melodies mingling with her grandfather's rich baritone voice.

Laura's throat tightened as she unwrapped another ornament—a wooden sleigh, carved by one of her students. The edges were rough, the paint uneven, but she cherished it. Lord, but she was going to miss those children and this town.

For the first time since the mine accident, tears welled in her eyes. She tried to swallow them but couldn't. The loneliness and despair slammed into her gut like a punch and tears came in an unwanted rush, streaming down her face. Sobs racked her body and the sorrow she'd brushed aside for so many weeks squeezed her heart to breaking.

She didn't know how long she cried or how long she sat on the cold floor, but a loud knock on her front door jolted her out of her trance. Her gaze darted to the clock. Six o'clock. Roman wasn't due until eight.

Laura scrambled to her feet and with her sleeve wiped the tears from her red-rimmed eyes. Pride had her pulling back her shoulders and running her fingers through her loose hair, pinching her cheeks for color. She produced a bright smile and opened the door.

Roman stood on her porch. A dark overcoat covered his warrior's body and he stood so close she was forced to tilt her head back to meet those gray eyes that seemed to miss nothing.

"You're early," she said as brightly as she could manage.

Worry deepened the lines on his face. "Your lights were on."

She sniffed and managed a smile. "I rose early today."

"They've been on all night."

She raised her chin. "How would you know?"

"My man reported back to me."

"What man?"

"I've had a guard posted outside your house since your grandfather died. A woman living alone is vulnerable." He pushed past her and moved into the house. "Now tell me why you've been crying."

Chapter Seven

Laura's fingers went automatically to her flushed cheek. "Nothing to worry about. I was looking at the ornaments and I remembered happier times. I'm fine now."

Without invitation, he strode over the threshold and closed the door behind him. He laid his hands on her shoulders. "I've never known you to cry."

There was strength in his touch and she felt oddly comforted by it. "First time for everything."

He swore, jerked off his coat and tossed it on the banister. "You don't look fine. Did you get any sleep last night?"

"Of course."

"Liar."

"I dozed in a chair." She tried to smile, but the gesture didn't seem to convince him.

He cupped her elbow in his hand and escorted her toward the kitchen. "I'll bet you haven't eaten, either."

"I ate."

"When?"

"Yesterday."

He grunted. "You've lost weight since the accident. You look as if a stiff breeze could knock you over."

"I'm fine."

Ignoring her, he guided her into a chair by the kitchen table. He moved to the stove where a kettle sat next to a platter of cookies. "Where do you keep the tea?"

"On the shelf beside the oven, next to the cups." She started to rise, wanting something to do. "Here, let me get that."

"Sit." The command brooked no argument. "You need food in your stomach before we head out today."

She swirled her finger in circles on the table as he fed the oven's red embers with kindling and located the tea. "I've been thinking about the tree. Maybe we don't need one this year. It's a lot of trouble and I doubt anyone would miss it."

He set the mug on the table, then sprinkled tea leaves on the bottom. "You love decorating Christmas trees."

She had once, but not anymore. It was simply too painful. "For me, it's more habit than anything."

He tore a chunk from a loaf of bread and set it on a plate in front of her. She took a bite and discovered she was hungry. When the kettle hissed, he poured hot water on the leaves. He watched her, waited until she'd eaten and drank.

"I heard you talking about decorating Christmas

trees in July at the Independence Day picnic,'' he said finally.

Startled, she wrapped her chilled hand around the mug. "I did not."

"You were at the July picnic, talking to Mrs. Hollis. You were wearing that yellow dress, the one with the pearl buttons. And you said something about covering the trees with red bows and pinecones this year."

He was right. She'd forgotten about the ribbon she'd bought in Denver that was still tucked away in her dresser. She started to feel better. "I didn't think you noticed women's dresses or cared about decorating."

He leaned toward her. "I don't. Unless you're wearing the dress or doing the decorating. I notice everything about you. I have since my first day in town."

The few rational thoughts she'd scavenged since his unexpected arrival vanished. "I don't know what to say."

Roman said nothing for a moment, his wolf-gray eyes assessing. But when she started to fidget, he rose from the table. "Nothing to say, not now anyway. Today, we're cutting a tree."

She couldn't go, not with her feelings in such turmoil. She dabbed at crumbs on the table with her finger. She scrambled for a convincing excuse as he guided her into the foyer. "It's too cold today."

He helped her into her coat, then wrapped a red scarf around her neck. "I'll bundle you up."

"It's going to snow."

He handed her her bonnet. "By the way the sky looks we won't have snow until tonight." Opening the front door, he added, "Now if you don't have any more lame excuses, we'll go."

"I raised valid concerns." She brushed past him into the blustering winds. Monday's snow had settled on the ground and frost crackled in the air.

Laughing, he closed the front door with a firm click. "Right."

Before she could summon another protest, she found herself nestled beside him on his sled. With a thick quilt and furs blanketing her legs, he snapped the reins and the horses went forward. Bells on their harnesses jingled as Roman guided them through town, past dozens of curious onlookers.

Jutting mountains scraped the cloudless sky as sunlight glittered on the fresh snow. The view was breathtaking and, amazingly, Laura found herself relaxing. The mountain air eased the tightness in her muscles. Lulled by the warmth and fresh air, she dozed.

When she woke, the sled's runners had cut through the snow. They were deep in the mountains. "I fell asleep," she said immediately, embarrassed.

"You needed it."

"Yes." She stretched, amazed at how refreshed she felt. Laura's focus shifted toward Roman. Everything about him drew her to him—his hands and the way he held the reins with easy confidence; the touch of his thigh against hers as the sled swayed through the snow; his woodsy clean scent.

What was it about this man? Without speaking a

word, he had the power to churn her resolve to mush and make her ignore well-laid, sensible plans.

"So where do you normally go tree hunting?" he asked.

Startled from her thoughts, Laura cleared her throat. "There's a valley about a mile outside of town. Grandfather and I always had the best luck finding trees there."

"How big of a tree are we looking for?"

"Eight feet or so."

He raised an eyebrow. "Kind of big, don't you think?"

"Not for the foyer. We always put it by the stairs." She hesitated, realizing he didn't know. He'd only been in Timberline seven months, yet it seemed he'd been here a lifetime. "You've never been to one of our parties before."

"This will be the first. I hear it's a party not to be missed."

"Everybody comes. Even the children. It's wonderful." Her lips curled into a smile just thinking about last year's party. Mr. Hollis and her grandfather had sung a duet while Mr. Warner struck a lively tune on his fiddle. The children had laughed and the ladies all drank and ate more than they should have. "Who did you spend the holidays with before you came to Timberline?"

"I've always worked on Christmas Day."

"You've never taken Christmas off?" The thought of him alone during the holidays saddened her.

"Holidays don't mean much to me—other than extra wages. More of an annoyance.'' No self-pity laced his words.

"How can you say that? The decorations, the smell of cakes cooking, hints of a special present—all that has got to be just a little exciting, even to you.''

"A time or two, I went to church, but the holidays are just a distraction.''

"That's it?''

"Yep. I grew up fast when my parents died.''

Somehow she'd assumed there was more in his life than work. To discover there wasn't gave her a new sense of purpose. "Roman, I am going to personally see that you enjoy this Christmas.''

He kept his gaze trained ahead, but she imagined the hint of a smile tugging the corner of his mouth. "That so?''

"Yes. And I'd like to give you a gift.''

He shook his head. "The only gift I want is you.''

A rush of heat warmed her body and it took an extra beat for her heart to stop racing so she could face him again. "I was thinking along the lines of a nice pocket watch or perhaps a new coat. But I want to do something special for you. You've been a good friend to me.''

"Friend?'' His ragged tone made *friend* sound like an obscenity.

"What's wrong with friendship?''

"Nothing,'' he said working his jaw. "In the right context.''

"There is no bad context for friendship.''

He glared at her sideways. "I want more. You know that.''

She moistened her dry lips. ''What if friendship is all I can offer?''

''Let's stop talking bloody friendship and find a tree.''

Roman pulled the sled to a stop on a snowy hillside next to a large stand of tall, proud fir trees. He tied off the reins, hopped down and walked around to Laura's side of the sled. He lifted her as if she weighed no more than a feather and lowered her to the ground.

With his body heat washing over her she found friendly thoughts difficult. Exercising a good bit of willpower, she stepped back. The sooner they found a tree, the sooner she could get away from him, and her mind would clear. ''There are so many lovely trees.''

He unlatched the ax from the side of the sled, took her elbow in hand and started toward the trees. ''Which one do you like?''

The man didn't know anything about Christmas. ''I need to inspect them first.''

''What's there to inspect? They're all tall. They're all green. Trees are trees.''

''They are all not the same. It has to be just the right height and not too wide.''

He stopped in front of a tall spruce. ''This one looks good.''

Indeed the tree's front did look full and lush, but as she walked around the side she noted a big bare spot. ''It won't do. No matter which way the tree is turned the hole will show.''

He cocked an eyebrow. "Turn that section toward the wall. No one will see it."

Men. "*I'll* know it's there."

He looked as if he'd argue but instead pointed to another tree. "What about that one? No bare spots."

She wrinkled her nose. "It has a crooked trunk. It'll fall."

"I'll tie a rope around it and nail it to the wall."

She laughed at the outrageous suggestion. "You can't do that!"

He shrugged. "It won't fall over."

The man's straightforward logic did have a certain charm. "Honestly, Roman. You've as much Christmas spirit as a tree stump."

Roman mumbled something about women then nodded toward another tree. "Now how about that one? Straight trunk, no holes, eight feet tall. It doesn't get any better than that."

She inspected its lush branches. "It is lovely. We'll keep it in mind as we look at others."

"Others?"

"We won't know if this one is perfect unless we compare it to other trees."

Shaking his head, he knelt down and laid the ax blade against the trunk. "This is a good tree. You like it. I'm cutting it." He whacked the trunk.

She quickly scanned the trees around them. "But there could be a better one!"

He paused and looked up at her. "That's your trouble, Laura. You're always looking for something better when what you need is right in front of you." He shifted his focus back to the tree.

Laura opened her mouth to argue then stopped. Roman was right. Living in Virginia she'd dreamed of adventure in Colorado. Now, she dreamed of the quiet life back in Virginia.

Roman stood and nudged her back a step. "Stand back." When she was clear, he gave the tree a hard shove. The trunk cracked and the tree hit the snowy ground with a whoosh.

He grabbed the trunk with one gloved hand, held the ax in the other and looked right at her. "You've got people who would do anything for you, and a classroom of adoring children whom you haven't told you're leaving. It doesn't get any better than that."

"You make it sound so black-and-white. My decision to move was the hardest I've ever made. I don't want to leave my friends behind."

"I understand fear, Laura." He spoke so gently that it nearly undid her. "I've had a taste of it more than once in my life. But it's a heartless master that will squeeze the life out of you if you let it. Don't let fear chase you away from those who care most about you."

Roman understood. "Death is everywhere in Timberline."

"It's everywhere period, Laura. You can't live your life waiting to die. Life's about living in the moment." He moved closer. "Here you aren't alone. You have friends who've not only weathered tragedy with you and shared losses, but who accept you as you are."

"My friends back east have been kind," she said in defense.

"Is that enough for you?"

His words touched at the heart of emotions she'd not been able to put into words.

Michael's letters had contained the right words of sympathy, but each had gently chided her grandfather for dragging her west. She'd tried to explain to Michael that moving west had been her decision—that it had been about wanting *more* from life than tea parties and needlepoint. Michael had jokingly suggested the mountain air had confused her thoughts.

Laura kicked the snow, remembering another one of Michael's barbs about Colorado. "The folks back east always thought I was an oddity."

The corner of his mouth tipped up. "Then they were fools."

She'd forgotten just how much she'd been a fish out of water back east. Roman seemed to know her better than she knew herself. "Where do we go from here?" She hadn't agreed to stay, but she no longer felt in a rush to leave Timberline.

He stared down at her, his face inches away. His gaze lingered on her lips and for a breathless moment she thought he'd kiss her. She rose ever so slightly up on tiptoe, hoping he would.

As if he'd read her thoughts, he grinned, then turned toward the sled to latch the tailgate. He started to whistle.

Feeling more than a little foolish, she stared at his muscled back. She'd all but melted at his touch and he knew it.

Why did the man have to be so right about everything? Why did she suddenly want him so much?

Vexed at him and herself, she knelt down and balled up a thick handful of wet snow. She took extra care to pack it tight, then hurled it right into Roman's back.

He whirled around with the speed of lighting. For an instant his eyes glinted like a hunter's. Then slowly a devilish grin lifted the edges of his lips. He bent down and scooped up a huge handful of snow as she started to back up.

Laughing, Laura stumbled back. "I—I was just kidding."

He tossed the snowball from hand to hand. "I'm not letting you off that easily."

Chapter Eight

"Don't you dare hit me with that!" Laura was giggling, backing away and shaking her head. Sunlight danced off her gold curls and her eyes sparkled with laughter. Damn, but Roman had missed her smile.

She'd been laughing when he'd first seen her.

He remembered the spring day clearly. He'd just refused Zachary Butler's generous offer to manage Butler's Folly—a rich, but poorly maintained mine. The rotting timbers creaked warnings of a cave-in and Roman had been around long enough to know Zachary's promises of wealth wouldn't do him any good if he were dead.

And then he'd seen Laura. She'd been standing in the patch of grass by the schoolhouse, surrounded by an army of children tugging at her lemon-colored skirts each vying for the ball in her hands. Her thick braid of hair glowed like spun gold and brushed past her narrow waist and gently rounded hips.

He'd stopped, leaning against the sun-baked wall of the title office and watched as she'd laughed and tossed the ball toward the other end of the field. The children had scampered after it like a gang of large-footed puppies and her laughter rang clear and bright as a church bell.

Roman had never seen a more beautiful woman.

He had returned to the mine and accepted the old man's offer on one condition. Profits for the next year would be sunk into mine repairs. The old man, faced with certain bankruptcy, had accepted Roman's offer without negotiation. Roman and his crews had worked around the clock to shore up the mines, but their efforts hadn't been enough to prevent the cave-in.

Laura's voice tugged him from his thoughts. "Why don't you just put that snowball down?" She'd edged around the side of the sled for protection. "It wouldn't be polite to hit me with it."

Laughter rumbled in his chest. "I'm not one of those fancy Virginia gentlemen." The sled now stood between them. Every time he moved right, she moved left. To add interest to the cat-and-mouse game, he scooped up more snow and gently patted it against the large snowball already in his hand.

She wagged her finger at him. "I'll get wet if you hit me with that."

He moved toward the back of the sled. "I've got a chunk of ice slithering down my back as we speak. I'd hate for you not to enjoy the same feeling."

Reading the intent in his eyes, Laura skittered toward the horses. "Roman, I mean it, don't you dare hit me with that snowball. I'm sorry I hit you, okay?"

He grinned. "Sorry doesn't cut it, princess." Moving as quick as a cat, he darted around the side of the wagon toward her. She squealed and took off running. Her black skirts skimmed the top of the snow as she ran toward a stand of trees. He overtook her easily, grabbing her around the waist and hauling her against him.

"Let me go!" Laughing, Laura tried to shove out of his embrace.

She felt good in his arms and as her bottom wriggled against him, he forgot all about snowballs and playfulness. His heart hammered in his chest, his body throbbed and he wanted nothing more than to lay her on the blankets in the sled's bed and make love to her.

Without warning, she lunged forward and broke out of his embrace. She started to flee, but the weight of her damp hem and the uneven snow threw her off balance. She fell forward into the snow onto her hands and knees.

She laughed in earnest now. "So much for my dramatic exit."

"Let me help." He grabbed her elbow and hauled her to her feet, turning her around to face him. He struggled to keep the tone light when all he wanted was to devour her.

Her bonnet had fallen back and her cheeks were bright red. Flecks of snow sprinkled her hair. She started to brush the snow from her skirt. "That's what I get for acting childish. I'll be lucky if my dress isn't soaked through by the time we reach town."

He wiped damp snow from her cheek. "I'll keep you warm."

The huskiness in his voice caught her attention and

she looked up with a blush. "There are furs in the sled."

He pulled her against him, sharing his warmth. Her breasts pressed against his chest. "Every time I hold you, you feel better than I'd remembered."

She made no move to struggle out of his embrace.

He smoothed damp curls from her face and lowered his mouth to hers. She tensed for an instant, then relaxed against him and her mouth opened. Her kiss was passionate, and its heat warmed his blood to boiling.

He groaned his pleasure, drawing her tighter against his body. If not for the cold and snow he'd have taken her right here on this hillside.

One of the horses nickered and pawed his hoof against the snow. Roman raised his head, drawing in a ragged breath as he touched his forehead to hers. "Tell me you still want to leave Timberline."

"I don't want to leave," she confessed. "But I have to."

A small victory, but a first step. Tomorrow would bring more challenges but he refused to worry. Instead, he kissed her. "Let's get your tree back to town."

She moistened her lips. "I'd forgotten all about the tree."

Male pride made him chuckle. "That's progress."

Something had changed between them in the mountains.

They sat nestled next to each other during the ride back to town. Though they didn't speak, there was a connection between them that went far beyond friendship and respect. She realized what bound her to him now wasn't Timberline, the miners, or Butler's Folly.

It was love.

And it scared the devil out of her. The idea of ever losing Roman to the mines frightened her beyond words.

They arrived at her house just after lunchtime. Wordlessly, Roman settled the horses in the livery while she changed into a blue dress with red piping. By the time she'd come downstairs, he had hauled the tree into the foyer and propped it against the corner.

Roman stepped back to admire the evergreen. "It'll fit just right when I stand it up properly."

She plucked a dead leaf out of the tree, acutely aware of him. "Yes."

He laid his hand gently on her shoulder. "Laura, I love you."

She smiled, her heart so full of emotion she feared it might burst. "And I love you."

Roman wrapped his arms around her narrow waist and pulled her against him. She leaned into the kiss, amazed at the power of her emotions. Her body hummed with wanting in a way she'd never dreamed possible. Her pulse raced and she was drunk with his taste and touch.

She felt so alive in this moment, she wanted it to last forever. She didn't want him to leave. "Make love to me," she heard herself say.

He stared at her long, tense seconds before he swept her up in his arms and carried her into the parlor. He laid her down on the thick carpet in front of the fire. He unfastened the buttons that trailed from her neck to her waist. He pushed open her bodice and kissed the top of her creamy breast, which peeked out over the top of her lace chemise.

He undressed her, taking his time, savoring every inch of her. Only when she lay naked before him, her clothes pooled on the floor, did he move away from her to quickly shrug off his coat and shirt. She rose up on her knees and marveled at the way the pale afternoon light glistened on his chest.

He tugged off his boots, then pushed his pants down over his lean hips. Her heart skipped a beat when she glimpsed his erection. Roman gave her no time to think. He covered her body with his, threaded his fingers through her hair and kissed her.

Instinctively, she opened her legs, forgetting about everything but the feel of him and the pressing need inside her.

His hand slid down her flat stomach, cupping her buttocks. She arched, silently asking for more.

And then he touched her between her legs. His touch nearly drove her mad with wanting. She sucked a breath in through her clenched teeth, torn between desire and shame. "Roman, what are you doing to me?"

He kissed the hollow of her neck. "Loving you."

She closed her eyes and moistened her lips. Speech was difficult. "I've never felt like this."

"Me, either."

He coaxed her legs wider then and straddled her. Positioning himself outside her, he slowly pushed inside her until he reached the delicate barrier. He hesitated then pushed through it with one quick thrust.

She tensed, overwhelmed by pain. Roman stilled, murmuring soothing words in her ear as she slowly grew accustomed to him. Then gently, he began to move inside her with long, deliberate thrusts. Discomfort faded to pleasure and soon Laura lifted her hips up and accepted all of him.

Breathing was a struggle as wave after wave of sensation washed over her. And then in a blinding flash, spasms overcame her, rippling through every muscle in her body.

Roman thrust into her, moving with the fever of a man possessed. He called out her name, then drove into her to the hilt, spilling his seed, before collapsing against her.

Later, Roman took her upstairs to her room. They stayed in bed all afternoon, making love two more times. Time suspended as they savored the erotic haze that shut out the world and all worries.

When the clock in the hallway chimed six times, Laura sat up. Roman lay on his back, his eyes closed, the sheet twisted around his narrow hips. A contented man.

Smiling, she swung her legs toward the edge of the bed. She was hungry and no doubt he was, too. She thought about the ham and bread in the kitchen and her mouth watered. She'd not been this hungry in months.

As she scooted to the edge of the bed, a long arm

wrapped around her waist and pulled her back. Laura shrieked.

"Where are you going?" he said, his eyes half-open.

"To get food. I'm famished."

He sat up. "I'll go with you."

"Stay in bed. I'll bring you up something."

He kissed her on her bare shoulder. "As tempting as that is, I better get up. The house is cold and I'd best check the fire in the parlor."

Laura reached for her robe, which lay on the trunk at the foot of her bed. Without his heat, her skin had quickly chilled and she wasted no time putting on the robe.

Roman pulled on his pants and shirt. His mussed hair softened his hard features, making him seem more approachable, vulnerable even. For her, he'd let down his guard.

Her heart clenched. "This moment is so perfect. I want it to last forever."

He smiled. "There will be a lifetime of moments."

But before she could speak, the distant sound of the mine alarm bell echoed in the room. The warning rang when there was a cave-in at the mine.

Laura clenched the folds of her robe. "Not again."

The softness in Roman's face vanished as he hurried to the bedroom window and pushed back the lace curtains. A stream of people, their lanterns glowing bright in the dusk, hurried up the hill toward the mine. The *clang-clang* of the alarm sounded louder.

"I've got to go." He pulled on his shirt and shoved on his boots.

Laura froze with panic. Memories of that horrible night in October returned, fracturing her short-lived happiness. "I can't go through that again."

He reached for his coat. "The choice isn't ours."

Panic and fear exploded inside her. She couldn't bear to lose him.

"Roman, please stay." Her cowardice shamed her.

He hesitated, his back to her. "I have to go." He strode out of the house toward the mine.

Chapter Nine

Laura dressed quickly and hurried to her front porch intent on going after Roman, ready to beg him to leave Timberline forever. She stopped when she saw the procession of her neighbors carrying lanterns and moving toward Butler's Folly. In the group were off-duty miners, women fearful for their husbands and sons, children praying they'd not seen their fathers for the last time.

She tried to remember who worked the night shift. Dan Owens. Paulie Mills. Bart Goodin. There'd be at least sixty men in the mine right now. Most with family in town, many with children in her classroom, all friends who'd stood by her when she'd buried her grandfather.

No one had turned his or her back on her when she'd been in need.

And she'd not ignore her friends now.

Fear be damned.

She put on her coat and gloves, then quickly made her way down snowy Main Street. Mentally she prepared a list of things to be done. Blankets to be gathered. Fires to be built. Coffee to be made. If this accident was like the last, it was going to be a long night.

As she made her way up the hill toward the mine, others joined her. Their faces tight with worry, they trudged in the ice-coated snow to the entrance. Large flakes started to fall from the starless sky.

No one spoke because no one had to. Everyone understood lives were at stake. The rescue workers would have to work quickly, as a team, to save the survivors trapped in the rubble.

Countless lanterns and torches lighted the mine entrance where men talked in agitated shouts, women cried and comforted each other. She'd tried so hard to forget that disastrous October night, but the scene triggered a flood of memories.

Her palms felt moist, her back tight with tension. Instinct told her to run even as she forced herself to put one foot in front of the other.

Laura spotted Roman's assistant, Fred Winters, and immediately went to him. The man wasn't much older than she, but the deep lines etched at his temples and the black soot coating his skin suggested he was a decade older. "Where's Roman?"

Fred shoved dirt-crusted fingers through his auburn hair. "He rode the bucket down. He's leading the rescue work."

Pride mingled with her fear. Roman never shrank from what needed to be done. It was one of the reasons she loved him.

She forced herself to concentrate on the accident. "What happened?"

Fred rubbed the back of his neck with a trembling hand. ''We was shoring up the number five shaft—it was the last needing repairs.''

She didn't hide her surprise. ''You were doing repair work this late at night?''

''Mr. Maddox insisted. Since October, shoring up the walls has been the number one priority.''

The pain and guilt in Fred's eyes nearly made her weep. ''Go on.''

''I was inspecting the work just like Mr. Maddox asked. One of the young lads knocked the wrong timber free and brought a whole section down.''

Laura straightened as she mentally bolstered her courage. ''How many men?''

''Six, seven. No one knows, exactly.''

But Roman would find out. He was doing what he could.

Now it was her turn.

She turned toward the women. Many were older than she, more experienced, but in their minds she was the mine owner. It was up to her to organize and direct. ''Ladies, it could be a long night. We'd best get to work.''

Sally Jenkins looked up from her handkerchief, her red-rimmed eyes desperately searching Laura's face for hope. She wasn't more than a year or two older than Laura, but she already had four children. ''My Henry's down there.''

Laura put her arm around Sally's shoulder. She pictured the tall man with the booming laugh and ebony hair. ''Roman's gone after him.''

Sally's relief was palpable. "He'll be all right then."

"You know Roman won't rest until all the men are out." Her gaze scanned the huddle of women gathering around. "We need to start fires, get coffeepots brewing."

Mrs. Warner raised her hand. "I'll see to the fires."

Laura nodded, then turned to three girls, each about fourteen. "Go to my house. There is enough food for an army in the kitchen."

"That's for the party, Miss Laura," one of the girls said.

"No sense waiting the three days if it's needed now. When the men working rescue come out to break, they're going to be hungry."

"John Murphy," she said to a tall, gangly boy of thirteen. "Go from house to house. Get as many blankets as you can and get the doctor up here. Likely with his bad hearing he didn't hear the bell."

"Yes, ma'am."

"Sally," she said. "Start the coffee."

The young woman sniffed back her tears and nodded. "I'll do it."

The formerly disorganized group of volunteers dispersed without question, moving with the direction and purpose of a well-organized army. Food was set up on sawhorse tables, blankets stacked and pots of coffee dangled on a spit over a large fire tended by two women.

The activity kept everyone calm and steady. And it wasn't until everything was in place that Laura's nerves started to fray. Minutes turned into hours as they all waited for the men to come to the surface.

At midnight, Laura stood by the bonfire warming herself when Sally shoved a warm cup of coffee in her hands. "Drink this. It'll warm your bones."

Laura managed a halfhearted smile. "Thanks."

Sally stared into the dancing flames. "I hate this part the most."

Laura nodded. "The fear, the waiting, the hoping."

Firelight glistened in Sally's tired brown eyes. "It takes its toll."

Laura studied Sally's pretty face. "Why not just leave this life behind?"

Sally shook her head. "My father was proud to be a miner, just as my Henry is. The work is in their blood. Mine, too, I reckon."

And somehow, Laura knew that the work, the mountains, the excitement of living in a mining town were now a part of her. Timberline was home.

The hoist, which lowered and raised the cage through all levels of the mine, started again. It had gone up and down dozens of times during the night but each time all activity stopped as everyone watched and waited for news.

This time, the bucket not only held an exhausted rescue worker but an injured miner. The man, slumped forward, was covered in black soot and blood oozed from a cut in his head.

Sally immediately recognized her husband. Tears streaming down her face, she ran to him. "Oh, dear Lord, it's my Henry."

Fred ran to the bucket, inspected Henry Jenkins and shouted, "He's fine! Bruised and battered, but alive."

Laura waited until they removed Henry Jenkins from the bucket before she approached Fred. "The others? Are they coming up?"

"They haven't reached the other trapped men yet."

Laura pressed her hand to her face. Unshed tears burned her throat.

Roman, be safe.

In the next fifteen minutes, five more men were brought to the surface. Like the first, they had minor injuries but would recover.

Laura sniffed and rubbed the tears from her cheek as the rescued miners hugged their wives and children.

Roman, come home to me.

As the crew lifted the seventh man out of the bucket, an explosion from inside the mine sounded. Smoke drifted to the surface from the caverns below.

Laura began to tremble. She thought she'd faint with worry. She ran to Fred. "Who else is left down there with Roman?"

"Roman's the last man unaccounted for."

"Drop the bucket," she ordered.

Frightened, he ran his hand through his hair. "That explosion was bad, Miss Laura. There's no telling if he made it or how far the bucket will go."

"Do it!"

"Yes, ma'am."

As the bucket dropped into the mine, smoke and dust billowed up from the hole. Metal clanged against rock, then the bucket stopped.

"How deep did it go?" Laura demanded.

"To the bottom."

Tense seconds passed. The rope remained still. Dust swirled in the air. Then the sound of a hammer pounding three times against the cage echoed up the shaft.

"I'll be damned!" Fred quickly reversed the machine and began the slow ascent.

Laura's fingers knotted into tight fists. She was barely aware of the cold or the silence that rippled through the crowd.

Finally, the bucket emerged.

And Roman was in it.

Black dust caked his skin and clothes and his head was bowed. He was exhausted. Laura's heart nearly shattered at the sight of him.

She wrapped an arm around his waist, uncaring that the soot covering him stained her dress. She helped him out of the cage. "I thought we lost you."

"I'm not so easy to kill."

The inches separating them felt like miles. "You're the strongest man I know." The crowd of people had backed away from them, but she sensed they were listening. "About what I said earlier—"

"I'm tired, Laura. And I don't want to go over that again now." He started to move way. He was building a wall between them, shutting her out.

Laura shoved aside her panic. "I was wrong."

He stopped but didn't face her.

"I want another chance."

He faced her and shoved his fists into his pockets.

"Laura, I was wrong. This life is hard. It isn't easy. You belong in Virginia, where it's safe."

"I don't belong in Virginia." She touched his arm, blinked away tears when he flinched. "Life out here isn't easy. It is hard. But I learned something about myself tonight."

Silent, he clenched his jaw.

"You were right about me all along. I wouldn't have moved to Colorado if my safe, predictable life had made me happy."

He pulled his hands from his pockets and flexed his fingers. "What are you saying?"

"I love you. I want to marry you. I want us to build our life together here in Timberline."

She waited, unable to breathe.

Roman stood stock straight as if he didn't believe what he'd heard. "You're reacting to the emotion of tonight."

"Tonight made me see what was in my heart all along. I love you, Roman."

His gaze bore into her. "Are you sure, Laura? There's no going back after this."

Tears spilled down her cheeks. "I don't want to go back. Only forward. With you."

A slow smile curled the edges of his lips and he scooped her up in his arms. "I love you, Laura Butler." He kissed her breathless, then let out a whoop of joy. "You've given me the greatest Christmas gift of all." He swallowed, his eyes glistening. "Fred, get the minister over here!"

Fred started at the sharp command and hurried toward Roman. "He's just started down the mountain toward home, sir."

Roman hugged Laura to his side. "Drag him back if you have to."

Fred scratched his head. "What for, sir? We didn't lose anyone."

Laura wrapped her arms around Roman. "We need him back here so that I can marry Roman Maddox before he changes his mind."

Fred grinned. "Yes, ma'am!"

Fifteen minutes later, the groom and his bride, still covered in black soot, stood before the Reverend Bower, who was breathless from his hike back up the hill.

Children roused from sleep, wearing only nightshirts, unlaced boots and overcoats, could barely stand still for all the excitement. Wives stood close to their husbands, holding hands. Young girls whispered of romance.

"Do you, Laura, take Roman?" the minister asked.

She grinned up at him. "I sure do. For better or worse."

"And, Roman," the minister said deepening his voice. "Do you take Laura?"

"That I do. That I do."

Reverend Bower peered over his glasses, grinning. "This is about the oddest wedding I've ever officiated at. But I haven't seen a happier couple."

"Just finish the job, Reverend," Fred shouted, laughing.

The minister looked down at Laura and Roman's

joined hands. "With pleasure! I pronounce you man and wife."

Roman swept Laura up in his arms and kissed her as the crowd cheered.

* * * * *

**Embark on the adventure of
a lifetime with these timeless
tales from Harlequin Historicals**

On the lookout for captivating courtships
set on the American frontier?
Then behold these rollicking romances
from Harlequin Historicals.

On sale January 2003

THE FORBIDDEN BRIDE
by Cheryl Reavis
*Will a well-to-do young woman defy
her father and give her heart to
a wild and daring gold miner?*

HALLIE'S HERO
by Nicole Foster
*A beautiful rancher joins forces
with a gun-toting gambler to save her spread!*

On sale February 2003

THE MIDWIFE'S SECRET
by Kate Bridges
*Can a wary midwife finally find love and acceptance
in the arms of a ruggedly handsome sawmill owner?*

THE LAW AND KATE MALONE
by Charlene Sands
*A stubborn sheriff and a spirited saloon owner
share a stormy reunion!*

Harlequin Historicals®
Historical Romantic Adventure!

FALL IN LOVE
THIS WINTER
WITH
HARLEQUIN BOOKS!

In October 2002 look for these special volumes
led by *USA TODAY* bestselling authors,
and receive MOULIN ROUGE on video*!

*Retail value of $14.98 U.S. Mail-in offer. Two proofs of purchase required.
Limited time offer. Offer expires 3/31/03.

See inside these books for details.

Own MOULIN ROUGE on video!

*This exciting promotion
is available at your
favorite retail outlet.*

Only from
HARLEQUIN®
Makes any time special ®

 MOULIN ROUGE ©2002 Twentieth Century Fox Home Entertainment, Inc.
All rights reserved. "Twentieth Century Fox", "Fox" and their associated
logos are the property of Twentieth Century Fox Film Corporation.

Visit Harlequin at www.eHarlequin.com   PHNCP02R

Two families...
Four generations...
And the one debt that binds them together!

BECKETT'S BIRTHRIGHT

The dramatic prequel in the **Beckett's Fortune** series from
Harlequin Historicals and Silhouette Desire!

Just as Eli Chandler is about to get hitched to a pretty con artist,
his intended bride is kidnapped! Determined to see justice done,
the honor-bound ranch manager sets out on a bold adventure that
brings him face-to-face with his new boss's tempestuous daughter,
Delilah Jackson. When all is said and done, will Eli be free to say
"I do" to the one woman who's truly captivated his heart?

Don't miss any of the books in this riveting series!

AUGUST 2002
BECKETT'S CINDERELLA by Dixie Browning
SILHOUETTE DESIRE

NOVEMBER 2002
BECKETT'S BIRTHRIGHT by Bronwyn Williams
HARLEQUIN HISTORICALS

JANUARY 2003
BECKETT'S CONVENIENT BRIDE by Dixie Browning
SILHOUETTE DESIRE

BECKETT'S FORTUNE

Where the price of family and honor is love...

Harlequin Historicals®
Historical Romantic Adventure!